B

T

# CONSTABLE UNDER THE GOOSEBERRY BUSH

Retiring after forty years as president of the Aidensfield Old Gooseberry Society, Joseph Marshall decides to nurture some prize-winning fruit. However, his health rapidly deteriorates and the people of Aidensfield raise funds to send him to Lourdes for a miracle cure, but the pilgrimage means Joseph cannot tend his beloved berries and Claude Jeremiah Greengrass, determined to gain revenge on Joseph for an earlier humiliation, grows a colossal berry. Meanwhile a crime wave involving stolen bicycles means that Constable Nick finds himself coping with a variety of problems in his own inimitable way...

# CONSTABLE UNDER THE GOOSEBERRY BUSH

# Constable Under The Gooseberry Bush

*by*

Nicholas Rhea

**Magna Large Print Books**
Long Preston, North Yorkshire,
BD23 4ND, England.

British Library Cataloguing in Publication Data.

Rhea, Nicholas
    Constable under the gooseberry bush.

    A catalogue record of this book is
    available from the British Library

    ISBN    0-7505-1501-5

First published in Great Britain by Robert Hale Ltd., 1999

Copyright © 1999 by Nicholas Rhea

Cover illustration © Barbara Walton by arrangement with Robert Hale Ltd.

Published in Large Print 2000 by arrangement with Robert Hale Ltd.

Magna Large Print is an imprint of Library Magna Books Ltd.

Printed and bound in Great Britain by
T.J. (International) Ltd., Cornwall, PL28 8RW

# 1

'I'm going to retire, Mr Rhea.'

I was sitting at a scrubbed wooden table in the sunny kitchen of Joseph and Mabel Marshall's delightful stone-built cottage in East Lane, Aidensfield. A coal fire was burning in the grate as a sooty black kettle sang on the hob. It was puffing miniature clouds of steam into the room as the lid bubbled and bounced with the fluctuating power of the steam. Their black cat, Sweep, was asleep on the clip rug in front of the fire and the mantelshelf bore an array of brass ornaments, all gleaming in the sunlight which poured through the windows. Some of the brassware caught reflections from the blazing fire too, all adding to the happiness generated by this room. Prominent among the ornaments was a pipe rack containing half-a-dozen briars, an indication of Joseph's love of his pipe and tobacco.

A dark wooden crucifix with a white plaster figure of Christ hung on the wall above the fireplace and there was an oval medallion of Our Lady on the rear wall of the kitchen, indicators of the strong, living Catholicism of this couple.

Sometimes when I called, a string of rosary beads hung from a hook on one of the walls whilst ever-present on the landing window ledge was a statue of the Sacred Heart, easily visible from the street outside. This visible display of faith was common in most of the Catholic homes of Aidensfield.

The kitchen table bore warm buttered scones, strawberry jam and a pot of tea along with plates, cups and saucers, while a vase of new daffodils stood on the window ledge. It was a scene of total rural contentment, something very normal but most enjoyable in my daily routine as Aidensfield's village constable. In this case, it was mid-morning and I was enjoying one of those delicious mouth-watering scones with a cup of hot fresh tea prepared by Mabel.

I'd come to discuss the plans for the next Aidensfield Gooseberry Show – it was several months away, but I needed to confirm the date for my diary so that I could reserve, through Ashfordly Police Station, a quantity of 'No Parking' signs and traffic cones, necessities for my formal part in the event. During the summer months, there were heavy calls on 'No Parking' signs and cones in our beautiful and heavily visited area of the North Riding of Yorkshire.

I was making plans well in advance because I had no wish for Aidensfield to be swamped or brought to a halt by tourists' cars and coaches being indiscriminately parked in the lanes and gateways. Cars especially were an increasing problem in the rural beauty spots, often through the thoughtlessness of visitors. To counteract their behaviour, I intended to ensure there'd be a formal parking area in a convenient field because the annual Gooseberry Show always attracted a crowd.

Most were serious growers from near and far, but as the populace had become more mobile, many additional people such as day-trippers and tourists turned up out of sheer curiosity. Their parking proclivities had to be controlled because many townspeople thought they could park anywhere in the countryside that did not boast a 'No Parking' sign, the vital work of country people had to continue in spite of waves of incoming visitors. Some of them seemed to think that the National Park was a theme park provided only for the amusement of tourists.

'I thought you *had* retired, Joseph?' I smiled, teasing him. 'You finished on the railway a few years ago, didn't you?'

'Aye, I did, but I'm talking of t'Old Gooseberry Society, Mr Rhea,' he said with all seriousness, removing his smoking briar pipe as he looked steadily at me. 'As president, I mean. Retiring as president. It won't be easy, giving it up, because I've been doing t'job all these years....'

'Forty years!' chipped in the formidable Mabel. 'Forty years he's been running that show. I've told him it's time he handed over to somebody younger! He's not just president either, he's secretary and chairman and weighman and publicity man ... the lot; he does all the running about! He shouldn't, not at his age.'

'A one-man band!' I smiled.

'Yes, but he should give jobs to committee members, Mr Rhea. He's done it all by himself, even putting chairs and tables out....'

'There's never been any complaints, Mabel, and every show's been a huge success, so he's obviously been doing a great job!'

Not wishing to take sides in this domestic skirmish, I selected another of her scrumptious buttered scones and smothered it with a thick layer of home-made strawberry jam.

'It's getting tougher now, Mr Rhea...' began Joseph, puffing at his pipe and filling the room with its distinctive aroma. 'And I'm beginning to feel my age, you know....'

'He's never won the Supreme Championship, Mr Rhea,' Mabel interrupted, determined to say her piece. 'Far too busy organizing things, that's his trouble. What with doing bits for St Aidan's like opening up and locking the church every day, and tidying up the graveyard and then being secretary of the Guild and helping out at the village hall, he's never got time for things at home – except them gooseberries of his!'

'Lots of village institutions would have trouble surviving if it wasn't for volunteers like Joseph,' I added feebly.

'Mebbe so, but so far as his gooseberry job's concerned, he's been neglecting his bushes so he could run things, rushing his work, forgetting to do things like pruning at the right time and not putting muck where and when it's needed. He's producing berries only half as big as he could do with just a bit of extra attention. He could have won the Supreme time and time again, but he never has! It's time he did, Mr Rhea,

11

before he's under six foot of soil. It is daft, isn't it? Him being the organizer, knowing more about gooseberries than them other lot put together, and yet never winning the main prize! By, I'd like to see his name on that trophy! So, Mr Rhea, I say it's time he packed in, handed over to somebody younger and got down to growing a champion berry. The Supreme Champion, I mean, the heaviest berry in the show. He could do that, Mr Rhea, if he set his mind to it – he could even win the world championship if he shaped himself.'

'It would be nice if he did have his name engraved in silver, wouldn't it?' I agreed. 'The year's Supreme Champion of Aidensfield Old Gooseberry Society.'

'I want him to do that, Mr Rhea, just once. He's quite capable but he'll never do it so long as he keeps doing all them jobs. That's what I've told him – I've said it's high time he handed over to somebody else, somebody younger, before it's too late.'

'My berries have allus been good ones,' Joseph managed to interrupt her as he produced another cloud of smoke. 'Nobody can say they were poor; I've allus been in the top few....'

'But never the top one, Joseph!' she

12

snapped. 'For all your work over forty years, you've never made the top. And it's time you did! It's time you took things a bit easier and concentrated on that prize. He is turned seventy-five, Mr Rhea, time's getting short....'

'He doesn't look it,' I felt compelled to say. 'He's obviously had a very contented life!'

'That's because I've tended him so well,' and she smiled suddenly, a surprisingly nice smile, and a proud one. 'He's never gone without his dinner and he's always had clean collars and shirts on Mondays, without fail, both when he was working and since he retired from the railways.'

'Everybody says he's a very lucky chap, having you around.' I knew that the people of Aidensfield regarded Joseph and Mabel as a devoted and happy couple even if she was rather domineering at times. There was always a warm welcome at their small cottage and they could often be seen walking together along the lanes and down the fields – friends as well as man and wife. Unless, of course, the walks were Mabel's idea of putting on a public display of wedded bliss. Certainly, she'd always been ambitious for Joseph, even if he had never become a station master or chairman of

13

British Railways.

Joseph was very popular in Aidensfield and district and was known locally as a Big Catholic. He was known equally well as a Big Gooseberry Man, but the terms did not necessarily mean the same thing. A Big Catholic was one who followed his or her faith with unswerving devotion, attending daily mass as well as Sunday mass and working for the church in various ways. A Big Catholic took the collection, helped with the cleaning and flower rotas, tended the graveyard, worked on the maintenance of the building, assisted the priest on the altar, never missed mass on Holy Days of Obligation, took communion regularly, went to confession, attended benediction and always responded to calls for help by the priest or any member of the congregation.

Joseph did all those things and more, because he was also chairman and secretary of St Aidan's Guild, a somewhat unique but very historic organization. Dating to pre-Reformation days, it was an ancient type of funeral club, one of the few of its kind to survive.

Its members paid a very low monthly subscription which was invested so that deceased members could be given a decent burial irrespective of their wealth or status. The guild also ensured that regular masses would be said for deceased members, particularly upon the anniversary of their deaths. In the event of a death, guild members would attend the funeral in their long grey cloaks with red sashes and linings. The guild would make all the arrangements for the funeral, even digging the grave and arranging refreshments afterwards, and thus no one need suffer a pauper's funeral. The long grey cloaks, worn by male and female members, were originally designed to conceal the clothing of poor and rich alike, thus being great levellers, and the cloaks were owned by the guild. When a member died, the cloak was returned for subsequent reissue to an incoming member.

Joseph Marshall was therefore a very Big Catholic, a term which had nothing to do with the size and shape of the person concerned. The word 'big' was also used on the North York Moors to indicate strength or status because I've heard of big winds, big rivers and big bulls, just as a renowned breeder of blackfaced sheep would be a Big Blackface Man or a famous pig breeder would be a Big Pig Man.

With that definition in mind, the term Big Gooseberry Man or Big Berry Man to be more precise, has two meanings. It means one who is keenly associated with the growing of prize gooseberries or with the aims of the Old Gooseberry Society, but it can also mean a person who actually grows very large gooseberries. Joseph Marshall was therefore both a Big Catholic and a Big Berry Man.

Mabel, on the other hand, had never had a job other than her household duties. They'd had three children, two sons and a daughter, now adults with families of their own. They lived away from the village but kept in close touch with their parents, but Mabel's love of her family had kept her fully occupied and totally content. That devotion was now focused upon her grandchildren although she was a granny who preferred children to be seen or not heard. Now in her early seventies, Mabel had seven grand-children who were frequent visitors and I knew she doted on them even if some regarded her as rather strict.

She was a short and rather stout woman with a round pink face and a head of pure white hair, always neatly styled. Around the house, she always wore a flowered apron over a blue skirt and white blouse, removing it only when she went outside or locked up for the night. She attended village events and functions, but in spite of her forceful views, had never accepted responsibility for anything outside her home, except helping with the cleaning and flower arrangements in St Aidan's Church. Like Joseph, she was also a Big Catholic who claimed she could clean a candlestick far better than any youngster, and that the flowers from Joseph's garden were better than any bought in a shop.

She was quite happy to be one of the crowd and not to take a leading role in any aspect of village life, although she had once been offered the post of president of the Women's Institute. Generally regarded as a very high honour, Mabel had not been tempted and had politely declined.

On this early spring morning, therefore, we continued to chat for a while with Joseph reminiscing over some of the highlights of his berry-growing career and, as he spoke, he filled the room with clouds of pungent smoke. Listening to him, though, I could sense that he would miss the involvement and excitement of his leading role in the world of giant gooseberries, and yet he was resolute in his decision to retire. I think Mabel was the force behind his decision, however, but it was probably a good thing for him.

'Have you told anyone else about your intention?' I did not wish to be responsible for spreading his news around the village until he had made it public.

'I'm doing it tonight,' he said softly. 'We've a meeting of the Old Gooseberry Society: I'm going to make it official.'

'I won't say a word until it is official,' I assured him, adding, 'It'll come as a surprise to them, won't it?'

'I should think it might,' was all he said, but I knew he'd never talk about such private moments in advance of his big announcement. It made me realize that I was rather privileged to learn of his decision in this way, then I wondered if he would also relinquish his church work and other voluntary commitments. Whatever he decided, he would be difficult to replace.

Before leaving the house, I obtained the formal date of the show from him – Monday, 3rd August which was Bank Holiday Monday. The show would be in Aidensfield village hall and the exhibits would be collected from 10.30 a.m. until 1 p.m. and weighed as they arrived.

Prizes would be awarded, the winner being determined by weight alone. The size and appearance of a berry was not a factor in deciding a winner and thus personal opinions could be discounted. So delicate were the scales that they were taken into the village hall on the day prior to the show so they could adjust to the temperature, and then they were tested for accuracy – they were even capable of weighing a pigeon's breast feather. No berries would be accepted after 1 p.m., and once they had been weighed, they would be laid out on the tables beside their exhibitors' names. They'd be separated into their classes and colours – yellows, reds, greens and whites – with certificates for the winners of each class, with the shining silver Aidensfield Cup for the show's heaviest berry – the Supreme Champion. The show would be open to the public from 2.30 p.m. until 5 p.m. That was the pattern every year and on this occasion there seemed to be no need to change that routine.

Although I could have guessed the date and timings (it was always held on August Bank Holiday Monday), I did need this kind of formal confirmation from Joseph just in

19

case there had been a sudden change of venue or opening times. I noted the facts in my pocket book and would later enter them in our events diary at Ashfordly Police Station, along with the name and telephone number of the organizer Joseph Marshall for this one final time.

'Right, thanks, Joseph.' I made my move to leave the happy home. 'I'll attend to the parking side of things, and the security of exhibits and so on. I'll be in touch a few times before the big day, but I hope your decision to retire is accepted, even though no one wants to lose you.'

'There's no such thing as an indispensable man,' said Joseph, with just the tiniest show of emotion and I guessed he didn't really believe those words. 'If you want to know how much you'll be missed, you put your hand in a bucket of water and when you take it out, the hole that remains is a measure of how you'll be missed. That's what my old dad once told me. And it's right! I mean, Mr Rhea, we've got used to being without Winston Churchill, haven't we?'

'We have,' I agreed. 'But he didn't run Aidensfield Old Gooseberry Society, did he?'

'And I'll bet he didn't know a Yellow Woodpecker from an Admiral Beatty,' grinned Joseph.

'Good luck, Joseph,' I said as I reached his garden gate. 'And thanks for the scones and tea, Mabel.'

'We'll see you at mass on Sunday, but come any time, Mr Rhea,' she said. 'Even when he does hand over to somebody else, you're always welcome.'

'Thanks,' I said, and left the Marshalls to their contented life. As I walked along the lane, I admired Joseph's beautifully kept garden with its range of fruit trees, berry bushes, vegetables and flowers, but his neat spread did seem heavily populated with well-pruned, bare-branched gooseberry trees. In sophisticated berry circles, gooseberry bushes are always called trees, and gooseberries are always called berries. Although Joseph had plenty to occupy him in his garden, I did wonder how he would cope without the absorbing interest of his berry society responsibilities to sustain him.

That same afternoon I had to visit Ashfordly Police Station to deliver some crime reports and when I walked into the cramped office, Sergeant Blaketon was chatting to PC Alf

Ventress over a mug of tea. Their conversation was deep and earnest, so much so that they did not immediately notice my arrival. Then Sergeant Blaketon realized I had walked in.

'You'd better pour yourself a mug, then listen to this, Rhea,' Blaketon boomed. 'It affects us all. You might have heard that Sergeant Bairstow is retiring but his departure will bring some changes to our section.'

'Well, fancy that! Old Charlie Bairstow calling it a day! I did hear rumours, Sarge; he'd been telling somebody he was thinking of packing in,' said Ventress. 'But I never thought he'd do it! I thought he'd have to be carried out of his office feet first.'

'Well, he's made his mind up. It's official now. He's put his ticket in and is retiring at the end of the month. There'll be a farewell party, of course, but as you know, he shared duties with me. Ashfordly and Brantsford sections have worked together for some time now, and his replacement will be Sergeant Craddock, Raymond Craddock; he's being posted here from Guisborough.'

'You don't mean Twinkletoes Craddock, the Welsh Wheeler, do you?' There was just a hint of alarm in Alf's voice.

'If you are referring to his ballroom dancing and cycling, then yes, Ventress, I am referring to the Twinkletoed Welsh Wheeler. He replaces Sergeant Bairstow which means he'll have responsibility for Ashfordly section in my absence.'

'It won't be the same, Sarge!' grunted Ventress.

'There's more, Ventress,' continued Blaketon. 'From what I hear, there is going to be much closer co-operation between sections – beats may close, gentlemen, sections may amalgamate. Changes are ahead. It might well happen that Ashfordly and Brantsford section merge with only one sergeant in charge of both.'

'Oh, blimey!' groaned Ventress. 'If Craddock comes here, it'll mean I'll have to get a haircut!'

'And you'll have to have your trousers pressed, and keep all that cigarette ash off your tunic! Sergeant Craddock is a fresh-air fiend, Ventress, a man who likes open office windows even in the middle of winter, and he's also keen on exercise and activity. For others, that is, not just himself!'

'Well, so long as he doesn't want us to have a session of physical jerks every morning.'

'He might just do that, Ventress, although he'll probably be happy enough just throwing all the windows open and stopping you smoking in the office.'

'Stopping me smoking? That's inhuman, Sarge! You can't prevent a hard-working chap from having his little pleasures....'

'What's a pleasure for you might not be a pleasure for others, Ventress!'

'Folks like him don't have any real pleasure, Sarge.'

'And,' continued Sergeant Blaketon with some relish, 'should I decide to retire, then the chances are that he would take command of both Ashfordly and Brantsford sections; they'd be put together to form one unit.'

'But, Sarge, I mean, did I hear that right?' stammered Alf Ventress. 'You're not thinking of retiring as well, are you?'

'It has crossed my mind from time to time, Ventress. I am no spring chicken. I'd rather go voluntarily than be told to retire due to my age, so, yes, if the right opportunity came along, I might just take it. A nice little village post office perhaps? Something to keep my mind occupied and to give me a reason for getting out of bed on a morning.'

'I can't believe I'm hearing all this...'

muttered Ventress. 'I just can't!'

'It's an option that's open to me, that's all. An option. But one I shall be actively considering.'

'I don't know whether I can stand all these changes,' muttered Ventress. 'I'm going to make another cup of tea. Why can't things stay the same, Sergeant? Things were going along very nicely here ... very nicely indeed....'

'Time and tide wait for no man, Ventress!'

'Yes, but can't we make things happen more slowly? In one fell swoop, you're talking about merging Ashfordly and Brantsford, creating large units, bringing in ferocious new sergeants who ban smoking and throw open windows on cold days, wholesale retirements of folks we've got to know so well ... it's all too much for a simple chap like me.'

'We can't afford to become complacent, Ventress,' grinned Blaketon. 'But nothing's set in stone. Our leaders might think of something totally different!'

'If I wasn't on duty, I'd have something stronger in my tea and I don't mean more sugar,' said Ventress. 'I just can't see why people want to keep changing things.'

'It provides work for admin. wallers at

headquarters for one thing,' smiled Blaketon. 'If you are the head of a department with nothing to do, you arrange something called a redevelopment strategy or performance assessment, or a survey on the utilization of capital assets, or a structured reorganization of personnel. That sort of thing keeps your staff busy for months and you get promoted at the end of it.'

'We call it empire building, Sergeant!' grumbled poor old Alf. 'That's what it is. Using us troops as mere pawns in the game.'

We could have discussed these matters for hours but I had to leave because I had arranged a meeting with a man who'd witnessed a road accident in Newcastle; I had to call on the gentleman, a commercial traveller, to obtain a statement for Newcastle police. He lived in Ploatby which was a tiny village on my patch, and so, after entering the date of the Aidensfield Gooseberry Show in our Events Diary, I took my leave of Sergeant Blaketon and the unhappy Alf Ventress.

But it had been a stimulating few minutes. A new Sergeant at Brantsford or even Ashfordly! Although I did not know the incoming Sergeant Craddock I felt it wouldn't be long before I did!

26

That following weekend, I received a report of a crime which, as it transpired, was to become the first of a long series of very puzzling thefts, or larcenies as the crime was then called.

As it was a Sunday, I'd been to early mass and had assisted Joseph with taking the collection. After mass, he'd hailed me and said, 'Well, Mr Rhea, I did it.'

'Made your retirement official, you mean?'

'Aye, handed my resignation in. So now I've nowt to do with next year's gooseberry job. It's funny, knowing I don't have to fret about organizing it the minute this year's is finished.'

'You deserve a rest,' I said. 'It's been well earned. But you'll still be doing your other jobs, here at the church and with the guild?'

'Oh, aye. Well, there's nowt to worry about taking the collection at mass, Mr Rhea, or making sure t'village hall's locked up at night. And t'guild doesn't take up a lot of my time.'

'Well, I hope the Gooseberry Society finds somebody to take over from you – and that you settle down to enjoy your new freedom.'

'I think things will work out well, Mr Rhea. I've nominated somebody I think'll make a good president, so voting papers are being prepared. I'll get it sorted out before I go.'

Joseph always called me Mr Rhea in spite of me knowing him so well, and I left him to finish off his Sunday church duties. I walked up the hill to my home and had just finished lunch when the telephone rang. It was a call from a kiosk in Crampton.

'Is that the Aidensfield policeman?' shouted a distraught voice.

'Speaking. My name is PC Rhea,' I acknowledged.

'I've had my bike stolen,' the man panted. 'Just now, well, within the last hour....'

'Where from?' I asked.

'Here, where I'm ringing from. Crampton. The CTC place where we have lunch, Riverside. Mrs Simpson said I should ring you.'

'Give me a description and I'll circulate it immediately on our radio,' I told him. 'Then wait there, I'll come and see you....'

He told me it was a Frejus make, a gents' Italian-built racing bike with 27" wheels, a silver-grey 24" frame and Derailleur ten-speed gears. The bike, a lightweight racing machine, had aluminium handlebars with blue tape around them; it was fitted with toeclips, a pair of lightweight blue mud-guards and a slim racing saddle with a small saddle-bag containing spanners and a spare tubular tyre. The caller said he used it for road racing as a rule, when it did not have mudguards, but the mudguards had been fitted for today's outing, a leisurely club ride around the North York Moors. The splendid and very distinctive bike was worth £245, a huge sum by some standards; clearly, it was an expert's pride and joy.

As promised, I rang Ashfordly Police Station with the news and ask PC Alf Ventress, the constable on duty, to rapidly broadcast news of the theft to all stations, with special emphasis on notifying police vehicles which were patrolling the vicinity. He said he would do what he could; then I explained I was on my way to speak to the loser and to obtain more information after which I would update my report.

The snag was that, with an expert rider aboard, the bike could be fifteen or even twenty miles away if it had been missing an hour; if it had been placed in the back of a covered van or lorry, of course, it could be forty miles away or more, and out of sight.

I felt the latter was probably the case – no intelligent thief would risk riding such a prominent machine along our country lanes although, to be fair, most thieves do lack genuine brain power. Sometimes, I wonder if that's the origin of the saying – as thick as thieves. However, a search of the locality, highly desirable by the loser, was really a waste of time although an element of luck might enable one of our patrols to quickly locate the bike and its unauthorized taker. It was a forlorn chance, I felt; nonetheless, we would do our best.

Having circulated details I drove to Crampton and made my way to the CTC café. This was Mrs Molly Simpson's Riverside Restaurant, a splendid place with beautiful gardens beside the water. During the summer, the lawns were adorned with lots of tables so that people could eat outside and there was even a small wooden jetty and a rowing boat which could be hired for trips on the river. The indoor restaurant was equally pleasant, with views of both the river and the garden. The café facilities had been approved by the Cyclists' Tourist Club and so the outer wall of the house bore the wheel logo; this meant it was patronized by lots of cyclists, especially during weekends, for they could be sure of a warm welcome and good food. On this occasion, being a cool day in early spring, the cyclists had chosen to eat inside but had left their machines outside the premises.

This was the normal practice. The bikes were all parked in a long row, three or four deep, on the short grass against the outer wall of the garden. Although they were, in effect, standing almost on the village street, none had been locked – at that time, such security measures were not considered necessary. It was a common Sunday sight to see dozens of cycles parked in this way outside cafés and I'd never been aware of a theft in such circumstances. I parked my Mini-van and walked into the grounds, passing the massed ranks of bicycles and eyeing them all, just in case the Frejus was among them, possibly having been overlooked. I guessed there'd be around forty bikes. I did not see the Frejus – but I realized that any one could easily steal a bike as they passed by and ride it or remove it quickly from the scene without anyone noticing. In this case, the owners had all been inside the café for their meal with their precious machines being beyond their vision – so was that something the thief had known in advance? Or had this been an opportunist crime?

As I entered the grounds of the garden restaurant, a tall man detached himself from the others and approached me. They had all assembled outside the restaurant now, awaiting my arrival. My man was clad in cycling gear – a woollen, short-sleeved vest in light blue with a pocket at the rear, dark shorts, cycling shoes with toe-plates on the soles and a peaked cap. He'd be in his late thirties, I reckoned, a slim but powerful man with black hair and prominent dark eyebrows.

'PC Rhea?' He came towards me, the anxiety showing on his face.

'Yes, it was your bike, was it?'

'Yes, any luck?'

'Not yet,' I had to admit. 'I've circulated a description to all our patrols, but if it's been placed in a lorry or van....'

'I know, all my pals here did a quick recce the moment I discovered it had gone. It's been spirited away, Constable. Not ridden, it's such a distinctive bike, I'm sure no one would risk riding it away.'

I established that his name was Larry Whittaker, aged 32, a draughtsman by profession, who lived at Stockton-on-Tees. He'd ridden from Stockton that morning with club members, the run being preplanned with lunch booked at Mrs Simpson's Riverside Restaurant. He'd parked his bike, along with the others, outside the restaurant at 12.30. They'd spent about an hour over the meal, chatting and enjoying the atmosphere as they prepared for the return trip via a different route – along to Scarborough and then back to Stockton through Whitby and Guisborough.

I learnt that his bike had been one of the last to be parked – and thus one of the first available to a thief. Luckily, he had a note of the frame number – FJ 180536 – in his pocket diary and I was able to add that to the details I would incorporate in my written crime report. That number would be invaluable should we find the bike, or even just its remains. Without it, we'd have difficulty establishing ownership – a new owner could claim it was his machine and we'd have problems proving otherwise.

I did have to undertake my own search of the village, just in case someone had hidden the bike as a joke. That was the sort of prank expected of a teenager, or even a jealous colleague.

After confirming that no other cycle had been stolen from this location, I conducted my half-hour hunt with Whittaker and some of his pals helping me, checking places like deserted sheds and barns, behind roadside walls, under the bridge, beside the river and even in the river itself, as well as all likely hiding places.

On that first recce, we encountered some of the residents of Crampton but none had seen anyone taking the bike. From our efforts, we were positive the precious bike had been spirited away from the village and I decided it would have to be recorded as a crime. I asked Larry Whittaker how he was going to return home and he told me Mrs Simpson had a suitable bike, one left at the restaurant months ago by a man who'd become ill during an outing. The fellow had never recovered and had given up cycling, saying she could keep the bike – it was a Rudge, a heavyweight touring cycle, but capable of getting Mr Whittaker back to base. He could return it in due course.

Satisfied that I had all the necessary particulars for my report, I told Mr Whittaker that I would remain in the village for a while, asking the local residents if they could help, with special emphasis on whether they'd seen anyone with a van or lorry around lunch-time, or noticed anyone riding the bike away. Whittaker did say his bike was insured and I told him to inform his insurance company and make a claim; in due course, they'd contact the North Riding Constabulary for confirmation of the crime. And with that, the cyclists mounted their machines and rode away, with Larry Whittaker looking somewhat uncomfortable on the heavy old Rudge. Compared with the lightweight racing cycle he'd lost, it was built like a tank and I reckoned he'd have a sore backside and aching legs by the time he reached Stockton.

I spent a couple of hours in Crampton, knocking on doors and hailing people walking in the streets, but no one had noticed anything remotely suspicious. The truth was, of course, they'd all been in their homes having Sunday lunch as the crime was being committed, but even if a truck had passed through, or if someone had ridden a cycle past their doorways, those actions in themselves would never be regarded as out of the ordinary. In short, my enquiries drew a blank.

From Crampton I drove into Ashfordly to register the crime at the police station, knowing it would be another black mark in our statistics, but at the same time, I accepted it hardly constituted a crime wave. Alf Ventress was in the office and told me he had broadcast details of the theft as I'd requested, but there'd been no results and so I settled down to complete the necessary paperwork. The recording of a crime invariably generated a pile of paper and it was while I was typing my official report that Sergeant Blaketon returned. He'd been visiting the rural constable at Falconbridge.

'Problems, Rhea?' he asked, as he eyed the report in the typewriter before me.

I explained what had happened and told him what I'd done and he nodded in satisfaction, adding, 'It's not just any old bike, then? Not some old heap of rust nicked for spares, by the sound of it?'

'Not at all, Sergeant,' I assured him. 'This is a specialist's machine, a top-grade Italian racing cycle, worth a lot of money.'

'But the thief might not know that,' countered Blaketon. 'If this was an opportunist crime, he'd lift the first bike he got his filthy hands on – and it just happened to be a special one.'

'Or it might have been someone who realized its value,' I added. 'Or it might be someone who knows that cyclists assemble at places like CTC eating-houses with special machines, keen cyclists who buy the best, and that such places are rich picking grounds for cycle thieves.'

'Are you saying there've been other crimes like this?'

'No, Sergeant; so far as I know this is the only one, certainly the only one in our area, but because the bikes are lined up against the wall as the cyclists eat their meal inside the place, they make easy targets.'

'A job for our crime prevention teams, then, to warn cyclists to lock their machines whenever they leave them unattended. Right, well, do what you can – and tell the café owner she ought to put a notice up, telling her customers to lock their bikes. And isn't there that annual church service for cyclists at Thackerston Minster next week? Have words with the vicar and get him to warn everyone who's coming. We don't want crime waves in Crampton and Thackerston, Rhea!'

'Right, Sergeant,' I said, thinking his suggestion was very valid. I should have thought of it myself, but in the rush of the moment, had overlooked Mrs Simpson's valuable crime prevention role although I didn't think the vicar of Thackerston could warn all his incoming flock of cyclists. They came from all over the North of England and even further afield.

'And have words with Greengrass, Rhea,' he added.

'Greengrass?' I puzzled. 'This is hardly his type of work.'

'He deals in second-hand junk, Rhea, spare parts for all sorts of things from washing machines to sewing machines by way of cars, lorries – and bikes.'

'I'll pay him a call,' I assured the sergeant.

'I'll bet he has a few old bikes tucked away among that stuff of his, and I bet he does a reasonable trade in spares.'

'He'd run a mile if anyone offered him that stolen Frejus,' I said. 'It's the sort of bike you'd see used in the Tour de France, not the sort you'd find on a butcher's round in Ashfordly. And any pieces removed from it would hardly fit your average sit-up-and-beg.'

'So far as I'm concerned, Rhea, a bike is a bike, and Greengrass is a rogue. Go and see him.'

# 2

'Have you any spare parts for bikes?' I was standing ankle deep in mud in the rubbish-strewn foldyard at Hagg Bottom, the untidy ranch of Claude Jeremiah Greengrass. The scruffy owner of that esteemed establishment was in front of me with Alfred, his equally unkempt dog at his side. Alfred was sniffing at my legs and I began to wonder if he thought I was a lamp post. I was prepared to beat a hasty retreat at the first sign of any suggestive leg-raising by Alfred.

'They're not putting you lot back in the saddle, are they?' Claude chuckled at the thought. 'Too expensive on the rates, are you, you and your flash little radio controlled Mini-vans? I'm all in favour of bikes for bobbies; it means you can't get anywhere in a rush and it means you get wet and cold with soggy boots and numb fingers and rain down the back of your neck....'

'And it means we can creep up on villains

39

in total silence and catch them red-handed in the act of committing their villainy,' I grinned. 'And bikes provide good exercise, they keep the lungs working and leg muscles in trim ... they're excellent generators of good health!'

'So are you buying a bike or summat? What's all this about? Why are you asking me about spare parts for bikes?' He blinked furiously as he began to ponder the real reason for my presence.

It was clear he was not keen to give me a straight answer – evidently he thought there was some kind of catch or a subtle underhand reason for my presence. In reality, of course, I never expected a straight answer from Claude Jeremiah Greengrass either, no matter how innocent my questioning. Perhaps I was being rather less than honest? But I was dealing with a rogue of renowned resilience!

'I just want to know if you've any good quality and reliable spare bicycle parts for sale,' I persisted.

'No, you don't *just* want to know that. You know very well I've got a shed full of spare parts – chains, gears, wheels, handlebars, pedals, frames, spare tubes and tyres – so what's all this mystery about? If you just want a wheel or a set of front forks, why not just ask for them instead of being so blatantly devious?'

'A bike was stolen earlier today...' I began.

'I knew it! The minute somebody comes onto your patch and nicks something, you think I'm the guilty party ... well, it's not me. I don't nick bikes and I don't buy stolen property. I buy and sell high quality spare parts for all sorts of machines, garden equipment and household gadgets, all obtained legitimately from my suppliers. Not that there's much trade in second-hand bikes or bike parts these days, not in these hills. Folks are turning to motor bikes and cars; bikes are becoming an endangered species round here.'

'This was a special bike, Claude. And I know you didn't take it. I'm not accusing you. It's out of your league, anyway. It's a racing bike, an Italian one, Frejus make. Worth over two hundred pounds.'

'Two hundred quid for a bike? If I pay a fiver for one, I think I've been robbed. At that price, it must be gold plated or mebbe it's jet propelled?'

'It's a specialist's bike, Claude. A racing cyclist had it stolen from Crampton today, at lunch-time. From outside Mrs Simpson's restaurant. I just wondered if you knew anything about a local trade in expensive second-hand bikes.'

'Not me, Constable. I can fix you up with top-of-the range rubber pedals or bells with a very beautiful ringing tone that won't frighten old ladies, or even front wheels that'll take ten times your weight, but not summat as flash as that.'

'But you'll keep your ears and eyes open, just in case you hear something during your travels, or perhaps an incautious remark from one of your wide range of valued customers?' I put to him.

'I'm no copper's nark,' he muttered.

'What's your lorry insurance say about carrying livestock?' I asked, changing the subject completely. 'I thought your insurance covered you for goods other than livestock. I'm sure I saw you carrying a load of sheep....'

'Well, in that case I might just keep my ears to the ground, Constable. Just between you and me, you understand.'

'Good man,' I beamed.

'Nothing promised, mind.'

'OK. And I might not ask to see your insurance certificate this very minute, but nothing's promised for the future! Like tomorrow,' I countered.

'Right, well, it seems we understand each other. But in all honesty, Constable, I can't see why anybody would pinch a bike worth as much as that. It's like pinching summat like the original *Laughing Cavalier* or the *Blue Boy*, or running off with the Crown Jewels – everybody would recognize the loot. Why would anybody risk pinching a bike like that?'

'My thoughts precisely, Claude. Either it's been taken by somebody who knows precisely what he wanted in which case it'll not be seen again in its present form, or else it's been nicked by an opportunist who had no idea what he's got his filthy hands on.'

'If an expert has nicked it, you can bet your bottom dollar it'll never appear on the roads again in the same colours. It'll be repainted, restyled, new bits fitted … and it might be sold for a fraction of its real value.'

'Spoken like a true connoisseur of crime, Claude!'

'Well, us *bona fide* second-hand dealers have to be very careful; we've got to know what's hot and what's not, otherwise we get your mates in the CID coming round to inspect our yards and stock. But if I got that bike offered to me, Constable, I'd not touch it with a barge pole, no matter what the asking price.'

'But you *would* give me a ring and you would note the name of the chap and take the registration number of the vehicle that brought it to you....'

It was now Claude's turn to balk at such a suggestion and to change the subject which he did very swiftly. 'So what's all this about old Joseph Marshall, eh? Giving up his gooseberry work.'

'He's not giving it all up,' I corrected Claude. 'It's just his presidency he's giving up. He wants to spend more time tending his trees; he intends competing in the future.'

'Well, I hope he never wins!' snapped Claude. 'For all his church-going and holiness, he once did me out of a first prize, did Holy Joe. When he was supervising the weighing, I should have had a winner with my Thatcher – in fact, I *would* have had a winner with that berry, but according to him, it was only worth second place. That's after he made me cut off a bit of its stalk ... that bit would have just put it in the winning place, Constable. Them extra few grains would have made all the difference, the weight of a magpie's tail feather it was. As narrow as that.'

'You're only allowed a certain length of stalk, Claude, you know that. Stalks do add weight to a berry. You can't include half a bush in your exhibits, that would be unfair. Joseph's as honest as anyone on this earth. He was just doing his job.'

'Exceeding his duty, you mean. Being officious. Getting his own back on me just because he said I'd once sold him a bagful of rotten apples, and that was an accident ... I've never been a fan of the gooseberry society since then; his holier-than-thou attitude put me right off. Fancy praying for a win and then chopping my stalk off! I am on the committee, you know, been there years and never been sacked. My name's

45

still there even though I never attend meetings these days ... being a successful self-employed businessman, I'm much too busy.'

'I had no idea you were a Big Gooseberry Man, Claude?' I was genuinely surprised at this revelation. I'd never seen him at any of the shows.

'I've been a member for years. Like my father before me and his father before that. I've grown some good berries in my time. I've got my trees round the back of the house, genuine Aidensfield trees grown from family cuttings. Come on, you can have a look at them, just to show you I can tell the truth!'

And before I could tell him I'd rather call back another time, he was leading the way to the rear of his ramshackle house, scattering squawking hens and quacking ducks on the way and opening the string-held broken gate to admit us to the back garden. I felt obliged to follow. Alfred the dog galloped ahead of us, probably hoping that something exciting was about to happen and then I found myself tramping through a spacious bed of nettles and briars as we made for a small area of cultivated ground. Immediately beyond that cultivated patch were some gooseberry trees, as yet without new foliage, and they occupied what I felt was a rather dark and shady corner of Claude's garden – if this rather unkempt patch could be called a garden. It looked more like a rough shoot to me or a portion of land the moor was about to reclaim.

The rear wall of Claude's house occupied one side of the gooseberry patch while another border appeared to be the wall of a wooden shed of some kind. The two other sides of the gooseberry patch were open and I could see there was about a dozen trees, but they were smothered with goosegrass, convolvulus and tall strands of dead grass. It was a miracle they produced anything.

'There you are, the Greengrass forest of gooseberry trees,' he beamed with obvious pride. 'My inheritance. Part of the family history.'

'You've done well to keep them alive and flourishing, Claude. So when did you last show a berry?' I asked him.

'A few years ago.' He frowned and blinked

as he tried to recall the actual time. 'I can't remember exactly, but it's not since I had to cut my stalk off. That ruined it for me, I lost all confidence in them powers-that-be.'

'You know Joseph's never won the Supreme Championship,' I commented.

'Too busy with his organizing, Constable. But now you mention it, I'll make sure Holy Joe never does win it!' grinned Claude. 'If I thought he was going to seriously have a go for the Supreme, I might be tempted to tend my trees a bit better and feed 'em with top quality muck, then do a bit of pruning and thinning before I submit my entries. Stalks or no stalks, I still know how to grow a big berry or two.'

'I've heard Joseph is going for it this year,' I smiled. 'The Supreme Championship, I mean. To mark his retirement. And he does know his berries – if anybody can grow a winner, it's Joseph,' I said.

'If that's what he's up to, then it'll be my aim to stop him and to win this year!' chuckled Claude. 'I can just see his face … and I'll make sure all his stalks are cut off! If Holy Joe thinks we're all going to sit back and let him win just this once because he's retiring, he's got another think coming!'

'He's a very decent and friendly sort of chap!' I defended Joseph.

'Joseph Marshall! He's not. He's as cunning as a cartload of monkeys, make no mistake about that. As deep as they come is Holy Joe, Constable. Don't you let yourself be fooled by his friendly rustic nature or his hands clasped in supplication.'

I decided to make my own judgement about Joseph as I changed the subject once again. 'Aren't your trees growing in too much shadow?' I commented. 'They won't get enough sun there, will they?'

'They've done all right so far.' But I was aware that, following my remarks, he did study them with renewed interest.

'Being in the shade like that, won't it encourage powdery mildew on your berries?' I continued. 'That shed's shielding them from most of the day's sunshine and I'd say they're a bit short of regular ventilation in that corner. A flow of regular fresh air and gentle moorland breezes wouldn't do them any harm.'

'It's my new hen house. I had it built there a few years back as there's nowhere else to put it. I know it's blocking the sunshine and obstructing the breezes, but I've never bothered because I'd given up showing big berries – until now, that is.'

'So if you can't move your shed, why not move your berry trees to a new location? Put them somewhere where they can get sun and better ventilation? Even if you don't intend showing the berries or growing giants that will astound the world, you'd be sure of a good crop, enough to provide for a tasty gooseberry pie or two.'

'Well, if I'm going to beat Holy Joe's berry this year, I'll have to do that, Constable. Freshly tilled ground with a spot of good mannishment might help an' all. And none of these fancy modern chemicals, they make your berries taste of nowt. I've a patch out there, in the sunshine, that used to hold my midden heap, it should be pretty fertile I'd say, virgin ground almost.'

'It sounds ideal,' I agreed.

'It is. I once grew a prize-winning marrow there. This could be a serious berry-growing year for me now that you've told me what cunning old Holy Joe's up to.'

'I wish you the best of luck!' I grinned at Claude's new resolve.

'I'll need it. Now I've got work to do, and I know you've got to find your cycle thief, and Alfred wants his tea....'

'I get the message. I've got people to see as well, Claude. Well, thanks for the guided tour of your berry patch, and I hope all your stalks are little ones. And don't forget to keep an eye open for stolen bikes!'

He grunted some sort of reply but did not accompany me off his premises and disappeared indoors to make a meal for himself and his dog. After spending some time wiping the mud off my boots, I motored away, intrigued by Claude's reaction to Joseph's impending assault on the Supreme Championship. I had no idea there was such feeling within the gooseberry world and wondered how many other people would want to defeat Joseph out of spite. Fair competition was one thing – revenge was quite another. I was becoming very interested in the outcome of this forthcoming contest and wanted to see the huge berries that would be featured. Every year there were hopes that a world champion would be produced – would that happen this year, I wondered? The world champion was, quite simply, the heaviest gooseberry ever grown in the world. In 1952, prior to my time as the constable of Aidensfield, that was achieved by Tom Ventress of Egton Bridge, a village deep in the North York Moors not far from Whitby.

He was renowned for growing huge berries, but his mammoth 1952 specimen weighed 30 drams and 8 grains. It was talked about for years afterwards – and still is.

But more immediately, I had other important things to concern me. A crime for example. First, I drove back to Crampton for a chat with Mrs Simpson; she'd already placed a large handwritten notice on the noticeboard of her café to warn her customers about cycle thefts and there was a note to the effect that bikes could be brought into her garden and parked on the inside of the wall rather than the outside where they were so vulnerable.

'I don't want my reputation or my income affected by thieves.' She was a small and rather independent woman whose husband had died in the war. She earned her living by making full use of the spacious family home as a café and doing most of the cooking and baking herself. She was renowned for her chocolate cakes and fruit loaves. Her hair was turning grey now but her pleasant round face usually bore a smile and she seemed very happy in her chosen work. Certainly, cyclists from a huge catchment area knew of her and her food but her establishment was patronized by other diners too. But cyclists were her favourite, possibly because she and her husband had been keen cyclists in their youth, albeit preferring to tour rather than race.

'I wondered if there is any kind of link between you and the other CTC approved places,' I asked, noting she had closed early for this March Sunday.

Nonetheless, she produced a mug of tea for me and a piece of apple pie and I settled at a table to enjoy myself.

'Not really,' she said. 'The CTC itself is the only link. Why?'

'I think all places where cyclists gather and leave their machines outside for a considerable period of time, should be warned about this theft, and the likelihood of others. And we need to warn cyclists who attend other events in large numbers.'

'Like Thackerston Sunday you mean?'

'Yes, that's one example, and I'm sure there are others in the region.'

'The man who lost his bike, Mr Whittaker, said he would ask the CTC to contact other places like mine, all their recommended cafés for example, and to warn all the affiliated clubs,' she smiled. 'And he said he would send a note up to *Cycling*, that's their magazine, but he didn't think his efforts would produce much in the way of publicity because his is the only bike to have been taken. As he said, it's hardly a crime wave, hardly a major problem.'

'It's important though, because I want to prevent a crime wave,' I told her. 'If people think they can steal bikes as easily as they took Mr Whittaker's, we might have a return visit or two by the villains. Other people running places like yours will suffer from thieves while some unfortunate cyclists will lose their pride and joy.'

'You really think that, Mr Rhea?'

'If someone steals and gets away with it without any real hassle, they'll try it again, Mrs Simpson. And good bikes of the kind your customers use will bring a lot of cash. We need to take this very seriously.'

'Yes, I agree. I'm pleased you are taking it so seriously,' she said.

'So, have you heard any more about the theft?' I asked. 'From the local people? They often see and hear things.'

'I hope the thieves leave me alone. I don't want them to keep stealing from here. I'd lose my reputation. But no, I haven't heard anything, although one or two locals have mentioned the crime but they saw nothing, Mr Rhea.'

I told Mrs Simpson about the steps I had taken, adding that I was going to call on the vicar of Thackerston later that night, and then I thanked her for her helpfulness, particularly in lending a bike to Larry Whittaker for his ride home.

'He managed to get home on it even if he was a bit stiff and sore,' she smiled. 'He has another lightweight bike; racing cyclists often have two or three machines. He'll return mine by van in the near future although I said he could keep it. He's heard nothing about his own bike, Mr Rhea; he seems to accept it has vanished into thin air.'

'We've had no other thefts reported,' I told her. 'But we do issue a Stolen Cycles Supplement which circulates all bike shops and dealers, so let's hope we can trace it through them.'

I remained for a short time, chatting about her children who lived away from Crampton and then left. I liked Mrs Simpson but had never discovered her Christian name. Everyone called her Mrs Simpson. Although it was growing dark as I continued to patrol my beat, I did park the van from time to time to make careful searches of several places where the Frejus might have been dumped.

After all, if a child had stolen the bike, or if some passing youth had taken a fancy to it, they'd probably find it difficult to control while riding, bearing in mind its racing frame with steeply angled front forks, its rat-trap pedals fitted with toeclips, its narrow saddle and its very hard rubber tyres. Riding this kind of sophisticated racing machine was a far cry from pedalling a sedate Hercules or Raleigh roadster.

I had to consider the likelihood it had been dumped, but I did not find it nor did I find anyone who had seen it. By the time I had completed that shift, I felt sure the bike had been spirited away from my patch by someone who would completely disguise it and I would endorse my crime report accordingly. Having completed that search, I decided to visit the Reverend Jason Chandler who was vicar of Crampton, but who held responsibility for the tiny ancient Minster at Thackerston, the venue of the annual Cyclists' Sunday.

The cycling clubs of Britain called it Thackerston Sunday and came in their hundreds to attend a special church service in the ancient minster, once a teaching centre for the Catholic faith, but now a tiny Anglican church. The event known as Thackerston Sunday had been held regularly since 1925, missing only one Sunday during World War II when the vicar suffered a minor injury through a piece of flying shrapnel as a bomb dropped on the moorland above the village. He'd been walking his dog nearby at the time and had narrowly missed death. The dog had fled, never to be seen again. In addition to attracting cyclists from all the northern counties and further afield, it also attracted top preachers, including the Archbishop of York, several politicians and other people in the public eye.

There was always wide publicity both before and after the gathering; once the morning service was over the assembled cyclists either made their long way home, or continued a tour of the moors after having sandwiches and flasks in and around Thackerston or perhaps calling at a local pub for a snack.

Although Larry Whittaker had promised to alert the CTC and all its associated clubs and members, I felt the Reverend Chandler should be aware of the risk because instead of attracting forty or so cyclists like Mrs Simpson, his congregation would be something like 300, or even more. The church could seat around 180 if they squeezed themselves into the narrow, ancient pews, and the rest would have to stand in the aisles and other available spaces, even spilling outside into the church grounds. Having allowed the Reverend Chandler time to complete his Sunday evening services, I drove into the vicarage grounds and rang the doorbell.

'Ah, PC Rhea,' he greeted me. 'Just in time for a sherry!'

He waved me inside, bidding me to leave my cap on the stand in the hall as he led me into his spacious lounge. A coal fire was burning and Mrs Chandler was knitting beside it, also with a large sherry at her side.

'Mrs Chandler,' I acknowledged her.

'Hello, Mr Rhea, do come in,' she smiled, and I felt I was welcome.

Without checking that I really wanted a sherry, Jason Chandler produced a large glass from his cabinet, poured a generous helping of dry sherry and handed the full glass to me.

'Sit down,' he invited, indicating an easy chair.

He was a man in his middle fifties, small and rather compact, with a head of fine grey hair, rimless spectacles and a keen interest in everything around him. He'd written a history of Crampton, for example, then a history of the local parish church, and now he was working on a similar history of Thackerston. 'You've met Pauline?' he referred to his wife.

'Yes, at the last garden fete,' I reminded him. 'You looked after me very well, Mrs Chandler – cool drinks on a hot day are ideal for busy policemen! But, now, well, first I must say I'm sorry to call so late in the evening.'

'Nonsense, it's only eight o'clock!' he smiled. 'So what can we do for you?'

I explained about the cycle theft at Crampton and told him what Mr Whittaker intended to do with regard to warning other clubs and individuals, but I then referred to the forthcoming Thackerston Sunday and asked if he could help in any way to advise the incoming cyclists to adopt some kind of security for their machines.

'I'm in daily contact with the organizers,' he assured me. 'All I can do, Mr Rhea, is tell them what you've told me and ask them to warn their club members. A high proportion of our congregation are not club members, they're individuals who come along for the day. I fear we are not going to be able to warn everyone.'

'I realize that, but if you could warn as many as possible, then I'm sure word would pass among them as they assemble for the service. I will come to patrol outside the church during the service, my uniform should deter any likely thief, and I would imagine the cycling clubs will recruit volunteers to guard their machines.'

'Right, I understand. Some do stay outside the church anyway, late-comers as a rule because we can't accommodate them all inside. But I'll stress the risks every time I speak to any of them during the coming week, whether they're organizers or just members of the congregation.'

'Thanks, that will be a great help.'

'Good, then before I commence the service – it begins at eleven o'clock by the way and runs for about an hour – I'll give members of the congregation a further reminder and enough time to pop outside to secure their bikes or to arrange guardians if they think it's necessary. Sadly, we can't warn everyone.'

'That's all I want, I couldn't ask for more

co-operation,' I smiled, sipping the sherry. 'I just hope that the Thackerston Sunday isn't a target for our cycle thief.'

'I shall pray for him,' smiled the vicar. 'Now, Mr Rhea, while you are here, perhaps you could settle a mystery for me.'

'Of course,' I told him. 'If I can. Just ask.'

'I've heard on the proverbial grape vine that Joseph Marshall has resigned as president of Aidensfield Old Gooseberry Society. To be honest, I can't believe it. I didn't get to the meeting, I had a church event to divert me. He's been there years, hasn't he? A true rock of foundation! I just cannot imagine Joseph being happy without some commitment to his beloved gooseberry show – and I must admit I can't imagine the show running without him.'

'Yes, he has decided to retire but he doesn't leave until after the next show,' I confirmed. 'It's a pity because he was a good president. He would always listen to others but at the same time always knew his own mind. He had acquired a lot of wisdom over the years, Mr Chandler. And he used it to good advantage.'

'It won't be easy to find anyone quite so good but I do accept that change isn't always a bad thing. So who's the new president going to be?' he asked.

'I've no idea, I haven't heard. I couldn't attend the meeting either; I was on duty that evening, doing a spell in Ashfordly,' I had to admit. 'The candidate has to be drawn from members of the committee, so that narrows the field somewhat, and I think there has to be a two-thirds majority in the voting. Only committee members can vote, too, and it's done on voting slips – secretly! Joseph has proposed a candidate, I believe. Anyway, it's clear you have a keen interest in the Aidensfield Old Gooseberry Society. Are you a member?' I asked, almost as an afterthought.

'Yes I am, as a matter of fact, although I've never shown my berries neither am I on the committee. In the years I've grown them, they've never approached anything like the required sizes, they're more for making pies than creating astonishment in the eye of the beholder. But I was thinking of having a go this year, oddly enough. Just the other week, I read that some gooseberries flourish under sycamore trees and the next day I discovered that a young sycamore had established itself in my garden. It's almost an omen, isn't it? It is now quite tall, and, Mr Rhea, my berries are direct descendants of genuine Aidensfield stock. Lord Kitchener variety, they are. White ones. So I do qualify to show my berries.'

'I sense there's a lot of interest this year,' I said. 'Perhaps Joseph's decision has focused a few minds on the society and its aims.'

'You could be right, but if we are members, we should really play our part. So this year I might just do a spot of judicious pruning, swot up on the best food for my trees and see about competing – with a bit of divine assistance from above! I think our local show is a wonderful thing. To concentrate solely on gooseberries is a marvellous idea, so unique – no flowers or vegetables or children's drawings or the work of amateur artists ... just gooseberries of immense proportions. Wonderful stuff!'

'From time to time, incomers try to change the rules so they include flowers and fruit and so on,' I told him. 'But we've managed to resist them so far – thanks to Joseph Marshall. He would never let newcomers change anything, even though some have managed to wheedle themselves onto the committee.'

'I wonder why incomers always try to change things?'

'It's usually those who are not genuine

country people,' I commented.

'Perhaps that's the reason. They come from towns and cities, and move into a village because they have a dream of what village life is like, and promptly try to change things so that we're downgraded into something dreadful like suburbia with street lights, traffic lights, no parking signs and speed limits. And they object to the smells and sounds and character of the landscape, like crowing cockerels, muddy roads and pig manure! It makes me wonder why they want to come and live here.'

'Well, a good winter with a few feet of snow and freezing fog often sees them rushing back to the city streets,' I laughed.

'It was good of you to call, Mr Rhea. And I do hope the new gooseberry president is worthy of his office, whoever he is,' said the vicar.

And on that note, I left, making a mental note to attend the Thackerston Cyclists' Service next Sunday morning. I felt I had done what I could so far as preventing further cycle thefts was concerned and after a final patrol of my beat, returned home at ten o'clock that evening and booked off duty.

In the week that followed, I learned that the new president of Aidensfield Old Gooseberry Society was Jacob Butterworth, a 59-year-old sheepfarmer from Rock Head Farm, Aidensfield. A sturdy man of medium height with broad shoulders and a thickset figure, his trade mark was a red waistcoat which he wore whenever he dressed up to leave the farm. He wore it with his sports jacket or with his best dark suit, and without exception he always loomed smart and well-dressed. Some said his ruddy complexion matched his waistcoats, for he did have a very weathered face, huge hands and whopping feet which he usually encased in brogue shoes.

Jacob specialized in the blackface breed which he ran on the open moors above his premises and he was chairman of the local branch of the Blackface Sheepbreeders' Association. Also a stalwart of the Old Gooseberry Society, Jacob was a popular choice who was known across the entire North of England as a very fair man with a deep knowledge of every aspect of rural life. An expert in many subjects, he was modest by nature and yet he was a highly successful farmer whose wife, Lorna, had recently been appointed secretary of Aidensfield

Women's Institute.

They were much involved in various other aspects of Aidensfield community. Their three grown-up sons were all working within an agricultural background – Stephen was a veterinary surgeon, Terry was a livestock auctioneer and Frank was a gamekeeper. It transpired that Jacob's stock records were due for their quarterly inspection by me and so, very soon after the announcement of his new appointment, I found myself sitting at the huge scrubbed wooden kitchen table enjoying a large mug of coffee and a plate of apple pie and cheese. This was my ten o'clock snack; all the farms in the area provided such snacks for all their callers. Jacob's stock register was on the table before me – it was up to date and in order, as I knew it would be, and so I added my signature beneath the final entry and then said, 'So you're the new gooseberry president, Jacob, I hear?'

'Aye, Mr Rhea, I am. I tried to tell 'em I was a bit too busy with other things, but our committee voted me in and said they thought I'd be the right bloke for the job. Anyroad, we've only a handful of meetings a year, and the annual show. And I shan't do every job like old Joseph did – as soon as

I'm in the hot seat, I'll be looking for a secretary and a weighman and a chairman of committee. I'll spread the workload around – there's plenty of blokes on that committee who've nowt to do. But they'll soon find themselves taking a bit of responsibility, or resigning!'

'The committee won't object to all those sudden changes, then?' I laughed.

'Not if they think it's their own idea!' he chuckled. 'I'll make sure they give their approval to it all – I've sat on a few committees in my time, Mr Rhea, and I know how to get 'em to do what I want! And another thing, I expect 'em all to set an example by submitting berries to the annual show.'

'A sort of do as I do and not do as I say,' I smiled.

'Aye, well, the way I see it is that it's no good being on the committee if you sit there and do nowt, that's my reasoning, Mr Rhea.'

At that moment, I thought of Claude Jeremiah Greengrass, a long-term committee member who never seemed to attend a meeting. I was sure there were others like him. But even now, I could see Jacob was going to make a good impact –

and I felt sure his work would strengthen the society, and not weaken it as would the introduction of fruit and flowers to the show tables. The committee had chosen well – and the society was going to be in good hands for the foreseeable future. With a forceful president like this, I might even try to grow my own giant berries!

The week passed without any further memorable incident. The following Sunday, I attended early mass at St Aidan's and again helped Joseph with the collection. I thought he looked rather pale and thinner around the face, but I passed no comment. He did not complain that he was feeling unwell and so, in spite of a twinge of concern, I refrained from drawing attention to his gaunt appearance.

Soon afterwards, I found myself heading for Thackerston in full uniform to perform my crime prevention duties outside the ancient, tiny Thackerston Minster.

Although the Cyclists' Service was not due to begin until 11 a.m., I decided to arrive around 10.15 a.m. because by that time, people would be assembling, even if they were merely chatting outside and renewing acquaintanceships from previous years. In spite of my early start, there was a gathering of about forty cyclists when I arrived, and they had assembled outside the little stone church to chat and sip coffee from their flasks. Their bikes were lined up against the iron railings which bordered the lane – Church Lane was about a hundred yards long with a car-park at the end and it would accommodate hundreds of bikes against its boundary railings. Some bikes were already chained to the railings and others bore padlocks and chains around their wheels. One group had a huge chain through several machines and this anchored them all to the iron rails behind. I wondered how on earth that chain had been transported here, for some of these cyclists had ridden a long distance – trips of more than a hundred miles were not unknown – but after parking my van in the church car-park, I moved among the riders, chatting and telling them about last week's theft.

I was pleased to learn that a considerable number had taken steps to secure their bikes, so clearly our efforts had borne fruit, although many did turn up without any form of security for their machines. My uniform would have to protect the vulnerable – that's if our thief did turn up. If he did arrive, however, it would not be easy spotting him among such a large crowd, particularly if he dressed in cyclist's clothing. The church's access road, the car-park and the church itself were thronged with colourful people, men and women of all ages and more than a scattering of children. In some respects, it was like a crowd of spectators at the Cup Final.

Just before the service started, however, the Reverend Chandler came outside and announced that the proceedings were about to start. The crowd dwindled as the riders filed in and I could hear the organist pumping forth her music as voices were raised for the first hymn – 'Ride On, Ride On In Majesty'. But several riders did remain outside, guardian angels for their friends' valuable machines and I spent some time chatting to them as the service progressed within. I patrolled around the exterior of the church making sure my uniform was highly visible to any lurking felon and eventually, as the church clock struck twelve noon, the service concluded with the final hymn, 'Return O Wanderer To Thy Home'. Eventually, the congregation filed out with lots of small groups forming; some cyclists rode off quite quickly, clearly having a long journey home while others debated whether to join forces for further conversations or to have their packed lunches here, or to pop into a convenient pub or café.

It took a long time for them all to disperse and although most of them departed within twenty minutes or so, I could not leave until the last cycle had been claimed by the last owner and that did not happen until one o'clock. I watched in some relief as the final rider went to retrieve the final cycle from its place against the railings, unlocked it and rode off with a cheerful wave. Every rider had a bike upon which to ride home! None had been stolen. I issued a long sigh of relief. Then the Reverend Chandler emerged from the church and smiled at me.

'Any problems?' he called upon seeing me.

'No, everything went fine! No thefts!' I must have sounded very relieved.

'Thanks for your attention today,' he called again.

'And for your help during the week,' I responded. 'Clearly, most of them came prepared. But it all went well. I can go home now and enjoy my lunch.'

'And me!' And so we parted.

Mary had my Sunday lunch ready although there was no hurry for me to consume it. There was no requirement for me to finish it within my permitted three-quarters of an hour meal break because I was working discretionary duties today. So long as I completed my eight hours on duty, it did not matter how they were organized; consequently, I settled down for a leisurely family meal of roast beef and Yorkshire pudding followed by apple crumble. All very fattening but all very nice for a busy working chap with a big appetite! But at 2.15, just as I was about to tuck into some cheese and biscuits with a cup of coffee, the telephone rang. Because it was a duty day for me, I answered it. Had I been off duty, then Mary would have accepted the call.

'Aidensfield Police, PC Rhea,' I responded.

'Ah,' said the voice. 'You are on duty, Constable?'

'Yes, I am … who's that? Can I help you?'

'You can. You can get yourself down to the Hopbind Inn at Elsinby because I have just had my racing cycle stolen. And it is a valuable one!'

'Oh dear,' I groaned. 'Yes, well, I'll come immediately. Perhaps if I had a description now, I could circulate it to our patrols?'

'Yes, right; well, here it is.' And the caller

provided me with the brief description of an orange-coloured racing cycle, Jack Taylor make with a 24 inch frame and fitted with a ten-speed Derailleur gear, narrow racing saddle, black lightweight mudguards, 27 inch racing wheels with tubular tyres, and a small saddle-bag containing tools and a spare tubular tyre.

'I'll radio our patrols immediately,' I promised the caller. 'And neighbouring police forces. Then I'll come and see you. You'll remain at the Hopbind Inn until I arrive?'

'Yes, I will.'

'And your name?' I asked.

'Raymond Craddock,' he said. 'Sergeant Raymond Craddock.'

And, inwardly, I groaned.

# 3

Sergeant Craddock was a tall and rather slender man with tidy light brown hair, a very fresh complexion surrounding sharp, fox-like features and quick grey eyes which never seemed to be still. He was dressed in a blue and white cycling vest with short sleeves, tight black shorts and black cycling shoes with toe plates beneath the soles. As I eased my official van to a halt outside the Hopbind Inn at Elsinby, I guessed his identity immediately because he was standing outside the pub, clearly awaiting my arrival whilst his companions were enjoying their drinks and snacks indoors. Even before I could clamber out of my little van, he came to the driver's door in a state of some suppressed agitation. I did manage to extricate myself from the vehicle, however, and stood beside the van as I prepared to deal with him.

'At last!' he said. 'You must be PC Rhea?' I could see he was striving to remain calm in my subordinate presence. I noted that his

74

fists were clenched as he spoke; clearly, the loss of his precious cycle had severely shaken him. I felt he would now have more sympathy for any victims of crime with whom he may have to deal.

'Yes, I'm PC Rhea. You must be Sergeant Craddock.'

'Yes, that's me. Soon to be a member of this section. So, PC Rhea, tell me what you've done to trace my cycle.'

I began to explain, but he interrupted, 'I paid a lot of money for that cycle, PC Rhea, a lot of hard-earned money – and some bloody toe-rag decides he has more right to it than me! I hope you trace it – well, what I mean is, I hope *we* trace it. All of us. All members of the constabulary.'

Although his words had a definite ring of the North Riding of Yorkshire in them, and their vowels, they contained more than a hint of musical Welsh, an interesting combination. I explained I'd already circulated a preliminary description of his cycle and referred to the previous theft, adding I'd earlier taken measures to bring the crimes to notice of the secretaries of all cycle clubs who were affiliated to the CTC. I stressed our particular emphasis on places where lots of cyclists left their machines unattended.

'Good, yes, very good. You could hardly have done more. And I was pleased to see you patrolling at the Thackerston service – the vicar did warn us all, you know, but who would think the thief would strike at a quiet pub like the Hopbind? It was my fault – I did chain my bike at the service because that's where I thought the thief would strike. But no, he did not – he fooled us, PC Rhea, he's a man of guile, mark my words, therefore we must use guile to catch him.'

'No one can be a hundred per cent secure against a determined thief, Sergeant.'

'And don't we all know it? But if I had followed my own advice and chained my cycle, well, it might have been a different story.'

'Then he might have stolen someone else's, Sergeant. Only a few of these are locked, even now.'

'All very true, very true indeed. Well, the dastardly deed's been done, so shall we get the formal bit over? For a start, you'll need my personal particulars for your crime report, won't you?'

We sat in the van as I obtained the necessary details and wrote the required statement. Next, I learned that his bike was worth around £180 and it was following those formalities that I discovered our local cycle thefts were not the first or only ones. Craddock told me there'd been a similar series in the north-east – Middlesbrough and County Durham had, between them, experienced a total of fifty thefts over the past twelve months or so, but my two crimes were the first in the North Riding of Yorkshire.

I had not been notified of those distant thefts because they were committed many miles away in different force areas although that information would have filtered to me in due course. Scant details of the crimes would appear on forthcoming Stolen Cycle Supplements which were distributed throughout the region. From what Craddock told me, it seemed all those cycles stolen in County Durham and Middlesbrough had been taken on Sundays from places where large numbers of cyclists had gathered and left heir machines unattended. Furthermore, all the thefts comprised expensive racing cycles. Beyond any doubt there was a pattern to these crimes and equally beyond doubt, they were being perpetrated by the same person or gang of thieves. Now that I was aware of those earlier crimes, I would actively seek further details about them even though they were not all local crimes – they were regional offences with at least three police forces involved.

So far as I knew, there was no co-ordinator for the enquiries with each force dealing individually with their crimes. Things had changed because a police officer was now a victim and I wondered if Sergeant Craddock might collate all the available information. His efforts would necessarily be limited by distance and lack of effective communications, but his current station, Guisborough, was very convenient for the Teesside conurbation. There, cycling was a thriving sport and pastime and he would have lots of contacts and cycling friends to help, but his new station, Brantsford was at the other side of the moors, a small market town some thirty miles or so from Middlesbrough and Teesside in general.

That would not help Craddock, but he seemed quite pleased with my actions and expressed an opinion that professional cycle thieves were operating. For that reason, the likelihood of recovering any of the stolen machines was remote. They were being stolen for a specific market, he felt; they might even be shipped to the Continent where cycle racing was a major sport. As we chatted, he calmed down and relaxed slightly, although he did continue to smart from the indignity of becoming a victim of crime.

Finally, I asked if he had any problems in returning home without transport. He said his wife was driving across the moors to Brantsford today, her mission being to measure the windows for curtains in their new home at Brantsford Police station house, and the rooms for new carpets. If a message could be sent to her to wait for him, then perhaps he could beg a lift to Brantsford with me? After all, he was not a member of the public wanting a taxi service, but a police officer.

It might even be said he was investigating a crime during the trip! Not wishing to argue about carrying off-duty officers in official vehicles on non-police business, first I drove him to my police house at Aidensfield from where I telephoned Sergeant Bairstow at Brantsford Police Station. Mrs Craddock, it seemed, had not yet arrived and so the arrangements were made for her to await her marooned husband. I drove Sergeant Craddock to Brantsford, still clad in his cycling outfit, from where he would be conveyed home minus his precious bike.

'So it's big-time crime, is it?' boomed Sergeant Blaketon at Ashfordly Police Station when later I broke the news to him.

'So it would seem, Sergeant,' I had to agree. 'If all the stolen bikes are worth as much as those taken from my beat, we're talking of over twelve thousand pounds' worth of stolen property. That's a big sum for our "Undetected Crime" statistics.'

'Well, we don't want those kind of crimes in our section, Rhea, so we'd better get ourselves organized to prevent them. Right, I'll have words with the rest of the men, and I'll get them to visit every CTC café and every haunt of massed ranks of cyclists. The least we can do is to frighten off our phantom bike thief.'

'And send him to work into another area? Maybe that's why he's given up in Durham and Middlesbrough?' I said. 'Maybe their preventative efforts have driven him down to Yorkshire.'

'Then we'll drive him back, Rhea! No itinerant cycle thief is going to ruin my crime figures!'

Later that day, I conducted further enquiries in and around Elsinby but no one had seen the thief or noticed anything suspicious. Most of the Sunday regulars at the Hopbind Inn had seen the party of cyclists arrive, itself not an unusual event in the village, but none had seen anyone surreptitiously making off with a bike. As one regular said, 'Blokes on bikes were coming and going all the time. Some alone, some in twos and threes, others in bigger groups.'

I tried to elicit any information about lone cyclists who had been seen riding away, but gleaned nothing of value – after all, Craddock's orange-coloured bike should be easily noticed, I would have thought, but no one could remember it. In the eyes of most beholders, it seemed, a racing bike was just a racing bike, rather like trying to identify one sheep from another in a large flock. I searched the lanes and likely hiding places in and around Elsinby, but there was no sign of the bike, and I made sufficient fuss about it so that if anyone did find it abandoned in their fields or gardens or barns, they'd contact me immediately. But, like Sergeant Craddock, I felt we'd seen the last of the orange-coloured Jack Taylor cycle, at least in its current form.

When I returned home, I made a note to

ring the admin. departments of the Durham Constabulary Crime Prevention office and its counterpart in Middlesbrough Borough Police Headquarters on Monday morning (such departments did not operate at weekends) with the object of being sent personal copies of their Stolen Cycle Supplements. Copies were distributed to Ashfordly Police Station but I wanted my own so that I could spend time, even my own off-duty time, studying them.

There just might be some valuable clues tucked away in those reports which, as Craddock had said, now went back a whole year.

With this kind of mystery to occupy my mind and my time, along with the more routine work I had to complete as a rural constable, I gave little thought to Joseph Marshall and his forthcoming retirement from the world of giant gooseberries. I did, however, see him regularly at mass on Sunday, although on most occasions I had to dash away without chatting to him. I did note, however, that he continued to lose weight – it was very obvious because his clothes were hanging so loosely about him. When I asked how he was feeling, he said he was fine and made no complaint about his health. As a passing thought, I did wonder if he was on a diet of some kind but didn't press the matter.

A month passed without any further cycle thefts in our area although there was one at Ripon in the West Riding of Yorkshire, one in the suburbs of Middlesbrough and another at Barnard Castle in County Durham, all with the hallmarks of the previous crimes. As with the other cases, all were expensive racing cycles taken from popular CTC eating-houses at Sunday lunch-time. Having studied the circulars I'd now begun to receive from Durham and Middlesbrough, I realized these thefts, like my two crimes, were part of a very sophisticated operation. Broadly speaking, one bike per week was being stolen, each being worth up to fifteen times the weekly salary of the average person. From that I deduced the thief was making a handsome profit from his enterprise. I began to think he wouldn't ride a bike as a hobby – through earning such huge, tax-free sums he'd be able to afford a flashy car.

As the brisk and chilly winds of March gave way to the milder weather of a beautiful green April, I happened to be passing Joseph Marshall's cottage. Glancing over his garden wall, I saw that his berry trees, carefully pruned, were sprouting their new foliage and that the earth had been neatly hoed between them. There was not a weed to be seen and it was evident that Joseph was preparing for his *coup-de-grâce* at the forthcoming show. It was around 10.30 on a Monday morning and I decided, on the spur of the moment, to pop in for a chat – I could always ask his advice about pruning my own berry trees!

But Joseph was not at home.

'He's gone to the doctor, Mr Rhea,' Mabel explained, and I could see the concern in her face and eyes.

'The doctor?' Although I'd never known Joseph to be ill, I was not too surprised at this news. His weight loss, if it was not a voluntary act, must be causing concern.

'He's not one for going to see the doctor as you know, so I had to force him to go,' she told me. 'He can be very stubborn at times, Mr Rhea, but there's summat not quite right with him. I thought he ought to get himself looked at.'

'A wise decision. So what's the problem? Any idea?' I asked her gently.

'Well, we don't rightly know, Mr Rhea.' She was already filling the teapot from the kettle on the hob. 'It's a bit of a puzzle, I must admit.'

'I don't want to pry.' I settled at the kitchen table as she pointed to a chair. 'But recently, I've noticed he's lost some weight and didn't think he was dieting.'

'You're not prying and he's not dieting.' She was moving around the kitchen, lifting a couple of cups and saucers from a cupboard, then a pair of matching plates and she arranged them on the table before me. Next she found some buns in a tin and a jug of milk from the pantry and soon, there was an appetising spread in front of me. I decided not to force the pace of my questioning about Joseph's condition and waited for her to react.

'I know you're concerned,' she said eventually. 'And it's nice for me to talk it over with somebody who's not family, someone who might be able to advise me. He's lost pounds and his clothes look all loose and wrong. He looks as if he's wearing somebody else's things. Anyway, help yourself to a bun, Mr Rhea.'

Knowing Yorkshire country folk as I did, I felt she would tell me whatever she wanted me to know, so I poured a cup of tea with milk, then helped myself to one of her buns.

'He's lost his appetite,' she said, as she settled in front of me. 'That's the funniest thing of all. He's always had such a good appetite; he loves roast beef and Yorkshire pudding but he doesn't want to eat his dinner nowadays and can't even face his breakfast. He even turns his nose up at black puddings and pork sausages.'

'It's not flu, is it?' I did not know how to react to her news, but in my limited knowledge of medical affairs, things did look very ominous. I must admit that I wondered if he had cancer.

'No, he's not got flu. I know flu when I see it. Anyway, Mr Rhea, he's got himself down to the doctor's.'

'There's no bleeding anywhere is there? Sickness? Internal pains?'

'No, Mr Rhea, I thought of all that sort of thing and asked Joseph, but he said no. I did have words with the district nurse as well, and she talked to him. Apart from going very thin, he says he's perfectly all right – no headaches, no sleeplessness, no dizziness, nowt like that, except now he gets very tired whereas before all this he was very active. He could garden all day without a break.'

'It's a real mystery,' was all I could think of saying.

'You're right. It is a mystery. Even Nurse Margot is baffled. I've told Father Simon and he's saying mass every day this week for Joseph.'

'Well, I'm sure Dr McGee will find out what it is, and then set about having it put right.'

'I hope so, Mr Rhea, I really do hope so. I'm not used to having an invalid in the place; he's always had such good health. And fancy this happening just when he decided to retire from being gooseberry president. I thought we were in for a long period of being able to do things together and go places instead of always worrying about berries and getting ready for show day.'

'You fancied travelling, did you?'

'I did, Mr Rhea. I've always fancied going to foreign parts, to Rome to see the Pope and to Lourdes or Fatima. And London and Edinburgh, and the Lake District, Paris even or Spain ... I had such plans for us, Mr Rhea. Such lovely plans.'

'You've got to look on the positive side of things.' I tried to help her cope with this. 'His illness might not be serious.'

'Oh, well, I'll just have to cope with whatever comes,' she said.

I had to try and raise her hopes just a fraction. 'People do get mysterious ailments from time to time and in most cases they clear up just as mysteriously as they arrived. It might be that he's just gone off his food for some obscure reason, and in a few days he'll be as right as rain.'

'But he's never been off his food in all his life, Mr Rhea. He's always eaten everything I put in front of him. Never picked and poked at it.'

'There's always a first time, and he is getting older. People's appetites do grow smaller, you know, as they get older.'

'Oh, I know all about that but this is different ... he looks so thin. I can hardly believe it's him. He's lost stones. That's the really worrying part. I do hope you'll say some prayers for him, Mr Rhea.'

'Of course I will,' I promised, knowing how much her faith meant to her.

In spite of her belief in the power of prayer, her face betrayed her very deep concern. I knew she was worried that he might have cancer – that was what most of the village thought was wrong with Joseph. Certainly, some of the signs were there such as the sudden loss of weight and lack of appetite, but at least he was not in pain and not suffering from any other visible signs. I remained with Mabel for another twenty minutes or so but it was not a happy respite from my daily duties although I did feel that my presence, and my chat with her, was of some assistance in her rather solitary vigil. I'd make sure the parish priest, Father Simon, was aware of the seriousness of Joseph's condition and I knew he'd pop in to comfort her.

I had to leave before Joseph returned from the surgery because I had another appointment but I did make a mental note to visit him as soon as possible. Later that same day, I popped into Joe Steel's shop-cum-post office, a courtesy call upon my daily round. His emporium was one of my regular calling points because he overheard most of the village gossip and saw most of the comings and goings of locals as well as visitors. From my point of view, he was a good contact in the centre of Aidensfield.

We chatted about local crime with me referring to the racing cycle thefts and Joe saying the GPO were getting worried about the increasing number of people who were managing to obtain free telephone calls from kiosks by various fraudulent means. And then he mentioned Joseph Marshall.

'Have you seen old Joseph recently?' he asked me.

I nodded, explaining I'd called at the house only that morning to learn he'd gone to see the doctor.

'He came in here for his pension and looked like death warmed up,' said Joe Steel. 'He's as thin as a rail, Nick, the flesh has just dropped off him. I asked if he'd been to see the doctor, but he wouldn't go....'

'He's there now,' I assured the shopkeeper. 'Mabel's persuaded him to go but I don't know the outcome.'

'I don't like the look of it.' Joe Steel shook his head. 'Losing weight as fast as that often means cancer, you know. It happened to an aunt of mine, poor old thing ... she was dead within six weeks.'

'Six weeks?' I asked.

'Yes, that's all it took – six weeks, and nobody could do a thing to help her. Not a thing. We just had to watch her fade away.'

'Joseph's symptoms could indicate something else,' I said, trying to sound more cheerful. 'I'm sure there are other things that cause a sudden weight loss and a lack of appetite. Some people can literally worry themselves into being ill.'

'It makes me think I should retire and take things easier before my number's up!' said Joe. 'Too many folks retire and then die before they can enjoy themselves. I'd like to pack up this post office and shop and have time to do a bit of travelling, to see the world before I'm too old. I'm beginning to think we all spend too much of our lives working.'

'I couldn't agree more. I intend to retire early. But if you do leave, you might like to know that Sergeant Blaketon was talking about taking over a village post office when he retires,' I said whimsically. 'He's got to retire from the police when he's fifty five – unless he gets promoted to an inspector and then retirement comes when he reaches sixty. But as things are, he'll still be young enough to take on another career. Maybe you should mention it to him?'

'Really?' He sounded very keen. 'I might just do that, Nick! It's not easy finding suitable candidates, especially for village post-office work. A lot of our dealings are confidential and there's the security aspects of the money we handle. An ex-policeman sounds like an ideal choice!'

As I left the post office-cum-shop, I realized that Joseph Marshall's sudden and dramatic change of appearance was causing wide concern around Aidensfield. He was one of the stalwarts of the village, a character known to everyone and liked by all. Like me, all the other villagers would be anxious to know the outcome of his visit to the doctor, but a further two or three days passed before I learned that Joseph was being sent away for medical tests. His first session had been arranged for the following Monday at Scarborough Hospital, any subsequent examinations being dependent upon the result of that one.

I gleaned this piece of gossip from Arthur Drake, the butcher, another of the gooseberry society's committee members; Arthur was a Big Gooseberry Expert, famed for his Yellow Woodpeckers. I decided to visit Joseph and Mabel and called one teatime, just before knocking off duty. It would be about half-past four when I tapped on the door and called out, 'It's PC Rhea.'

'Come in.' Mabel's voice came from the kitchen.

I found her alone in the kitchen, ironing some bed linen.

'The kettle's boiling, I'll make some tea,' she offered.

'No thanks, Mabel,' I declined on this occasion. 'I'm heading for home and my own tea will be ready in a few minutes. I don't want to spoil my appetite with your scrumptious buns and cakes.'

'Is it Joseph you want?' was her next question.

'I just came to see how he is,' I said.

'He's not very well at all.' She spoke very softly and I thought I detected a tear in her eye. 'He's very tired and he's gone for a lie down, Mr Rhea.'

'Well, don't disturb him. I'll call again. I just wondered how things had gone at the doctor's.'

'Doctor McGee couldn't find anything wrong with him, Mr Rhea, so he's sending him to a specialist. He goes on Monday, to Scarborough. His heart and lungs are all right, there's no blood coming from anywhere and no blockages in his innards and he's not rheumaticky, so Dr McGee is quite baffled. He can't say what's wrong with Joseph; it's a right mystery, but he's told Joseph to stop smoking his pipe.'

'That won't please him! But I'm sure we'll soon know what it is, Mabel, as soon as the specialists have had a look at him. Then they can start to put him right.'

'I wouldn't be too sure about that, Mr Rhea. From what I know, it looks as if he's got cancer somewhere, in his insides mebbe, intestines or stomach or somewhere like his lungs with all that smoking. It's eating away at him, I think, and if that is the case, there'll be nowt anyone can do. Except God. Only God can work miracles, not them doctors, but Father Simon's going to say a mass every day for Joseph....'

'Even cancer can be treated, if it's caught early enough.' I was touched by her simple faith but felt I had to add a practical note. 'So you mustn't be too gloomy.'

'No, I know I should keep cheerful for Joseph's sake but when I see how much weight he's lost, Mr Rhea, it makes me think he must be riddled with the disease. Mebbe he's had it for years without anybody realizing, not that he's ever shown signs of it, mind. He's never short of breath and has never coughed up blood.'

'That's encouraging,' I smiled. 'So how's he getting to Scarborough on Monday? Can I help with a lift perhaps? Or is he going by ambulance?'

'My son's taking him in his car, thanks. Alan that is. Joseph has to stay in hospital until the results come through, and then they'll decide what to do. Our Alan will collect him when it's all over.'

'I hope it all goes well, but don't be frightened to ask if you need help. Tell Joseph I popped in,' I said, and left the sorrowing Mabel as, full of my own sadness, I made my way home to the police house on the exposed hilltop at Aidensfield.

Over our evening meal, Mary told me she'd heard about Joseph's condition from someone in a shop at Ashfordly, so it seemed that Joseph's plight was being shared by his friends and acquaintances. That news, as news does in a small community, was rapidly passed around and prayers were being said in all the local Catholic churches. Had Joseph been just a retired railwayman there would not have been such great interest – it was his role as the Big Berry Man of Aidensfield and as a Big Catholic too, that had endeared him to so many. Everyone wished him well during his stay in hospital.

It was during this time that the Stolen Cycle Supplements began to arrive on a regular basis from Durham Constabulary, Middlesbrough Borough Police and the West Riding Constabulary due to their Ripon theft. Happily, I could secure back copies dating to the beginning of the series of crimes and in my spare moments, began to study them.

I hoped they would provide me with some extra clues but those early readings did not produce anything of particular value. No suspects nor even any vague descriptions of suspects had been listed, from which I deduced none had been observed, and no known thieves or receivers of stolen goods were suspected. I knew that all known cycle thieves and receivers would have suffered more than one visit from their local CID and uniform patrols, and I began to consider that the crimes were the work of someone without a criminal record. It could be someone unknown to any police officer and someone who had all the outward appearances of being honest and trustworthy. The crimes presented an interesting mystery and so I retained the circulars and filed them with the intention of having another look at them in due course. There must be some clue there, I felt, but it might take time for me to recognize it.

On the Monday following, Joseph Marshall went into hospital for his tests. I do not know their precise nature nor do I know what the medical experts were seeking, but I do know that they found nothing wrong with Joseph. Mabel was horrified at the negative news because she rang me to say that Joseph had asked her to inform me.

I was not sure why I had been selected for this chat, but said I would pop down to her cottage without delay. As always, the tea was mashed and the cakes were placed on the table; it was after normal tea-time when I made this visit, around six o'clock on an early spring evening with the birds singing and the leaves bursting from the boughs.

There was a hint of the marvels to follow in the shape of May blossom and acres of colourful wild flowers which would coat the floor of our woodlands and decorate the edges of the moor. Wood sorrel, violets, vetches and bluebells would dominate the coming weeks with the season's daffodils dying away after their early spring offensive. The tiny wild daffodils of Farndale and other moorland valleys would become history yet again, while the damp meadows would produce buttercups while speedwells adorned the footpaths and byways.

'So what's the news?' I asked Mabel.

'Joseph said he wanted you to know and

Nurse Margot. I tried to get hold of Margot,' said Mabel, 'but she's out on a case, so I thought you might help. I don't understand all this official jargon. I think that's what's bothering Joseph. With your legal background, he thought you'd under-stand things.'

'What jargon?' I asked.

'Well, this chap rang from the hospital to say Joseph could come home. I think he said there was nowt wrong with him,' and with that she began to weep. I put an arm around her shoulders in a clumsy attempt to comfort her and she rapidly gained control of herself, blowing her nose loudly and wiping her eyes on her sleeve.

'So what did the man say?' I asked gently.

'Well, Mr Rhea, I can't remember exactly, but he used a lot of big words and medical terms which meant nowt to me but I somehow got the impression they'd tested Joseph for cancer and heart problems and stomach trouble and found nowt. So they want him to come home. I've got to ring our Alan to go and fetch him tonight.'

'Well, that's very good news, Mabel. He's coming home and they've found nothing wrong with him. It must be good news.'

'But they *can't* be right, can they? Those

98

experts. You know and I know that everybody who saw Joseph said he was ill. He was as thin as a rail, he'd lost very near half his weight and he wasn't eating. There must be something seriously wrong with him, mustn't there? How can they say there's nothing wrong with him?'

'Who was the man you talked to? Can you remember?'

'Yes, he made me write his name down and his telephone number, in case I wanted to know more.'

'Right, I'll give him a ring right now. I'll say I'm a friend of the family just clarifying the situation. Can I use your phone?'

And so I found myself talking to a Mr Forbes who was a consultant of some kind. He was most helpful and affable, but explained, in medical terms which I found baffling, that no one could find anything wrong with Joseph Marshall. No cancer had been found and his lungs were clear. There were no problems with his digestive system or heart or blood or liver, kidneys and spleen. For a man of his age, he was remarkably fit and healthy, even if he was as thin as a rail and rather weak with no appetite.

I listened to this fellow, quizzed him about

the role played by other specialists and concluded that everything possible had been done. It was clear that those who had examined Joseph had concluded he was not suffering from any known disease or illness.

I thanked Mr Forbes, adding that Mrs Marshall was making arrangements for Joseph to be collected this evening by private car. Next, I asked whether the family could have a formal statement detailing the examinations and he said a complete account would be sent to Joseph's GP, Dr McGee of Elsinby. I knew nothing more could be done at that stage and rang off.

'They say there's nothing wrong with him,' I reiterated to Mabel. 'Or to be precise, they can't find anything wrong with Joseph. So let's have him brought home where you can keep an eye on him. You can see if he improves his weight or eating habits, and if not, have another word with Dr McGee. He might call for a second opinion at another hospital.'

'There must be somebody somewhere who can tell us what's wrong, Mr Rhea?'

'I'm sure there is, but let's get Joseph home first.'

'Right, it'll be nice to have him here, however ill he is.'

'Watch him carefully to see if he loses more weight. If he does, I think the worries will renew themselves. If he remains static and starts to gain a few pounds, then it might mean he's on the mend. And keep in regular touch with your doctor.'

'Yes, but to lose all that weight, Mr Rhea, there must be something wrong somewhere ... that's what I am trying to say, that's what I'm trying to tell those medical people.'

'They know that, Mabel. They accept that but the crux of the matter is that their tests don't show anything wrong. So we must watch and care for Joseph and, if necessary, get a second opinion. And have words with Father Simon about all this.'

'Right, well, thank you, Mr Rhea. I do appreciate your help ... I'll ring our Alan right away.'

And so the arrangements were made for Joseph Marshall to come home.

# 4

Joseph's homecoming was rather discreet. Although his friends in Aidensfield and elsewhere wanted to show their concern, they realized he would want only peace and quiet for a while. He'd want nothing more than the companionship of his wife in the familiar surroundings of their home. Wisely, they refrained from calling, if only for a couple of days.

In spite of his temporary isolation, however, news of his condition filtered into village gossip because one or two people had in fact been to visit Joseph. There was the butcher's delivery van driver, Ted Fryer, Margot Horsefield, the district nurse, Father Simon, the parish priest, and Joe Steel from the shop who'd popped in with a few groceries. His neighbours, Ron and Ethel Collins, had called too and Mabel had had a few close friends and relations to see her. The information they'd all gleaned entered the village's rapid-communications system and enabled us all to learn something of Joseph's current condition – even if accuracy was not a particularly strong element.

The truth was there had been little change in his condition since coming home. His weight had remained fairly static with no further dramatic loss, and his appetite had failed to return. The news that surprised everyone was that no serious illness or disease had been found, and although that should have been regarded as very welcome and positive, most of us greeted it with scepticism.

Everyone *knew* Joseph was seriously ill – you had only to look at him to realize that, consequently a feeling developed that the hospital had sent Joseph home to die peacefully among his friends and family. People rallied around to help him achieve that.

After a period indoors, ostensibly recovering from his ordeal in hospital, Joseph did venture down the village. One of his first outings was to resume his attendance at mass at 7.30 each morning and soon afterwards, his Aidensfield excursions increased. They included visits to the post office for his pension, popping along to the shop from time to time, looking in at the village hall to ensure things were running smoothly and going to the pub where he enjoyed a couple of pints on a Friday evening. This was the routine he'd followed before his illness and even if his appetite had shrunk, he could still enjoy a pint or two of best bitter with his pals. It was clear that Joseph had no intention of allowing his sickness to confine him to the house and it didn't take long for the villagers to become accustomed to his rather wasted and haunted appearance. Few discussed his health with him because they assumed he was dying slowly from cancer, and everyone agreed he was doing so with great dignity. They adopted a simple greeting 'Now then, Joseph, how are you today?' to which he would invariably reply, 'Not so bad, thanks.'

I do know that some were looking forward to a Guild funeral – it would be a spectacular affair with cloaked, red-hatted members accompanying Joseph's hearse and walking beside the coffin to the edge of the grave as they joyfully sang all the famous Catholic hymns, some of which upset the Protestants.

Joseph, meanwhile, showed no sign of quitting this world. His condition did not improve but neither did it appear to deteriorate, and each of these signs was regarded as rather ominous. Perhaps the most revealing aspect of his condition, so far as members of the old Gooseberry Society were concerned, was that his little patch of gooseberry trees appeared to be very neglected. Weeds were flourishing between them and even with my limited horticultural knowledge, I wondered whether they should have been further pruned or given extra manure as the growing season got seriously underway. Joseph must be very poorly if he was neglecting his trees, but in spite of that, they did produce a fine array of flowers in the first flush of spring and there were no spring frosts to damage the new blossom.

His general appearance at that time was dreadful with his gaunt features, skeletal figure and baggy clothes. One local wit remarked he'd seen healthier looking corpses and I must admit I began to wonder whether Joseph had abandoned any hope for the future. His deep religious faith would have prepared him for death, but did Joseph know more than us? Had he been given some truly bad news by his consultants, news he had decided to keep to himself? It looked a distinct possibility and I wondered if he had decided to conceal the truth from everyone, including Mabel and his family. I did not think Joseph would be quite so devious, although he might regard a diplomatic silence as a way of shielding his loved ones from the hurt and sorrow which would follow. I could imagine him not wanting to burden anyone with his worries – after all, he was accustomed to doing almost everything by himself.

If he did have cancer or some other grave disease or illness, I felt sure he would want to fight it or deal with it entirely alone. He wouldn't expect help from other people and I didn't think he would relish any overt sympathy or shows of deep emotion.

It was during the height of that concern that I had to call on Jacob Butterworth, the incoming president of the Aidensfield Old Gooseberry Society. It was a routine matter – the renewal of his firearm certificate – but it offered me an opportunity to discuss Joseph's condition.

'I've been to see him,' Jacob informed me. 'I'd heard about him going into hospital for that check-up and coming out looking like a skeleton, and I wondered if he wanted me to look after this year's berry show.'

'A nice gesture,' I commented.

'Aye, I thought it would take the load off his shoulders. He can do without that kind of pressure. There's a lot of things to finalize between now and August, adverts for the newspapers, posters, that sort of thing, and I thought he might want a helping hand.'

'And did he?' I smiled.

'Not him! He said everything was in hand and he could cope. He said he had no intention of missing this show, because it's his last one as president. He's determined to be there and to do all that's necessary to make it a good event.'

'What did you think of his general condition?' I put to Jacob.

'It's hard to say.' He shook his head. 'He's lost all that weight and reckons he's lost his appetite, yet he seems fit enough even if he is a bit slow and tired. He's out and about the village, doing what he used to do before he got whatever he's got. That's good for him. Once, you know, I had an old ewe like that. She went as thin as a rail and stopped eating, and she stayed like that for weeks. Then all of a sudden, she got better, started eating and became fitter than she was before. I'd had the vet in to look at her, time and time again, but he found nowt wrong. It's a mystery even to this day.'

'I've heard Joseph's neglecting his berry trees,' I said. 'That's unlike him. It shows he's far from well.'

'I don't think he's neglecting them, Nick. There's time enough yet for feeding them and doing whatever pruning or thinning out he thinks is necessary. And he did have a cracking show of blossom. If he's intending to win the Supreme this year, he's mebbe being a bit crafty, leading folks up the garden path, in a manner of speaking, and letting 'em think he's not interested when I'll bet he's got other trees behind the house, out of sight, with potentially monster berries on them. He'll be tending them as if they're his beloved bairns, you'll see. I've known Joseph long enough not to be bamboozled by a few neglected berry trees!'

'That sounds devious to me!' I laughed.

'Berry growers are like that, Nick! Up to all kinds of tricks.'

'Even so, I think lots of people in Aidensfield would like to help Joseph in some way, even if it means seeing to his berry trees if he becomes too ill to cope.'

'I don't think he'd allow that, Nick. If he has got cancer, like most folks seem to think he has, then he's in the hands of God – and his doctors of course. I reckon he's best left alone to get on with life as he thinks best.'

'So you think we should all stop fretting about him?' I put to the dour sheepfarmer.

'I do, Nick. I think it's best. Let him be. Joseph's happier left to his own devices. And if he wants a helping hand, Mabel will make sure he gets it!'

I had to admit that was my assessment too. I respected Jacob as a man of great wisdom and common sense, and decided to make an effort to stop worrying about Joseph Marshall and his big gooseberries.

In the meantime, Sergeant Ray Craddock had arrived to take charge of Brantsford Police Station upon the retirement of Charlie Bairstow. We'd given Charlie a fine retirement party at the Brantsford Hall Hotel, along with a gift of a pair of binoculars, something he wanted. The superintendent had spoken of the loss we would all feel upon his departure and he'd had his photograph taken for the *Brantsford Chronicle*. Charlie told us he was retiring to Scotland where he hoped to follow his hobbies of bird watching, salmon fishing and drinking malt whisky.

Owing to his own duty requirements, Sergeant Craddock had been unable to attend Charlie's farewell party and I did not encounter him for some time following his posting.

His main responsibilities were in Brantsford and he would cover Ashfordly Section only when Sergeant Blaketon was away for a considerable period, such as a spell of annual leave, or on a course, or perhaps if he fell ill. There might be an occasional visit by Craddock when Blaketon was enjoying one of his weekly rest days, but that would generally occur for a specific reason. Ashfordly and Brantsford were about eight miles apart, each with their own clutch of rural beats surrounding them, but with the advent of more motor vehicles and better communications, it did seem sensible to share the supervisory work of these two neighbouring sections.

During the past weeks, there'd been no further racing cycle thefts in my area although there had been several in other parts of the north-east. They had occurred at roughly the rate of one every weekend, some in our county and others in neighbouring areas. Once in a while, however, there was no such theft. As with the previous cases, each stolen machine was a valuable racing cycle which had been taken on a Sunday from an assembly of similar bikes left unattended. Still anxious to solve the two crimes which had occurred on my beat, I continued to scan the Stolen Cycle Supplements as they arrived, but they recorded nothing which helped my investigation. One problem was that each stolen cycle was described in very scant detail with no real information about the actual mode of the theft.

For my own peace of mind, I continued to make a search of likely hiding places on my beat while asking people like gamekeepers, farmers and ramblers to maintain a look-out for abandoned bikes in isolated areas, but it was all to no avail. No one found any abandoned bikes.

I knew that none of the missing bikes had been traced either. Quite often, 'borrowed' bikes were found abandoned somewhere and restored to their losers but these fine machines had completely disappeared. I did not receive any call or visit from Sergeant Craddock to further discuss his missing bike – clearly, he knew about my lack of success but understood the difficulties of solving such crimes. Furthermore, he was in an ideal position to know how all the enquiries were progressing.

The fact of his arrival in Brantsford had momentarily slipped my mind, but very soon afterwards I did get a call from him. It was a summons by radio while I was in my Mini-van patrolling the moors above Briggsby. He instructed me to proceed immediately to Stovensby where he had halted a suspicious character on the edge of the disused airfield. He told me to head for the main entrance where I would see his official car, adding that my presence was required because the detained man had given my name as a referee to his good character. Clearly the sergeant doubted the fellow's claims and so Craddock wanted me to confront him to confirm or deny that claim.

Stovensby was around fifteen-minutes drive away. It was a small hillside village with a chapel and a pub but little else other than a single street of stone cottages. Spread across the base of the valley to the immediate south of Stovensby was a disused wartime airfield comprising the remains of the runways, a deserted air-traffic control tower, empty and damaged dormitory blocks, and assorted other neglected buildings such as hangars and workshops.

At the mention of Stovensby and suspicious characters, I thought he must be referring to Tin Lid Talbot, the petty thief and scrap dealer who operated from a scrapyard on Stovensby airfield. Until recently, Tin Lid had lived in a prefab at Crampton but had just moved to new accommodation on the old airfield, close to his emporium of rust and rattles. He'd managed to buy, for a rock-bottom price, one of the old deserted workshops which he'd converted into a primitive kind of dwelling house. It reclined among his piles of scrap metal and assorted junk, and I think he paid the landowner a modest rent for the rest of his establishment.

I knew Tin Lid Talbot very well – his real name was James Edward Talbot who was in his late forties. He was a stooped, thin man of medium height and build, with dark, greasy hair, bad teeth and filthy fingernails. He always wore wellingtons, winter and summer alike, and had acquired his nickname from his old habit of collecting metal lids from almost any kind of container, ranging from dustbins to treacle tins. He never seemed to sell his collected lids, for the pile grew larger and larger on the old airfield, and he never stopped adding to it. I have no idea what he intended to do with his mountain of tin lids.

He was a sneak thief, too, but when he was caught, he always denied his involvement while simultaneously admitting his guilt. I've given a longer account of his crimes in *Constable by the Stream,* but this is an example of his behaviour. If he sneaked into someone's house and stole cash which resulted in an interview by the police, he would say, 'You don't think I stole Mrs Brown's money and used it to pay off my grocery bill, do you?'

A visit to the grocer would confirm he'd done exactly that. Or he might say, 'You don't think I stole those plant pots and sold them to that market gardener at Whemmelby, do you?' or 'You don't think I stole those silver spoons and hid them up my chimney, do you?'

In spite of his frequent confrontations with the police, Tin Lid regarded me as a friend because I'd once secured his freedom. I'd achieved that because I knew the way he framed his denials, and on that occasion I knew from the words he used that he was not guilty of the offence for which he was the prime suspect. So had Craddock caught Tin Lid Talbot in possession of stolen goods?

Those were my thoughts as I gave an ETA of fifteen minutes, but Craddock closed the transmission without providing any further information. I arrived to find Sergeant Craddock, tall and smart in his uniform, standing beside a red lorry which, even from a distance, I knew belonged to Claude Jeremiah Greengrass. I eased to a halt and climbed out of my Mini-van whereupon Claude materialized beside me. He was not in the happiest of moods.

'Constable Rhea,' he bellowed, 'will you explain to this little Hitler that I am a law-abiding citizen in business on my own account, and I buy and sell second-hand goods which are not stolen....'

'Ah, PC Rhea, we meet again,' beamed the new sergeant as he strode forward to begin his account of this confrontation.

'No news of your cycle, Sergeant?' I asked.

'I've resigned myself to the fact that I shall never see it again.'

'I know nowt about stolen bikes!' shouted Claude. 'We've been through all that!'

'So, Sergeant,' I addressed Craddock very formally. 'What's the problem with Claude?'

'You do know this man?' asked Craddock.

'Yes, I do,' I had to admit. 'He lives on my beat, at Hagg Bottom. He describes himself as a self-employed businessman. I've known him since I came to Aidensfield.'

'And would you say he is a person of good character?' There was a cold smile on Craddock's face as traces of his Welsh accent sounded strange against this York-shire background.

'Claude is not a thief and he is not a violent man.' I tried to sound diplomatic in the presence of the subject of our discussion. 'But I think he would admit that he has had a few brushes with the law in the past, minor matters involving motor vehicles such as no insurance or excise duty, one case of speeding I believe, and another of no driving licence, as well as no dog licence, trespassing on the railway, malicious damage to a rhubarb plant, illegal distilling of whisky and, if my memory serves me right, one conviction for being drunk while playing billiards.'

'That's juvenile stuff, done when I was young and daft. I'm not a criminal!' Greengrass bellowed at the sergeant.

'No convictions for receiving stolen goods, then? Larceny? That sort of serious crime?'

'Not to my knowledge,' I had to admit.

'No, I've not!' shouted Claude.

'Except for one case, Claude!' and I

recalled one such conviction. 'Receiving a load of stolen manure....'

'That was dumped on my land without my knowledge, and I got the blame because some copper found it and I couldn't explain where it had come from. And I still don't know who put it there, but the magistrates confiscated it and used it on the court-house rose bushes. I hope they wilted and got greenfly!'

'Hmm,' said Craddock. 'Not exactly a criminal record of the top league, is it? No burglaries, arson, armed robberies, embezzlements or housebreakings ... it's all very petty stuff, Mr Greengrass.'

'That's what I was trying to tell you before Constable Rhea turned up. I'm not a big-time criminal. I might have been a bit daft in my younger days and made mistakes, but all I'm doing now is trying to make an honest living.'

'So, the question is,' – Craddock walked across to the rear of Claude's old truck – 'what are you doing with all these barrow wheels?'

When I peered into the back of the wagon, it was full of barrow wheels. They were piled high in no identifiable order and comprised large ones and small ones of every conceivable colour and style. There must have been hundreds, but there was not a wheelbarrow in sight. Some time ago, I'd noticed a pile of such wheels in one of Claude's outbuildings. This load was probably that very same pile.

'What am I doing with them? I'm taking them to a customer, that's what I'm doing. I told you that before you called in cavalry reinforcements.'

'Who, Claude?' I asked. 'Who's your customer?'

'Tin Lid Talbot,' he said. 'Me and Tin Lid go back a lot of years, and he has markets for things I collect. Like second-hand barrow wheels. And he does a good trade in second-hand weathercocks, used drain pipes and old frying pans.'

'So where have they come from, these wheels?' asked Craddock.

'From barrows I've rescued from scrap heaps, rubbish dumps, gardeners who want rid of 'em and anywhere else you care to think of. Folks bring their wheels to me, Sergeant, when their barrows fall to bits. I'm renowned for the quality of my second-hand barrow wheels. Some barrows will outlast their wheels and some wheels will outlast their barrows. But it means there's a big market for second-hand barrow wheels – barrow wheels collapse or crumble after years of work in gardens, but can folks get replacement wheels for their old barrows? 'Course not. You try finding a wheel to fit your old barrow – your barrow will have years of life left in it, if only you can find a wheel. But you can't get them in the shops because styles and sizes change, so it means spending money on new barrows – but I can fill a gap in the market. I can refit old barrows. Me and Tin Lid can find wheels for almost any make or model of *old* barrow you care to mention, even those dating to before the war. Old wheels for old barrows, Sergeant. It's a very good line of business.'

'So you sell yours to Tin Lid?' I said.

'We work together; he sells 'em for me and I pay him a bit of commission. He has contacts, you see, in the gardening and horticultural world.'

'Like market gardens where he nicks plant pots and garden rollers?' I said.

'I know nowt about his private life,' said Claude. 'All I know is that he's pretty good at selling second-hand barrow wheels. He'll get rid of this lot before next weekend and his customers will be begging for more.'

'So what do you think, PC Rhea?' asked

Sergeant Craddock. 'Do we arrest this man on suspicion of larceny or even for receiving stolen goods, or do we believe his story?'

'Arrest? It'll be false arrest and I'll sue the lot of you!' snapped Claude.

'I believe Claude.' I had to be honest. 'I've been to his premises and have seen the growing pile of barrow wheels ... they're not stolen goods, Sergeant. I'd stake my career on that.'

'Well, I am pleased your local knowledge is so thorough, PC Rhea, and that you are so well informed about the people on your beat, especially those of interest to the police,' smiled Craddock. 'Well, Mr Green-grass, this looks like your lucky day. You may go.'

'Lucky? I don't call it lucky being held up for half an hour and having to justify my trading techniques to snoopers like you!'

'You are lucky that PC Rhea was able to respond to my call so quickly, and to speak on your behalf.'

'I'll buy him a pint next time he's in the pub!' said Claude, but as he turned to climb back into his driving seat, Craddock called to him.

'Mr Greengrass?'

'Now what? My tax disc is up to date, my

brakes are in full working order and I got a new exhaust pipe last week....'

'I'm sure everything is just as it should be,' beamed Craddock. 'But I am interested in that red barrow wheel, the one near the tailgate of your truck.'

'What about it? It's not been nicked!'

'No, but I need a wheel for my old barrow, you see. Fifteen-inch diameter with a six-inch spindle and a solid rubber tyre ... now that looks perfect....'

'Does it now?'

'I've tried all the gardening shops and hardware people in this area, and no one can supply me with the right size or type of wheel. Mine is rather an old barrow, you see, inherited from my father.'

'That's just what I've been trying to explain! I'm a specialist in old barrow wheels, Sergeant Craddock. So how much are you prepared to pay, seeing it's not stolen property?' beamed Claude.

'I was thinking of something about £1,' said Craddock.

'I am thinking more like £5 for that wheel, and you can measure it to make sure it fits. And I'll take it back if it's not suitable and I'll even find you one that does fit.'

In a trice, Craddock had pulled a retractable tape measure from his pocket, the sort we all carried for measuring the scenes of road traffic accidents, and he was leaning over the side of the lorry to measure the wheel. It was exactly what he wanted.

'Two pounds,' he said to Claude.

'Four,' said Claude.

'Three,' responded Craddock, and so the deal was done. Claude passed him the wheel, pocketed the three pounds with a wide smile on his face, climbed aboard his wagon and started the engine.

As Claude drove past me, Craddock was placing the barrow wheel in the boot of his police car a short distance away, so Claude slowed down, leaned out of the window and whispered, 'That's two pints I owe you! Oh, and next time you're in my part of the world come and look at my gooseberries! You should see the size of 'em already! Filling out nicely they are. There's weeks to go, I know, but they're on course to be winners, mark my words. Just you go and tell Holy Joe, tell him to watch out for Greengrass world beater, a Thatcher it is, the best ever, even without a stalk – and I'm not going to divulge my secret recipe for feeding 'em.'

And with that, he drove away, chuckling at the outcome of this confrontation and happy that he was going to score one over Joseph Marshall. I then realized that Claude probably had no idea of Joseph's sickness, but decided it was not the right moment to inform him.

'It's odd how things work out,' said Sergeant Craddock, when he returned to my side. 'Here am I halting a man I believe to be a thief, and I finish up buying something I've been seeking for ages ... I'm pleased you could confirm I was not dealing in stolen property, PC Rhea.'

'Claude sails close to the wind, Sergeant,' I said. 'But he's not evil, just a bit of a rustic rogue.'

'So he doesn't deal in stolen cycles?' grinned Craddock.

'No, I tackled him about that. Those racing bikes are way out of his league.'

'Well, it was an interesting way of meeting your Mr Greengrass, and I'm sure our paths will cross in the future. Now, PC Rhea, what are the outstanding issues on your beat just now?'

And so, standing on the side of the lane near Stovensby's ancient airfield, I provided the new sergeant with a brief résumé of Aidensfield beat and some of the matters currently affecting my work. I did not refer to Joseph Marshall, of course, because his illness was not a matter for the police, although I did provide an outline of the forthcoming gooseberry show and our role in ensuring there was a smooth flow of traffic on the day. Craddock chuckled at the notion of whopping berries being shown for prizes, and I suggested he make an effort to attend, if only to have his education broadened. I told him of the man whose gooseberry was so huge that it rested on the ground, and when he harvested it, he needed a wheelbarrow to carry it. When he placed it in the barrow it collapsed beneath the massive weight, then the berry rolled away and burst as it fell to the ground.

The massive berry never reached the show table, I told him, and so the world never witnessed that giant of giants. Other than its grower, no one saw it, even in its damaged state, because the birds came and pecked up the remains before anyone could reach it, and so there was not even a tiny seed left as proof. Every piece of evidence of the world's largest gooseberry had been lost – except for the broken wheelbarrow which was placed in the hall during every annual show.

Sergeant Craddock laughed at this old piece of berry lore and I felt he had a sense of humour, even if I was rather unsure how to regard him at this juncture. He departed with a cheery wave, saying he'd meet me again in the near future, but as I watched him leave, I did not know whether he was a keen disciplinarian or a fresh-air freak as had been suggested. What was not in doubt was that he was a very practical policeman. The fact he had stopped and interrogated Claude was an example of that. Lots of supervisory officers would shrink from that kind of operational police work. I began to look forward with some interest to his forthcoming role in the work of Ashfordly Section and Aidensfield rural beat.

During the latter weeks of that springtime, which was rich in blossom, colour and sunshine while being devoid of troublesome frosts, I toured my beat as I undertook a variety of routine duties. As I motored around or sometimes patrolled on foot, it became very evident that there had been a massive increase in local enthusiasm for growing big gooseberries and I was not sure what had generated this passion in Aidensfield.

During my patrols in and around Aidensfield, I did get the impression that everyone, apart from Claude Jeremiah Greengrass, thought Joseph should – and would – win this year's Supreme Championship. How they thought that might be achieved was never revealed because there was no way the result could be fixed in Joseph's favour – not that he would allow that to happen anyway. It might be possible for everyone to withhold all berries heavier than Joseph's finest and send them to the Egton Bridge show. But no one would know that weight in advance. Their mere absence might ensure he won, in which case he would never suspect a plot, but he would be aghast if any hint of corruption tainted the society over which he presided.

Everyone knew it was impossible to forecast a winner – berries were weighed on the day of the show, and in any case, most of the competitors concealed theirs from the opposition, except for Claude Jeremiah Greengrass. And he would take immense pleasure in defeating Holy Joe. Furthermore, I don't think any of those lapsed members were regarded as a genuine threat but that did not dampen their enthusiasm. My regular visits to farms, cottages, households and allotments did show an inordinate number of berry trees under severe cultivation even if I did not catch a view of their best berries, but I did get the impression that the whole district was keen to partake in this year's annual show. There would be a fine turn-out for Joseph's last event.

By mid-summer, the Aidensfield berry trees were showing their paces. It was probably at this stage that the greatest skill and care had to be displayed.

By now, the early pruning had been done and the bushes were producing their crops. By dint of carefully removing a selection of surplus berries, the growers sought to encourage only the finest to remain on the tree. The secret was knowing which berries to remove and which to retain, how many to leave on the tree and how many to remove. If the grower achieved the right balance, the remaining fruit would flourish by utilizing the food generated by the tree, and they would become very large, handsome and heavy specimens. Also, big berries could be encouraged by feeding the trees with secret potions such as sheep droppings mashed in moorland spring water, pigs' dried blood, fish meal from off-shore catches at Whitby, potash or top quality cow manure that had matured for months. It was also necessary to protect the berries from heavy rainfall as well as troublesome insects and birds. There were many close secrets in the berry-growing world, ranging from blowing pipe tobacco smoke on to them later in the year to ward off wasps, and covering them with little umbrellas to stop the raindrops from knocking them off the trees. It was unwise, however, to grow one's berries under glass because they would be ready long before the date of the show. They had to be nurtured in the open air, and the trees had to be tended with loving care, even with their owners sitting up all night with them as the date of the show approached. And, as that date grew closer and closer with astonishing speed, the berry growers of Aidensfield realized they had only the remaining days of June and the whole of July to achieve their targets. The excitement began to mount.

And then Joseph Marshall took a turn for the worse.

# 5

It was a Wednesday morning when Father Simon told me about Joseph's relapse. I was visiting the Aidensfield Garage because I wanted to ascertain from the new owner, a lanky, somewhat cadaverous fellow called Bernie Scripps, whether a car stolen overnight from nearby Maddleskirk had called there for petrol. In all probability, the garage was closed at the time of the theft, but sometimes passing thieves broke the locks on Bernie's pumps at night to fill their vehicles. Another trick was to syphon a gallon or two from vehicles on the forecourt, but on this occasion he knew of no such attempt. If there had been, I would have arranged for a Scenes of Crime officer to search for fingerprints on the vehicles or pumps, a good set being such a useful asset in the detection of any crime.

I told Bernie the stolen car was a dark-blue and rather battered Ford Anglia which had been stolen from outside a council house in Maddleskirk and provided him with the registration number. He said he knew the car – he'd serviced it from time to time – and added he was sure it hadn't called during his opening hours. He did promise to look out for it although we both felt it would be miles away by this time. I suggested it had been taken by opportunist joyriders rather than professional car thieves because it was not the sort a professional thief would want to try and sell.

My own view was that the thief could be someone from the locality who'd used it to take himself and his pals home from the pub and I felt it would have been abandoned fairly soon after being stolen. I'd make a thorough search of my beat – it was something to occupy me for the rest of the day.

At this early stage of Bernie's arrival in Aidensfield, I did not know him very well, chiefly because one of his staff usually filled my petrol tanks (police and private) when I called. In spite of that, I was interested to see how he would cope with running a village garage because prior to buying this thriving little business, he'd been an undertaker in Strensford. It was an unlikely switch of career, although there was just a hint he might establish a chapel of rest and coffin-making emporium in the unused space at the rear of the garage. I was not sure about that idea – I did not feel that people would want to say farewell to their dear departed against a background of cast tyres, rusting exhaust pipes, scrap cars and vehicles awaiting repair. But there was no accounting for taste – indeed, Bernie had brought his old hearse with him, and that now stood, temporarily unused, at the back of his garage. Even if he did not start his own undertaking business, he could hire his hearse to others. I could imagine Bernie wanting to capitalize upon his assets and make full use of his ample space.

When I emerged from my chat with him, I found Father Simon busy at the petrol pumps. Dressed in tattered old jeans and a well-worn sweater, and looking most unholy, he was filling a can with petrol. It was intended for the parish lawnmower and, as was customary here, he was serving himself.

When he paid Bernie, he would buy a can of oil to mix with it, hopefully to incorporate precise proportions of oil and petrol to produce the correct two-stroke mixture. The cheerful little priest used a new invention for his steeply sloping lawn – it was a Flymo, a lawnmower whose whirring blade operated like a horizontal propeller to produce a cushion of air upon which the lawnmower floated as it cut the grass. This made it extremely manoeuvrable as it flew over footpaths and other irregularities to produce a lawn as smooth as a bowling green, even on steeply sloping areas of grass. The finely chopped pieces of cut grass were deposited back on to the lawn to form a useful mulch, especially in dry weather. The Flymo, a futurist device of great interest to conventional gardeners, was ideal for St Aidan's lawn because it sloped steeply from the walls of the building down to the ecclesiastical car-park below. But if the ingredients of the two-stroke mixture were incorrectly calculated to the slightest degree, the temperamental (or finely tuned) mower invariably refused to start. And that was enough to test the saintliness of any parish priest, even one who was a casually dressed monk from nearby Maddleskirk Abbey. The trick was to produce exactly the right mixture of oil and petrol – I knew the perils in attempting to do that because, on occasions, I took a turn in cutting the church grass. When Father Simon spotted me, therefore, he came over to me with the petrol can in his hand and I thought he was going to ask if I could cut the lawn. But his face showed concern and I did not miss its message.

'Ah, Nick,' he spoke softly in his gentle Irish brogue. 'You've heard the latest about Joseph?'

'Latest?' I knew from the tone of his voice that the news was not good. 'No, Father, what's happened?'

'He's back in hospital,' the priest told me. 'He was admitted yesterday. To Scarborough again, for more observations.'

'Poor chap, what's brought this on?' Knowing Joseph as I did, I was anxious to find out as much as I could and Father Simon was perhaps the best source outside Joseph's immediate family.

'Well, it seems he was having stomach cramps or pains of some kind and for a while he ignored them. You know what men are like for not making a fuss about such things. So far as his other problems are concerned, he thought he was not getting any worse. That was a good thing, he felt. Being no worse is almost as good as getting better. Anyway, when he started with tummy problems, he said nothing to his wife because he thought it might have been caused by forcing himself to take in bigger helpings, or different food.'

'Sudden and drastic changes in one's daily routine or diet can cause stomach trouble,' I added. 'Usually we blame it on the water!'

'I think Joseph was thinking along those lines. He had tried more fruit, you see, and vegetables and a range of food without fat in it, even rice instead of potatoes... Anyway, Nick, it seems he was getting stomach pains, more severe than just wind or indigestion, but the truth is he'd been suffering for some time before Mabel realized.'

'So how long has he been having the pains?' I asked.

'Sure, no one knows for certain, Nick. You'd think a man like that, suffering from some dreadful debilitating illness, would have the sense to call in his doctor the minute other things started to go wrong. But he didn't, so we've no idea how long his stomach has been causing problems. It was Mabel who called in Dr McGee; she caught him doubled up with pain, his face tortured and his hands holding his stomach ... he was in his garden, at the time, would you believe, doing something to his precious gooseberry trees.'

134

'He'd not collapsed, then?' I asked.

'Oh, no, but he was in severe pain so Mabel called the doctor and he was there in minutes. He didn't waste time examining Joseph, he said it was an immediate hospital job and rang for the ambulance straight away. Joseph was on his way to Scarborough within the hour.'

'You've been to see him, Father?' I asked.

'I have, yesterday afternoon. He's having a comprehensive range of tests and he'll have had several by now. They're examining his stomach, so I was told, but while they've got him, they'll check the rest of him, all over again, especially his internal organs and waterworks. So far, though, they've not found anything. I did manage to elicit that snippet from one of the doctors.'

'And Dr McGee? Has he any idea what might be wrong?'

'He has no firm opinion, even though he's examined Joseph as well as he can. At least, that's what he told Mabel. He's been attending Joseph at home but he's only a GP. We mustn't forget that, he's not a specialist.'

'I hope Mabel appreciates that.'

'I'm sure she does. None of us must expect too much from him and I doubt if he could confirm or even identify Joseph's problem. But he's a good doctor with lots of experience and I respect his opinions. I know he suspects cancer but we must respect his patient confidentiality and not quiz him too much. But I can talk to Mabel. As indeed I have.'

'So how long is Joseph likely to remain in hospital, Father? Has the hospital given any indication?'

'The authorities won't commit themselves. He'll be there for a few days of close observation and tests and I think the cancer specialists will take another very careful look at him.'

'Well, let's hope he comes through all this,' I said.

'We shall pray for him at mass every day,' said Father Simon. 'But no one can interfere with the Lord's will – if God wants Joseph to join Him and grow berries in a heavenly gooseberry patch, then Joseph will have to obey that call. God's will must be done, you see, even if we do not like it or understand it.'

'Thanks for telling me, Father. I'll pop in for a word with Mabel,' I said.

'She'd appreciate that,' the priest smiled. 'I must get this lawn cut – I've a baptism on

Sunday and want the place looking smart for my visitors. See you later, Nick.'

As Father Simon went to pay for his two-stroke mixture, I prepared to resume my patrol and decided I had sufficient time for a quick visit to Mabel Marshall.

It was the least I could do in the circumstances. Parking my van outside the cottage, I noticed her in the garden where she was hoeing between those of Joseph's gooseberry trees which were visible from the roadside. She was wearing her usual household apron but had short red wellington boots on her feet. They were caked with the damp earth as she pushed the narrow-bladed hoe between the trees, taking care not to damage their roots or stems. She worked with considerable speed and precision. One of my first thoughts was that Joseph would be proud of her.

'Good morning, Mabel.' She had her back to me as I called over the garden wall.

'Oh, hello, Mr Rhea,' she turned and smiled as she saw me. 'Come in, I was just thinking of breaking off for a cup of coffee.'

'Don't stop on my account,' I said. 'I've just heard about Joseph and thought I'd pop in to see how he was, and to see if I can help.'

'I want to sit down for a few minutes and I'd love a cup of coffee,' she insisted. 'My old legs get a bit tired these days and my throat's as dry as dust ... so do come in.'

As she busied herself in the kitchen, producing mugs and plates, some buttered scones and a pot of strawberry jam, a jug of milk and a bowl of sugar, the kettle was bubbling and singing on the fire. Soon she was handing me a hot coffee and inviting me to help myself to some scones and her homemade jam. We chatted about inconsequential things until she was ready to join me at the table and, when she was settled, I said, 'Father Simon's just told me about Joseph.'

'It's all so worrying, Mr Rhea.' Her eyes were moist. 'I do know Joseph's not a young man and I am wise enough to expect illness and disease and even death at our time of life, but it's all so puzzling, no one being able to find out what's wrong with him. I just wish they would give me some idea. No one will tell me, you see, not even a hint. I mean, I reckon he's got cancer of the bowels or stomach or something. Losing all that weight, and his appetite, and now those terrible pains in his stomach ... well, I think it all points to that. I just wish somebody would have the courage to confirm it, then we would know what the future holds.'

'So they've not given you any idea what the problem might be?'

'No, nothing. Not the slightest hint. That's what's so upsetting, Mr Rhea, not knowing. Nobody will commit themselves. Even Joseph has no idea what's wrong with him.'

'He's said that, has he?'

'He has, Mr Rhea. He says no one's told him anything, except to say they can't find anything wrong.'

'Doctors and specialists like to be absolutely sure before committing themselves. They don't have much choice; it would be wrong to give you misleading information or a rushed diagnosis. But if they cannot find anything wrong, they will say so.'

I tried to ease her worries but knew it was impossible and I could appreciate the dilemma she was experiencing. She could not accept there was nothing wrong with Joseph.

Being left in that kind of vacuum was worse than knowing it was a fatal disease. If terminal cancer was diagnosed, she could prepare herself to cope. There was very little I could do to help, but I wanted her to know that all of us – the whole village in fact – were sympathizing with her at this cruel time. I suspected that Joseph knew more than he was admitting, but no one could force him to reveal his knowledge. There was one small thing I could offer by way of assistance, however.

'What about getting to see him? I'll be happy to take you through to Scarborough,' I offered. 'With the sort of hours I work, I am often free during the afternoons, when visitors are allowed. Sometimes, it's hard for friends and relatives to get time off in the afternoons.'

'Thanks, Mr Rhea. I'll let you know, but I'm all right at the moment. My sons can take me, and Ron next door has offered, and Father Simon ... everyone's so very kind.'

'Well, don't be frightened to ask.'

'No, I won't,' she assured me.

'I'd like to see Joseph myself but don't want to get in the way of any family visitors. If I do go, you can come with me, so don't be afraid to ask.'

'Thank you, Mr Rhea.'

'I noticed you tending his berry trees,' I smiled.

'He's determined to compete this year,' she said, sniffing back a tear. 'He said how nice it would be if he could win the Supreme just this once, in his last year as well, his last year as president that is. But, apart from what I've seen him do in the garden, I know nothing about growing prize berries, Mr Rhea. I've already left it to him.'

'He'll tell you what to do, though?' I put to her. 'He'll make sure you always do the right things.'

'Oh yes. Even from his hospital bed, he keeps reminding me of jobs. He's had no strength lately, he got tired in no time so I helped him before he went to Scarborough. The main thing is to keep weeds down so they don't take up any of the nourishment intended for the berries, and so they don't block out the sunshine or stop air from circulating through the trees. Joseph's already done a fair bit of manuring and pruning; he managed his March pruning. Now, I've got to make sure his trees have enough moisture, not too much though, but the berries have formed now, Mr Rhea, the blossom's gone. It was a good spring without any hard frosts and the bees got busy fertilizing the flowers, so the trees are now full of very presentable young berries. Lots of them. Now I know Joseph always picked a lot of them off – he did his first thinning back in late May and was very careful which ones he left on.'

'There's where the skill comes in!' I agreed.

'You're right. He always seemed to know which ones to take off, so those left behind would grow to their biggest possible size. There's more thinning to do and some more netting to fix, against the birds.'

'You can do that, can you?' I asked.

'Oh, yes, I think so. Thinning's the tricky bit, Mr Rhea, knowing which ones to leave on the tree to the very end, and where to leave them so they get the best of the sun and so they're out of the wind and away from birds and wasps and so on. And there's sometimes a bit of summer pruning which has to be just right to let the air and sunshine in, and keep mildew off. Joseph has always said the right amount of pruning at the right time and in the right place is the secret of berry success but everyone has different ideas.'

'You've a lot to remember.' I smiled at her concern.

'I have!' she expostulated. 'I don't know how I'll cope if he's in hospital for any length of time.'

'You could get help. I'd say some of those

jobs need the services of an expert,' I suggested.

'And I'm no expert!' She sounded worried at this realization.

'You could always ask another grower to help,' I suggested, and the moment I uttered those words, I knew it was a crazy suggestion.

'Nay, Mr Rhea, I can't do that! I can't let competitors see how Joseph's berries are coming along, and I mustn't let any of them near his berries.'

'I realize that now ... it was silly of me....'

'They might nobble them, Mr Rhea,' she went on. 'You've no idea the dirty tricks some of them serious berry growers get up to. If somebody sets his heart on winning, he'll not let anything stop him, least of all the berries of another grower ... it's the easiest thing in the world to brush against a rival's best berry and make it drop off the tree when it's ripening fast, or puncture a really big one with a thorn or a needle ... or just pick the best off when nobody's looking and pretend it's the birds....'

'And has Joseph got a few secret bushes with big berries tucked away in a hidden corner of his garden?' I laughed.

''Course he has! They're out of sight from

the road, in that far corner of our back garden near the compost heap, gated off with nets covering them, but he's not had much time to bother with them this year. That's always been his problem, Mr Rhea, being too busy to deal with them special trees and being ill hasn't helped. There's still a lot of grass and nettles and other rubbish growing around them, stuff that should have been moved months ago, but I'm not going to touch them. I wouldn't dare. Joseph wants me to tend those in the front garden. He wants folks to see those berries, so they think all his berries are like that, not very big ones. He aims to lull them into a false sense of security, so he said. Well, I can see to these few trees with no problem.'

'But he doesn't want you to touch those in the back garden?'

'It's more than my life's worth, Mr Rhea. I'll just leave them alone. Anyway, he might be out of hospital soon, then he can tend his own berries. There's still a few weeks left ... and if anything'll get our Joseph out of his sick bed, it's the thought that he's going to miss the berry show.'

We chatted for about half an hour, with Mabel reminiscing about past happy memories in her long marriage to Joseph, referring to her children and grandchildren as her eyes misted over while she talked. She mentioned her unfulfilled desire to travel overseas, their closeness to the church and Joseph's Guild membership, but refrained from referring to the Guild's role in funerals. As she chattered, it was almost as if she was talking to herself, as if I was not in the room. I did not interrupt because I felt it would be good for her to unburden herself in this way but suddenly she realized what she was doing and halted her flow of words. I smiled, thanked her for her hospitality, reminded her about my offer of transport to Scarborough Hospital, and left. I walked away from the cottage with a distinct feeling that Joseph Marshall's wife was coming to a swift conclusion but hoped he would survive long enough to see his berry win the Supreme. And I just hoped he would die without any of the terrible pain that sometimes accompanied cancer. Feeling that I should be offering more solace but not knowing how to go about it, I climbed into my waiting Mini-van and drove away, heading for Waindale where a man wanted to renew the firearm certificate which authorized him to possess an elephant gun.

While Joseph was in hospital during the heat of that June, my normally peaceful patch at Aidensfield experienced its third bicycle theft. Like the previous occasions, it happened on a Sunday, but this time the crime was committed in a very remote area, high on the moors above the hamlet of Lairsbeck.

I received a telephone call from the kiosk in Lairsdale, a lonely valley deep in the moors comprising a scattering of farms, the tiny hamlet of Lairsbeck with little more than half-a-dozen houses, a telephone kiosk, a chapel and a thriving community of large wood ant-hills under a forest of pine trees.

As on previous occasions, I asked for a brief description of the bike so that I could swiftly circulate details of the crime to our mobile patrols and was not surprised to learn the missing bike was an expensive racing model, this time built by a small specialist manufacturer called Stratton Cycles. It was a gents' lightweight machine with a 24 inch frame coloured sky blue with silver lettering on the down tube; it had drop handlebars with blue handgrips, silver-coloured lightweight mudguards with the rear one bearing a red reflector, a racing saddle, rat-trap pedals fitted with toe-clips,

27 inch alloy racing wheels fitted with tubular tyres and a small saddle-bag containing the minimum of tools, a spare tubular tyre, some tomato and cheese sandwiches and a bottle of blackcurrant juice. The value was high, around £220, and it did not require a genius to associate this theft with the earlier ones. I assured the caller that I would immediately circulate the details and asked him to wait beside Lairsbeck kiosk, stressing I would meet him there in about twenty-five minutes. Next, I radioed Alf Ventress at Ashfordly Police Station with a request that he circulate the details as soon as possible, and adding that I was *en route* to meet the victim of the crime.

As I approached the kiosk, I saw a tall, thin man waiting nearby. He was standing against one of the pines which surrounded this part of the hamlet, and when he saw my police van, he hurried towards me.

I could see he was more upset than angry, so I settled him into the seat of the van and recorded the necessary details. As we talked, I explained I had searched the roads during my long journey up the dale, and that all my patrolling colleagues were already in possession of a description of his missing cycle. We had done everything possible up to this stage.

His name was Philip Henderson; he was 27 years old and worked in a processing plant at ICI, the giant chemical factory on Teesside. The cycle was the product of years of saving from his wages, and he'd only had it for two months; he was devastated by the loss. I asked him to show me from where it had been taken and he said it was some distance away, at the foot of Napier Howe. Napier Howe was a hill on the moors above Lairsbeck, almost two miles from our current position and so I drove him there. Leaning against a dry stone wall at the base of that hill were dozens of colourful bicycles, some expensive racing models like the one that was missing, and others of the tourist type. I couldn't see that any were locked or secured in any way, but their owners were sitting on the ground about halfway up the hill. They were having a picnic and Philip had left them to run all the way to the kiosk to break his bad news to me.

'So it went from there, did it?' I pointed to the wall against which the others were resting.

'It was at that end of the wall,' he said, indicating the right of the line, the point nearest any approach from the lower dale.

'Locked?' I asked.

'No, there's never been a need.'

'So, where were you, and the others, when the bike was taken?' I had to ask.

'We were on the hilltop,' he said. 'Or, to be precise, assembled around the summit, perhaps a little lower than the actual top. You see, we had come to pay a tribute to our club founder – Alan Bannister. We're the Napier Wheelers, that's the club he founded. He died in 1958 and he wanted his ashes scattered on Napier Howe because it was one of his favourite places. He named the club after the hill. So every year, we come here on the anniversary of his death.'

'And every one of you was on the hill – how long were you there?'

'One of our members is a vicar, so he said a few prayers. I'd say we were on the summit for about three-quarters of an hour. No more.'

'And your bike was taken in that time?'

'Yes. I parked it there when I arrived about half past ten; the little service of commemoration started at eleven and my bike had gone by twelve. I noticed it had gone when I came to get my lunch out of the saddle-bag. I couldn't find my bike; I

149

thought it might be hidden by some others, but it wasn't. It's gone, as clean as a whistle.'

I asked if he had seen anyone near the machines during their short service, but he shook his head. Then I approached the others and asked them the same question, but none had noticed anyone lurking nearby, nor had any vehicle been heard or seen. Somehow, the thief had managed to locate these bikes, steal the one of his choice and spirit it away within yards of the assembled club members.

I did tell Philip about the other thefts – he admitted that his club secretary had told members about the crimes but no one thought the thief would strike in such a remote place as Lairsbeck, especially with the owners so close to their machines. I asked how he intended getting home, and he said he had phoned his brother from the kiosk and he was already on his way by car to collect him.

The interesting thing about Lairsdale was that the moorland valley did not contain a through-road. A narrow lane meandered along the bottom of the dale, passed through Lairsbeck and then petered out some three miles ahead. From that point, it became an unmade moorland track which led to several farmsteads; then, even further into the hills, it degenerated into a footpath capable of being used only by hikers and ramblers. No motor vehicles or even a cycle could negotiate the narrow, rock-strewn route through the hills. This meant that, if the thief had used a motor vehicle to spirit away the cycle, he must have returned the way he had come. Even if he had ridden it away, he could not have escaped through the head of the dale. From that, I deduced the thief must be making use of a motor vehicle to carry off his trophies – and it was probably one which concealed the load, such as a covered pick-up truck or van. As we had never received any report of more than once cycle being stolen at a time, I realized that a solitary bike, with its wheels removed and handlebars twisted around, could even be accommodated in a saloon car. That was another possibility.

I began to wonder if I had passed the thief *en route* today but felt not.

This crime, with all the hallmarks of a professional job, would surely have been committed very soon after the group had arrived at their destination and that would have allowed the villain to be clear of the dale by the time the theft was discovered.

But how did the thief know the cycles were at this remote place? It was not the sort of place anyone would pass by chance – you had to make an effort to get there.

Clearly, the thief knew the movements of the cycling clubs on their Sunday outings – another indication of his professionalism. A list of meetings must be in circulation somewhere. As I pondered that aspect, I realized that someone must have seen a vehicle or a lone cyclist heading down this dale on the stolen machine. I'd call at the farms and cottages along the roadside to ask the occupiers if they'd seen anything remotely capable of spiriting away a stolen bike. Thus I had another crime and another puzzle to solve.

Leaving Philip Henderson to await his brother, I drove back to Ashfordly Police Station to enter the crime in our records, and to instigate the necessary procedures for circulating details of the theft. It was important that our patrols and all local cycle dealers were notified as soon as possible. Once I'd attended to the paperwork, I would return to Lairsdale to continue my enquiries, but inwardly felt it was a futile exercise. Whoever had stolen that bike would have ensured that no one saw him, as he'd done countless times already. However, once I began to talk to the people who lived beside the road, I did elicit a snippet of useful information. An isolated stone cottage with a thatched roof stood on the edge of the road midway up one of the steeper inclines some two miles from Lairsbeck.

It was called Heathercroft and occupied by a gamekeeper and his wife, the keeper working for Lairsdale Estate. He was John Hebden and his wife was Margaret. Margaret, a jolly red-faced woman in her late forties, had been weeding the little garden she'd created outside the gate of the house as a vehicle had approached up the steep hill. It was just before 10.30, she recalled, because John often popped home for a coffee and a chocolate biscuit around then. As the vehicle had driven slowly past, she'd straightened up, easing her back after a session of weeding. She described it as slightly larger than a Morris 1000 pick-up but smaller than Claude Jeremiah Greengrass's old truck. She thought it was a Ford but couldn't be absolutely sure. However, it was a maroon colour in fairly good condition, and it had a covered rear section without any back doors. She'd noticed that the back contained what looked like an old green tarpaulin; it appeared to have been thrown inside because it was not folded neatly, but in that state it seemed to fill the back of the little truck. She had seen it quite clearly as the truck had chugged past her.

'But the thing is, Mr Rhea, I did not recognize the van. It doesn't belong to anyone living in the dale, and I have no idea what it was doing here. I can't remember seeing it before, but we do get strangers driving along the dale on Sundays but this one didn't look like someone on a Sunday outing. There was a man driving, but I didn't really see him except that he had dark hair. I'd say he was in his late twenties or early thirties, but that's all. Anyway, the funny thing was the van came back about half an hour later which made me think he was looking for a house or a farm. But he didn't stop to ask directions. I thought that was strange, particularly if he was lost, but when it passed me that time, it was going much faster. I watched as it drove away from me. The tarpaulin was still in the back and the same man was driving.'

'Was he alone?' I put to her.

'Yes, I'm sure he was. I didn't see anybody with him.'

'Could you say what clothes he was wearing?'

'No, sorry. I couldn't really see him very well, the light was reflecting from the windscreen.'

'I understand. So can you remember the registration number?' I asked in forlorn hope.

'Sorry, no, I never thought to memorize it.'

'Now, you mentioned a tarpaulin, or something like a tarpaulin. Could it have been hiding something underneath? I'm thinking of a cycle lying on the floor of the truck and being covered with that tarpaulin.'

'Well, it did look as if it had been disturbed that second time I saw him. I wondered if something had been taken out from under it....'

'Or placed under it?' I did not want to plant ideas in her mind, but at the same time felt I had to press for some kind of more detailed opinion.

'Yes, I suppose so. The way it was lying there, yes, something could have been underneath it. But you know how it is, Mr Rhea, with agricultural vehicles and trucks used by farmers, they carry all sorts in the back, logs, sacks of this and that, shovels and spades, tools of all kinds, rolls of wire or netting, even dogs and sheep. One thing just gets thrown in on top of another.'

'So do you think it was a farmer's vehicle?'

'I don't think so. It was too clean and even the tarpaulin or carpet or whatever it was, looked clean. There were no names or lettering on the truck, by the way, so I don't think it was a delivery van of any kind, or a tradesman's run-about.'

I quizzed her for a few more minutes until it was clear she could not provide any further information, then thanked her. I told her she'd provided the only clue to date in a long-running series of cycle thefts. Before leaving, I asked her to ring if she ever saw the truck again and, if possible, to note its registration number. She assured me she would – she felt she would recognize it another time. After leaving, I called at more houses and farms along the dale, but no one else could provide any information. One farmer made the point that on Sundays, all kinds of vehicles passed along the dale – tourists, hikers, day-trippers, bird-watchers and so it was difficult to identify any which were behaving suspiciously.

'Besides,' he reminded me, 'whatever goes

up that dale must come down again, except walkers. And us local chaps know all the vehicles kept in the dale – and there's not a maroon truck among 'em.'

I asked the residents whether any had had a visit from the man in the maroon-coloured truck, but none had. None was expecting any kind of workman or a delivery of goods, so I felt increasingly sure the truck had been used to carry off the stolen bike.

Very pleased at this development, I hurried back to Ashfordly Police Station from where I could circulate a description of the van; I would also notify the other police forces which had suffered similar crimes so that they were aware of this possible link.

'Well done, Rhea,' said Sergeant Blaketon, who came into the office as I was completing my report about the suspicious truck.

'It was a bit of luck, Sergeant,' I said.

'It was good police work.' He seldom praised anyone, so this gave me a small feeling of pride. 'But before you circulate a description of that truck, it might be wise to contact the CID in the other forces, just to check no one's keeping such a vehicle under observation. For all we know, there might be a target criminal somewhere with a truck just like that, and there could be some kind of scheme to catch him in possession of stolen goods. It might be that he must not be alerted to our interest at this stage.'

It was good and very practical advice. I rang the other police forces involved and discovered there had been no other reports of such a vehicle nor had any suspect come into the frame. After discussions with the relevant officers in charge, we decided it would be useful to circulate a description of the suspect vehicle, albeit with a request that its registration number be recorded and its location noted without any interviews of the driver – unless, of course, a cycle had very recently been stolen nearby and there was high possibility of catching the thief in possession of it.

The main purpose was to discover the name and address of the owner, and then to monitor his movements and his contacts. Later, we would raid any premises he frequented with a view to catching him in possession of one or more stolen cycles. If he was the guilty party, it was vital that we obtained the evidence necessary to secure a conviction.

The following Tuesday, Mabel Marshall asked if I could drive her to Scarborough to visit Joseph that coming Thursday and, after checking my duty sheet, I said I could take her to the afternoon visiting session. She told me that Joseph's specialist wanted a word with her in private during that visit.

And so on Thursday, with Mabel beside me in her best hat and coat, and clutching a basket of cakes and fruit topped with some Get Well cards, I drove the winding route to Scarborough's fine brick-built hospital along the Whitby road. During the journey she chattered about her family and grand-children, interspacing her comments with tales about Joseph including his likes, dislikes, church work, Guild activities, reluctance to visit new places and his hobby of growing giant gooseberries. Judging by her non-stop chatter, I got the impression she was trying to keep herself cheerful as she approached the hospital. I must admit I did not say a great deal simply because I rarely had the opportunity, but I wondered what she expected to learn when she arrived. Had she been warned to expect some kind of unpleasant news?

Interested though I was, I decided not to press her for too much information in case I triggered a bout of tears or overt misery, so I endured her one-sided conversation. In due course we arrived in the car-park and I accompanied her to Joseph's bedside. Joseph was sitting beside his bed in an easy chair and was clad in a heavy dressing-gown and slippers. His unused pipe lay on top of his bedside cabinet. His thin face lit up at the sight of Mabel. I ushered her in first and she planted a kiss on his cheek as I acquired some chairs for us.

'Now then, Joseph,' I said, shaking his hand. 'I thought I'd pop in to see how you're getting on.'

'And Mr Rhea drove me through, Joseph, it's very kind of him.'

'Thanks, Mr Rhea.' Neither of them would relinquish their formality and I did not embarrass them by suggesting it. 'It's good of you.'

'So how's things?' I asked. 'How are you feeling?'

'Well, as a matter of fact, I'm feeling all right now and my stomach pains have stopped. Nowt but a bit of belly ache, they said, caused by summat I'd eaten. I'd had the runs for a day or two, but things have cleared up now. Apart from that they've pushed all sorts of tubes and things into me

160

from all ends, and sampled my water and my blood and had me spitting in jars, but they've found nowt. I'm still as thin as a rail, I know that, and I don't weigh much more than one of my berries. I can't work up an appetite, not even for that roast beef and Yorkshire pudding they put on this dinner-time.'

'There's no pain anywhere else?' I asked him.

'Nay, lad. I'm not in pain. Never have been, apart from that belly ache.'

'So what do they say, Joseph?' Mabel asked, the concern showing in the lines of her tired face.

'Nowt,' he said bluntly. 'They say they can't find owt wrong with me. I've had all sorts of important-looking folks in here, looking in my eyes, down my throat, up my bum and then giving me stuff to drink and pass through for testing, but they've come up with absolutely nowt.'

'Does that mean you can come home?' she asked.

'I've got to wait for the result of one more test, it'll be ready tomorrow, so they say. If I pass that, I'll be allowed home later in the day.'

It was then that an important-looking

doctor in a smart white coat came into the ward, shown towards Joseph's bed by a nurse.

'Good afternoon, Mr Marshall, nice that you could have some visitors.'

'My wife,' said Joseph. 'Mrs Marshall. And our local bobby, Constable Rhea.'

'You're not in trouble with the police, I hope!' smiled the doctor.

'Nay, Doctor, he's given my missus a lift in to see me.'

'Well, that is very kind. Now, Mrs Marshall, my name is Hindmarsh, I'm a consultant and first, I'd like a word with you,' he said. 'In private. There's a consultancy room just outside the ward. This way please.'

And so, looking at me as if for support or succour, she followed him like an obedient little dog.

'What's all that about?' asked Joseph, as the pair vanished into the corridor.

'We'll know very soon,' I said softly. 'Now, I've got some nice berry trees in my garden, so what can you tell me about growing a prize-winning berry?'

# 6

Mabel returned to Joseph's bedside after some twenty minutes. She was alone, the consultant having continued his way on other business. Reaching her chair, she settled down without a word, the expression on her face telling me she had received something of an unwelcome shock from Dr Hindmarsh.

'That chap, Dr Hindmarsh, he says he's been to see you quite a lot of times while you've been in here,' she addressed her remarks directly to Joseph and so I stood up and prepared to leave. The forthcoming discussion was clearly something of a very private and personal nature.

'No, sit down, Mr Rhea.' She waved me back to my chair. 'I'd like you to hear this.'

'Well, if it's something very private, perhaps I'd better not...' I began.

'No, it's not private. In fact, I ought to tell the whole world how wrong these folks are...' she said, and I could see the anger in her eyes and in the way her cheeks were highly coloured as she clenched her teeth. 'I've never come across such a lot of incompetents and such a bunch of ignorant folks in all my life. Really, I haven't. And they call themselves experts! They know nowt, Mr Rhea, absolutely nowt.'

'So what's brought all this on?' I asked.

'He should know!' Somewhat accusingly, she pointed to Joseph. 'That Dr Hindmarsh says he's been to see you a lot of times, Joseph, and given you all sorts of tests and examinations and he says he's already told you what he thinks.'

'He has,' agreed Joseph. 'I've never seen so much of one chap in such a short time. He always seemed to be examining me, wanting X-rays and prodding and poking about on my belly and my chest and private bits, taking samples of blood and water and asking questions, then checking what I said against what other experts have said, reading their reports about me. It makes me feel like summat in an antique sale.'

'And after all that, what did he tell you?' demanded Mabel.

'Well, he said they couldn't find owt wrong with me,' said Joseph, with a mixture of embarrassment and disbelief.

'That's right. He said you'd been told this

164

morning, and that's what he wanted to see me about. So he's just told me. They say there's nothing wrong with you!' she snapped. 'And do I believe a word of it? No, I do not! How can that be right? How can they say there's nothing wrong with you? I told that doctor you've not been right for weeks and how much weight you've lost and your appetite has gone and then there was them belly aches, but he said there's no reason for all that. Your heart and lungs are very fit and well, there's no cancer in you, according to their tests, and there's nowt wrong with your insides either or your waterworks.'

'That's what he told me.'

'And,' she continued, 'your blood pressure might be a bit on the high side, but it's nowt to get worried about, not at your age. It's nowhere near being too high. In short, Joseph Marshall, everything's working as it should be and you're not ill. According to them, that is.'

'Well, that's good news, isn't it?' said Joseph.

'It is, if it's true. And they said that stomach upset was nowt to get worried about. It was due to something you ate, and they think that's cleared up. He says you've one more test and if that turns out all right, you can come home.'

'Yes, I had to pee into a bottle this morning, before breakfast,' Joseph announced. 'It's being tested today somewhere.'

'What are they looking for?' I felt I ought to contribute to this discussion.

'No idea, Mr Rhea. But it's summat they wanted to check out as a last resort, in view of my stomach upset. To make sure whatever had upset me has gone clean out of my system, I think.'

'Did they give any indication of what time the result will be known? I'm thinking that we could take you home today if they'd allow us to. I'd be happy to wait.'

'No, it won't be ready until tomorrow morning, they said,' Joseph told us. 'My sample has to go off somewhere to be looked at and it'll take a full day to get it there and back.'

'They're not doing their jobs, Mr Rhea!' It was obvious that Mabel was unable to agree with the verdict of the hospital authorities. 'I've known Joseph very near all my life, more than sixty years, and I know him well enough to realize things are not right. How can they be, with him losing all that weight? It's not natural, and even if they use big words as they try and convince me he's all right, I know deep down he's not.'

'Can you recall exactly what Dr Hindmarsh said?' I wondered about the language he'd used to relay this information to her.

'Words I've never heard before, Mr Rhea, all jargon and incomprehensible to me, but I reckon they think he's imagining things.'

'Imagining things? Me?' Joseph sounded mortified at the suggestion.

'That's what they're trying to say, so it seems to me. But how can you imagine you're losing weight when it's dropping off pound by pound like it has? There's no imagination about Joseph's loss of weight, Mr Rhea, anybody can see it for themselves. And his lost appetite is not imagined – it's as real as I'm sitting here.'

'I'm just not hungry these days,' Joseph added for good measure.

'I've tried feeding him up with Yorkshire puddings and suet dumplings and plenty of mashed potato and gravy, along with some good stews and roast beef, with black puddings and bacon and sausages for breakfast, but he's like a child, Mr Rhea, leaving half of whatever I give him. That's not imagination, not when you've got to chuck out platefuls of good dinner. Them cats living near us have never had such a good time.

'What do you think I should do, Mr Rhea?' Mabel turned to me and I could see she was concerned at this unexpected development.

'This is what will happen,' I told her. 'When the hospital has done all its tests and got them analysed and assessed, they'll write to your doctor – Dr McGee that is – and he'll call Joseph into his surgery for a chat. That will happen as soon as his final test has been assessed. I think all you can do is wait until Dr McGee has a word with you, that is – and then decide what happens after that. If nobody can find anything wrong with you, Joseph, then it might just be a question of giving you time to regain your weight and find your appetite.'

'That hasn't worked so far,' mumbled Joseph, unconvinced.

'Well, I can't understand all these modern notions,' Mabel added. 'So far as I'm concerned, he's ill and there's no question about it. It's not in the mind – fancy saying a thing like that! Just look at the fellow, he's as thin as a scrawny old hen and that's no imagination. But I'll do as you say, Mr Rhea, I'll wait to hear what Dr McGee makes of all this. Mebbe he can explain things when he's got all the papers in front of him.'

'You could always seek a second opinion,' I suggested. 'From a private consultant, that is.'

'We're not the sort to go rushing off to private doctors, Mr Rhea, not with Joseph being a big man in the NUR when he was working, the unions don't like private medicine, but if it's a matter of life and death, then mebbe we should consider a second opinion. But I think it's a case of wait and see just now.'

'I think you're right,' I smiled. 'Wait and see what he's like when he gets home.'

During our journey back to Aidensfield, Mabel continued to express her disgust by reciting cases she knew of people dying from all kinds of fearsome ailments which had been ignored or not identified by so-called medical experts. I must admit that, in the short time I had known Joseph, I had never regarded him as one of nature's worriers, but I accepted that such a condition could manifest itself through a combination of factors, with advancing age and concealed stress being two of the most likely constituents. On the other hand, illness caused by a condition of mind was something Mabel utterly failed to comprehend. I delivered her back to her little cottage, telling her not to worry too much because Dr McGee would ensure that her husband received his closest attention whatever the comments from Scarborough Hospital, and I added that I would help her to visit Joseph again if she needed any further trips to the hospital.

Then I went home and got changed into my uniform for a late tour of duty.

Joseph came home the following afternoon, his final urine test not revealing any additional problems and the next time I saw him he was digging furiously in his garden. I was driving past at the time, therefore I did not stop, but I did wonder if he was trying to prove he was not ill. Certainly his garden had been slightly neglected during his incapacity, in spite of Mabel's attention to it, and now it seemed he was attacking it with considerable gusto.

I wondered if he was trying to make up for lost time – another reason for not interrupting him. Although I caught only a glimpse as I passed, I thought he looked thin, pale and rather weary. I hoped he wasn't overdoing things, and made a resolution to pop in when I had more time.

It was during those summer weeks that further expensive cycles were stolen from venues around the north-east of England. The crimes were not reported in any of the local newspapers and there was never any Press suggestion of a crime wave even though a substantial amount of money was involved. The odd bike stolen from widely separated areas was hardly likely to make news, and my only means of becoming aware of the continuing crimes came through my determined studies of the Stolen Cycle Supplements. Unfortunately, they were issued on an irregular basis, usually when there were sufficient reports to fill a couple of sides of paper. Consequently, it was sometimes a month before I learned of such a theft in a distant part of County Durham or from a CTC café near Middlesbrough. Each entry was very short and comprised only a very few lines with the minimum of information. This made it difficult to isolate racing-cycle thefts from the mass of more mundane matter – most of the stolen bikes listed were ordinary roadsters. A surprising number of black gentlemen's cycles were stolen, although I noted that a small pink girl's cycle had been stolen from outside a girl guides' hut and that a large, green, old-fashioned lady's cycle had been stolen from outside a shop in Redcar. I wondered what a large, green old-fashioned lady looked like.

By this stage, I had begun to compile my own register of stolen cycles by abstracting information from the supplements, but listing only those crimes which appeared to be the work of the man in the maroon pick-up truck. Whenever I discovered a note of such a crime, I contacted the local office of the CID to explain my interest and obtain background details. Sadly, I learned little more than I already knew, but my research reinforced my belief that all our villain was stealing were bikes which were expensive racing machines, many hand-built rather than being factory produced. It appeared that the thief was very knowledgeable and discerning, but he had no favourite colour because machines in a variety of colours were stolen.

One factor was that all the cycles had crossbars like gents' bikes, even though one loser was a woman. Nonetheless, her machine did have a crossbar – indeed, lady cyclists who were keen tourers or racing enthusiasts did use gents' cycles or, to be precise, cycles with crossbars. Apparently, that design of frame made the machines more stable and responsive to fast and powerful riding in races and on long tours. Another common factor, one which I had already identified, was that the machines were invariably taken from places where a large number of cycles were assembled. At first, I thought all such places were meeting points of CTC members but this was not always the case. Some were gatherings of local club members such as the Tees Valley Wheelers, The South Durham Road Club, the Hambleton Road Club, or events like our local Thackerston Sunday. It was clear, therefore, that the thief knew about such gatherings in advance because he seemed to arrive very soon after the cycles had been temporarily abandoned by their owners.

It was almost as if he followed them there, or was even a member of the party – or that he had an accomplice within the organization. But the thief was not a member of one single club because he appeared to have information about the activities of several different clubs or events which attracted large numbers of cyclists, whether or not they were members of particular clubs. He knew where they met, what time they gathered and possibly how long their bikes would be left unattended. Beyond doubt, he was very familiar with the north-east cycling scene – and all the crimes were committed around Middlesbrough, albeit extending into south Durham, the Yorkshire Dales and the North York Moors.

It was almost as if the thief lived or worked in Middlesbrough and ventured out of the town in a different direction each Sunday, to commit his crimes. I did examine a map of the area, marking upon it the locations of all the crimes and every one of them was within a forty-mile radius of Middlesbrough. That was another common factor I could not ignore.

In compiling my own register, I realized I had become a self-appointed collator but being totally efficient was not easy due to the number of different police force divisions and local officers involved. The fact that I was not party to the investigation of crimes beyond my own boundaries was also a hindrance. To gain the necessary assistance, I had to rely on other officers, probably with less commitment than myself and that was never wholly satisfactory. Nonetheless, I felt I was doing my best and wondered whether Sergeant Craddock was also conducting his personal enquiries.

I persisted with my local enquiries and my continuing search of the countryside, but apart from that one snippet of information about the maroon pick-up, I discovered absolutely nothing. And none of the other investigations had revealed the presence of a maroon pick-up in the vicinity at the time. I must admit I began to think the thief was skilful enough never to be caught or identified.

Then I had a piece of luck.

Margaret Hebden, the gamekeeper's wife, who had seen the suspicious maroon pick-up in Lairsdale, rang me rather breathlessly one Wednesday afternoon to say she was sure she had seen the same truck only half an hour earlier. It had been motoring along the lane which bordered the disused airfield at Stovensby but she'd been too far away to obtain the registration number. It had been around 3.30 p.m. when she'd seen it. Fortunately, I was at home when she rang and immediately jumped into my van and hurtled through the lanes – Stovensby was about twenty minutes' drive from my police house at Aidensfield. If the pick-up had been driving away from the area when

Margaret had seen it, it would have something like a fifty-minute start on me – which meant it could be more than twenty miles away by the time I arrived. But I had to visit the scene – it might still be in the locality.

I drove through all the lanes, peering into likely parking places such as farmyards and lay-bys, but saw no sign of the truck, and then decided to visit my old foe, Tin Lid Talbot, at his scrapyard on the old airfield at Stovensby. I thought the van might have been *en route* to visit him. As usual, I found him sorting through a pile of junk in one of his untidy sheds.

'Now then, Tin Lid,' I said. 'How's things with you?'

'Busy as ever, Mr Rhea,' he said. 'It never stops.'

'You've been behaving yourself lately?' I had to ask the question. He expected it of me.

'I have, Mr Rhea, never touched anything that I haven't obtained legally.' That was one of his stock answers.

Normally, I'd tackle him about some petty crimes for which he was a suspect, but not on this occasion.

'Good,' I smiled at the scruffy fellow.

'That's what I like to hear.'

'Something happened then?' He looked at me quizzically and I could see he was worried about my presence. 'Something happened to bring you here like this? It's not often you call without a reason.'

'That's very observant of you.' I could see he was in a good mood and, if as he claimed he had not stolen anything recently, then he should not be unduly worried about my presence, unless he was thinking I suspected him of receiving stolen goods. 'But I do have a reason for calling.'

'I thought you might,' he muttered. 'But I've done nothing wrong. Not that I know of, anyway.'

'I'm not suggesting you have, Tin Lid,' I smiled. 'It's a van I'm interested in. It passed this way less than an hour ago. I wondered if it might have called here.'

'A van, Mr Rhea?'

'A maroon one, with a covered back. Like a pick-up with a roof over the rear part but with no back doors.'

'Ah, yes. That van. Yes, I must confess the driver did call here, but I never paid a penny for those lids.'

'Lids?' I asked.

'Paint-tin lids. He brings them to me, lots

of them. I'm sure they're not stolen, Mr Rhea.'

'I doubt if anyone would deal in stolen lids from paint pots, Tin Lid. A regular supplier, is he?'

'On and off, Mr Rhea. He knows I deal in lids, and fetches his unwanted ones to me.'

'Free of charge?'

'Yes, free of charge, Mr Rhea. He just wants rid of them. They take up a lot of space, do unwanted tin lids.'

'Is he a regular visitor then? Weekly? Monthly?'

'Oh, no, Mr Rhea, nothing as regular as that. Once or twice a year mebbe, or mebbe up to three or four times. But not weekly. Oh, no.'

'Can I see them?' was my next request. 'The lids, I mean.'

'Well, I never thought I'd see the day when you were interested in second-hand tin lids, Mr Rhea, but yes, follow me.'

He led me into the shed where he kept a massive pile of tin lids in every conceivable shape, size and colour.

I began to wonder about Tin Lid Talbot's mania for collecting these things because he never seemed to dispose of any. There was the strong scent of paint too, enamel paint,

I thought, although the background pong might have been a mixture of anything sticking to the lids, ranging from baked beans to garden fertilizer.

'So which lids did he bring?' I asked, gazing down upon the collection of filthy lids, some of which were coated with unknown and unidentifiable filth.

'Them there.' He pointed to a heap of round tin lids, all of which seemed to have come from paint tins. There was about five dozen or so I guessed, all of the same size and all showing grey as the colour of the contents. Some of the colour adhered to the underside of the lids, and some of them bore a patch of colour on the top, to identify the contents of the tin – but all revealed the same shade of light grey.

'There's a lot of paint tin lids!' I noted.

'Yes, Mr Rhea. A lot. He always brings a lot when he comes.'

'And they've all come from tins containing grey paint?'

'They have, Mr Rhea, yes, they have. All from tins of grey paint. I think he likes grey paint, Mr Rhea.'

'I think you're right, Tin Lid. Now, the paint on them smells like enamel,' and I sniffed the air to make my point. 'What sort

179

of things would he paint with this?'

'Metal things,' he said. 'Cars, bikes, farm equipment, kitchen things mebbe. Probably be spraying it on.'

'Bikes, you said?' I asked.

'Yes, bikes, Mr Rhea. The chap said that. He paints bikes.'

'Does he?' Now I was getting very interested in these lids. 'What sort of bikes?'

'Grey ones, Mr Rhea.'

'I had worked that out, Tin Lid. Why does he paint bikes grey?'

'He builds bikes, Mr Rhea. He once told me a long time ago. Second-hand ones, and then he sells them.'

'I might want to buy a nice bike.' I decided not to reveal my genuine interest to this fellow. 'So who is this man? Where's he come from?'

'No idea, Mr Rhea,' he said. 'I've never known his name or where he comes from. He just turns up every so often with a sackful of tin lids which he lets me have, and then he goes.'

'And he comes alone, does he?'

'I've never seen him with anybody else,' Tin Lid confirmed.

'Always in his maroon pick-up?'

'Always, Mr Rhea. Never uses anything

else. He's had it years.'

'So where's his workshop, Tin Lid? He must have left some clues with you.'

'Search me, Mr Rhea. I have no idea. He never says much about himself. Just drops the stuff off and goes.'

'But he did say he painted bikes? Or is that something you dreamed up?'

'No, he definitely said that. He told me when I asked him where his tin lids came from. He said he buys tins of fresh paint for his work. He used a lot, he says.'

'So why does he bring the lids to you?' I asked. 'And what happens to the empty tins?'

'Search me, Mr Rhea. I've no idea what he does with his empties but he knows I deal in tin lids, you see, he knows I'm the premier dealer in tin lids in this part of the world, so he lets me have those he doesn't want. It's very good of him, especially when he brings them to me. I mean, I don't have to go and pick them up myself.'

'I find that very curious,' I said. 'Coming all this way especially to deliver a few tin lids to you. Unless he doesn't want you to know where he lives or works.'

My gut reaction was that the thief was concealing evidence of his clandestine work by spreading his used paraphernalia around widely separated places so that nothing could be traced back to him. But in that, he was wrong. For one thing, he must have a supplier for all his grey paint! Not many people would buy such quantities, unless they wanted to paint a battleship or two. With a bit of luck, the chain of evidence might be traced back to him.

'I think he comes here when he's got business hereabouts,' Tin Lid explained. 'I don't think he makes a special journey to see me.'

'You mean he sells his bikes somewhere in this area?'

'Some of them, mebbe. Not all of them. I believe he has a good name for bikes, Mr Rhea, sells them far and wide, he does.'

'Does he? They're special bikes, are they?'

'Oh, very. Expensive and smart, Mr Rhea, racing bikes. The best. Handmade for big cyclists.'

'So you think keen cyclists buy them?'

'Well, if what my mate at the bike shop says was true, only the really keen types would try to afford them. Not for the ordinary chap, they aren't.'

'So your contact with the maroon van is an expert at his work, Tin Lid?'

'Oh, very, Mr Rhea. I think he's one of the top experts at his job. It was me that put him in touch with a dealer, a local chap you see, and he was capped to bits with the bikes he got. That's why I'm in their good books, both of them, in a manner of speaking. That's my reward from the bike man – those lids, a regular supply.'

'So which bike dealer are we talking about, Tin Lid? The one who likes you.'

'I used to shift all his scrap metal, Mr Rhea.'

'Used to? You don't do it now?'

'He retired, Mr Rhea. He used to have a shop at Eltering, but he closed it a few years ago. When he was on the go, he sold bikes, new and second-hand, and did repairs. Eltering Cycles in Finkle Street, that was the shop. I always did well with gear wheels and bottom bracket spindles from there.'

'And now? What's the situation if that shop has closed?'

'No idea, Mr Rhea. I don't think there's a cycle shop in Eltering now, but that chap still comes this way now and again as I've told you, but not as regular as he used to.'

'What's he look like? If I want a bike from him, how do I contact him?'

'A youngish chap, very tall, thin as a rail.

Dark hair. I've no idea what he calls himself. It's funny that, I've known him all these years yet never known what his name is.'

'I believe you, but specialists and true artists are like that sometimes,' I said with tongue in cheek. 'Very guarded about their work, never advertising, always playing hard to get. Now, Tin Lid, if I wanted to borrow one of those tin lids to see if it's the sort of grey I want, would you let me take one? If necessary, I'll pay your price,' I added.

'Take as many as you want, Mr Rhea,' said Tin Lid. 'There's mebbe a slight variation in different brews or batches, so you can take a few. Fetch 'em back when you've decided. I know I can trust you to do that.'

'So you can! I've no real personal use for second-hand tin lids.'

I wanted to examine the lids away from his scrutiny in case they carried the name of the shop from which they had been obtained. From that, I might be able to trace the man who bought them. A further and perhaps remote likelihood was that they might bear the thief's fingerprints and so, in the event of this man's cycle factory being discovered, we could match the lids to the paint, and the paint tins to him via fingerprints. It was a long shot, but worth trying. I found an old hessian sack hanging on a nail and placed a small selection of the lids inside, watched by Tin Lid. At that stage, I had no idea whether Tin Lid was being honest with me or whether he knew I was trying to catch a thief.

He might be making a deliberate show of going along with my wishes and opinions in order to keep himself in my favour and at the same time shield the identity of the thief. I had a gut feeling that he knew more than he was saying – and if that was the case, the cycle thief might be alerted to my interest. But that was a risk I had to take – I could not lose the opportunity that Tin Lid had provided.

Upon leaving Tin Lid's premises with my bag of paint tin lids, I decided that a swift visit to Eltering was necessary. I wanted to trace the owner of the former cycle shop in Finkle Street. Parking in a side street twenty minutes later, I donned my police cap and set about my enquiries, noting there was now no cycle shop in that street. It didn't take many minutes of questioning the staff of a gentlemen's outfitters to establish that Adam and Eve's fruit and vegetable shop occupied the premises of the former Eltering Cycles. It had closed three years ago upon the retirement of the proprietor. He was called Sidney Suggitt and upon hearing this name, I thought Eltering Cycles was a better name for his shop than Sidney Suggitt Cycles. I also learned he had retired at the age of seventy and now lived in Pikelands Road. A quick check in the telephone directory at the gentlemen's outfitters then established he lived at No. 45. Within minutes, I was knocking on his door. A rather stooped old gentleman responded. Had he been standing upright, he would have been over six feet in height but he was very bent with either osteoporosis in his back, or some type of rheumatic problem. Or, of course, his back was bent through years of riding bikes with dropped handlebars or stooping while effecting decades of repairs to his customers' machines.

'Mr Suggitt?' I asked.

'Yes,' he said, screwing his eyes to peer up at me. He was wearing poor quality, creased, grey trousers, an old cardigan and carpet slippers.

'PC Rhea from Aidensfield,' I introduced myself. 'I have been trying to trace you, through your shop in town.'

'I don't do repairs now, Constable, if that's

what you're wanting, and if you're going to ask if I'll fit a new tyre to that police bike from Eltering Police Station the answer is no. The front wheel rim's buckled, I've told 'em that time and time again, so it's a waste of time, mine and theirs, to bother with it. Tell them to get a new one, Constable. A new bike, I mean, not a new wheel. That bike must pre-date the First World War; riding it is like trying to steer a tank around town.'

'It's a long time since we had to use our official cycles,' I smiled. 'But I'll have words with our new sergeant at Brantsford, he's a keen cyclist.'

'I think somebody should open a new shop in town,' he muttered. 'There's nowhere to get cycles maintained. I keep getting folks coming here wanting punctures mended, pumps repaired, or gears readjusted and ball bearings renewed. It's all general maintenance really but I just don't do that sort of thing now.'

'I'm not wanting you to do work for us, Mr Suggitt,' I said. 'I'm trying to trace someone you used to deal with.'

'Oh,' he said, and there was a long pause as he struggled to come to terms with the fact I was not seeking his specialized services and I wondered if he was just a little disappointed about that. 'So who is it you're looking for?'

At this stage, I did not want him to think I suspected a former business acquaintance of being a clever thief, so I had to choose my words carefully.

'There was a man who used to deliver second-hand cycles to you, for you to sell,' I began.

'Oh, well, you'd better come in, Constable. Excuse the mess, I live alone now my wife has died. I can rustle up a coffee or cup of tea if you fancy one. It's nice to get someone calling.'

And so I opted for a coffee and as he pottered into his kitchen to prepare it, I looked around his lounge. Filled with cheap, wartime furniture, it was full of cycling memorabilia ranging from photographs and certificates to cups and medals he'd won. As he waited for the kettle to boil, I occupied myself by admiring ancient photographs of Mr Suggitt on his cycle, sometimes in racing mode and sometimes standing in picturesque places with a touring cycle. He was shown either with friends, a woman I took to be his wife, or club members. Then he returned with two mugs of coffee, each wobbling dangerously in his shaking hands; I relieved him of one and he told me to sit down. An electric fire was burning in the grate, but it was casting out very little heat and I wondered how he kept warm in winter.

'I miss my Cynthia,' he said, referring to a photograph I'd been admiring upon his return. 'She was very supportive in my work, and liked to get into the countryside on her bike. I'm too old now, Constable, although I still have my old Wyvern. Hand-built it was, because of my height. I'd have a job getting my leg over now let alone balancing the thing – and coping with modern traffic.'

I allowed him to reminisce for a while as we sipped our coffee, and then he asked, 'So who's this man you're looking for?'

'I don't know his name, nor do I have a very good description,' I admitted. 'But he drives a maroon pick-up type of truck which has a covered back, but no rear doors. Quite distinctive in its own way. He's a tall young man with dark hair, and I'm told he builds racing cycles, specialist ones possibly. I was told he used to provide you with cycles from time to time.'

'And who told you that?' he frowned at me.

'Tin Lid Talbot,' I said.

'Ah, Tin Lid! What would I have done without him? He removed all my unwanted scrap metal, Constable. Whatever surplus bits and pieces I had from my repairs or renewals, Tin Lid Talbot would remove them free of charge.'

'He's good at removing things!' I laughed. 'Although he doesn't restrict himself to scrap metal!'

'Well, I can only speak as I found him. He was very reliable, calling at least once a week. What on earth he did with the stuff, I shall never know. But he did put me in touch with that young man you mention.'

'And then the young man supplied you with cycles?'

'From time to time, yes. Over the years, I obtained most of my general stock and spare parts from well-established manu-facturers like Raleigh, Rudge, Elswick, Humber, Hercules, Whitworth and Sturmey-Archer, but sometimes I was asked for a racing machine, or even a special, built to order. And that young man could supply them at a very competitive price. I didn't keep a stock of racing bikes, you see; really good ones are too expensive for me to lay out cash for, so I supplied them to order.'

'What sort of specials were you usually asked for?' I put to him.

'Lightweight racing bikes of superior quality, hand-built most of them, and made-to-measure like suits, generally catering for very tall people. It's often difficult getting a satisfactory rigid cycle frame for someone more than six feet three or four inches tall. But that young man would make bikes for tall people, Constable. With large frames. The bikes, I mean, had large frames. Not the people.'

'Ah!' I had a glimmer of a recollection that all those stolen racing bikes had twenty-four inch frames ... it seemed he was stealing specialist cycles for tall people, repainting them and selling them to shops like Eltering Cycles.

And Tin Lid Talbot had mentioned something about big cyclists – not big as in Big Catholics or Big Gooseberry Men, but big in terms of physical size. 'So who is this young man, Mr Suggitt? I'd like to have words with him.'

'He's not in trouble, is he?' asked the old man. 'He seemed such a pleasant young fellow.'

'Good heavens no, he's not in trouble! It's just that one of our new sergeants is a keen cyclist; he's a tall chap and wants a large-framed, lightweight machine. He's asked us all to keep our eyes open. Tin Lid thought you might help me find this specialist builder.'

'Well, to be honest, Constable, I do not know who he is. He never once said what his name was or where he came from. I would place an order for, say, a twenty-four inch racing machine with certain features, and he would supply it within four or six weeks. Beautiful cycles, they were; he called them Wyvern after the winged dragon of European mythology. Customers had a choice of saddle, handlebars, type of gear, number of gears, mudguards or not, light-weight wheels, tubular tyres ... the lot in fact, all supplied on request.'

'Did they have a choice of colour?' I asked.

'No, they were all light grey. That was his trademark, Constable. Pale grey, the colour of the dragon's skin, but with red lines and highlights, and a red-coloured dragon logo.'

'Your cycle is a Wyvern, you said?'

'Yes indeed. It was the first I obtained from him. I wanted something to test the quality of his work, and that was it.'

'And you are happy with the bike?'

'Well, I got it about seven years ago, not

long before I retired and haven't had much of a chance to enjoy it. It's a young man's cycle, Constable. I was rather too ancient to make full use of it, but yes, it is a very good machine, a quality cycle, and a marque I was happy to sell. I've never had a single complaint from any of those customers.'

'Did you sell many?'

'No, only a few. As I said earlier, they were special orders, Constable, not the sort of thing your average bike buyer would want. All handmade. So far as I know, the fellow did not employ any staff, he did the lot himself. He turned out very few machines, but each was a masterpiece. He was a true artist, Constable.'

'So it would appear, but even so, you must have had a business arrangement with him, such as invoices, a telephone number or contact address.'

'No, Constable. He insisted on cash deals on every occasion, and never said where he operated from. The only way I could get in touch with him was when he called at my shop. He called regularly, every fourth Wednesday.'

'Didn't that strike you as odd?' I had to ask. 'No paperwork, no contact address.'

'Yes, it did, as a matter of fact. I wondered

whether he was trading in stolen cycles, and although I checked his work carefully, I never found any evidence of the bikes being stolen property. I did get the North Riding Constabulary's Stolen Cycle Supplements, you know, and furthermore, Constable, I did study them. Not once did I find any reference to any cycle I'd bought from him.'

As he told me that, I thought it very feasible that the thief could steal a cycle in County Durham, take it home, respray it in grey paint, fit different parts, rename it Wyvern and sell it seventy miles away. Thus, someone studying the North Riding Constabulary's Stolen Cycle Supplements would never know of that original theft, while linking a cycle stolen in one county with one sold in another in a different colour and under a different name would be virtually impossible.

I began to think that poor old Mr Suggitt had been dealing in stolen cycles without ever realizing the fact.

'I'm surprised he managed to keep his name and business address such a secret,' I said. 'Even Tin Lid said that. He's seen the man and the truck he uses, but had no idea of his name or where he comes from.'

'Clearly he wanted to be anonymous,

Constable, and there is nothing criminal in that. Actors and authors make use of pseudonyms in their business, and lots of shopkeepers never make use of their own names, so that dealer is doing nothing unethical or illegal.'

'If he was supplying you, then he must be supplying other cycle shops,' I said. 'He must have lots of outlets for his work.'

'Oh yes, he did supply others. I once rang a friend of mine who has a shop at Guisborough, and he said he bought the occasional special from Wyvern. But he had no idea who the manufacturer was.'

Hearing this, I now began to realize that our cycle thief could be cheerfully supplying stolen cycles to a range of shops across the north-east of England. He was operating a cash-only system and all his machines were disguised to such an extent they'd never be recognized, even by their losers. If this man was ever to be caught, it seemed that the CID would have to be brought into the investigation and that some kind of trap or exercise would have to be generated to capture him. He'd been operating for years without being caught and seemed clever enough not to have grown careless in his evident success.

I began to feel that such an exercise was way beyond the capabilities of a country constable operating alone. I felt that a chat with our cycling Sergeant Craddock might be wise.

Before leaving Mr Suggitt, I had a look at his Wyvern and it was a superb machine. Lightweight but strong, with a beautiful grey frame adorned with red lettering and lines and a red motif in the shape of a winged dragon, it had all the trappings of a top-quality racer. It stood in his garage covered in dust and I felt Sergeant Craddock would love to get his backside on that slender saddle. But I also thought the CID might like to examine the machine in greater detail – if it had been stolen, it might still be possible to identify the real cycle beneath that covering of smart grey and red. But I could not seize the machine as evidence of a crime because I had no proof it had been stolen. Suspicion, yes; proof, no! Besides, I knew it would remain in Mr Suggitt's house for a long time yet. It would be there should I need to have it examined.

I left Mr Suggitt after thanking him for his help and his coffee, then drove back to Aidensfield to decide my next course of action. But, as I drove towards my police

196

house, I saw Father Simon's car approaching from the opposite direction.

He stopped and waved me to a halt.

'I'd like a word, Nick, if I may,' he said as I went to meet him. 'It's important and quite urgent. It's about Joseph Marshall.'

# 7

Worried that the priest had some really dreadful news, I led him into the house. As he was a friend, I took him into the lounge rather than the more formal surroundings of the police office where Mary offered him a cup of tea. He declined, as he also declined our offer of a seat.

'No thanks, I'm in a desperate hurry. I've a lot of people to see, so I'll have to say no.'

'So, Father,' I asked. 'What's this about Joseph?'

'Well, Nick, it arose out of the fact the hospital will not do anything for him–'

'Hang on, Father.' I wondered how much gossip of this type had reached the ears of the priest. 'That's not right. The hospital hasn't *refused* to do anything for him.'

'Well, should I have said *"can't"* do anything? Is that a better turn of phrase?'

'No, it's not; if anything it's worse. Each of those phrases implies his illness is so advanced or serious that nothing can be done,' I said. 'It sounds as if he has no hope of ever getting better, and that is not the case.'

'Well, I must admit that's the way I see it, Nick,' said the priest. 'I understand he's terminally ill.'

'I don't think so.' I felt I had to express my views. 'None of the experts in the hospital can find anything physically wrong with Joseph. That's why he's been sent home, Father.'

'Well, I must beg to differ, Nick. My understanding is that the hospital has decided nothing can be done for Joseph. They've sent him home so that he can end his days in the peace and comfort of his family.'

'It's a question of interpretation.' I tried vainly to explain my understanding of the hospital's verdict. 'The fact is he's not suffering from any fatal disease or illness. They've given him a very thorough examination and have concluded there's nothing physically wrong with him. That's the outcome of his tests.'

'You're sure about that, are you?' he put to me.

'I am. Lungs, liver, stomach and bowels, heart, all his natural functions – everything is all right, except perhaps for a little high blood pressure. That's what they mean when they say there's nothing they can do for him. They're saying he is not physically ill or diseased.'

'That's not what Mabel told me,' he said.

'So what did she say?' I asked.

'She said there's nothing they can do for him.'

'There is nothing they can do for him!' I said. 'As I said before, Father, it depends upon the interpretation of those words. The truth is that his problem could be in his mind; he could be worrying himself sick about something. He could be suffering from some psychosomatic problem.'

'Not Joseph, surely?'

'Yes, Joseph, our calm and unflappable Joseph. He's worrying himself sick about something. Physically there is nothing the matter except he's lost weight and won't eat.'

'Well, I'm not so sure about your interpretation, Nick, but Mabel told me she'd spoken to a specialist called Hindmarsh at the hospital, and he said there was nothing he could do for Joseph, so he's better off at home with her. That's a pretty clear indication to me that he's terminally ill.'

'Mabel must have been too worried to listen carefully. She was fearing the worst, Father, she thought Joseph had cancer. I think she's interpreted the specialist's words accordingly.'

'We all think he's got cancer, Nick, even though no one has said so.'

'I don't,' I had to say. 'Not now. After hearing what transpired at the hospital, I am more convinced he's not physically ill, Father. That's what Joseph was told himself – and he told me.'

'But if Mabel has put the wrong interpretation on the specialist's words, then so could you,' he put to me.

'That's a fair comment,' I admitted. 'So, Father, I think a word with Dr McGee might be wise. As Joseph's GP, he could get a positive answer from the hospital, and it would be sensible to establish the facts before too many rumours get flying around Aidensfield.'

'The rumours are already flying around,' he said. 'That's if they are rumours. The whole place is buzzing with the story that Joseph has some unmentionable and fatal disease, that he's been sent home to die, and that there is no hope. And I've already had Guild members reminding me they haven't

201

attended a funeral for years. I think they're looking forward to it. Robes are being found and washed, sashes ironed, hats aired ... plans are being made, Nick.'

'For his funeral?' I was aghast at this and groaned audibly. 'This is awful ... the poor fellow's not dead yet! Is that why you've come to see me? About the funeral arrangements?'

'Not directly, no. But it is to do with his state of health,' and I could see I had dented some of the enthusiasm he had engendered prior to this visit.

'In other words, you believe the rumours?' I felt I had to put this to him.

'What else could I believe? I understood Mabel had got the verdict direct from Joseph's consultant,' he said firmly. 'And that fitted in with what we all dreaded. So, as I said, that is why I am here.'

'All right, Father,' I said. 'So what can I do for you?'

'When we – the parishioners of St Aidan's that is – heard about Joseph's condition, we felt that if the medical profession could not or would not help, then God might, through use of course, through the parish that is, and by the intercession of the Blessed Virgin Mary.'

'Go on.' I was intrigued now.

'Well, so that God can help through Mary's intercession, there would have to be some visible sign of faith from Joseph, over and above his normal religious activities, something more than his attendance at daily mass, saying the rosary and so on.'

'I can understand that,' I nodded.

'So the parish felt we should send Joseph to Lourdes,' he said. 'As a gift; we would raise the money as a gift. A surprise, even. Now, I'm sure he cannot afford the fare to the shrine in France, so a small sub-committee has been formed to raise the necessary funds.'

'In the hope he'll receive a miracle cure?' I smiled. 'That means there's no need to muster the Guild just yet!'

'Yes, Nick. Exactly.'

'But he's not ill, Father. There is nothing wrong with him. That's the point I've been trying to make. So why send him to Lourdes?'

'I think the state of his health is a matter for God to decide.' Father Simon appeared just as stubborn as me on this matter. 'He has lost weight, he is not eating and the medical profession is baffled by his condition. In my books, Nick, that is an indication that he needs urgent treatment and help, and if the National Health Service won't give him that, then I'm sure Our Lady of Lourdes or Saint Bernadette will intercede on his behalf.'

'If his problem is his state of mind, then a visit to Lourdes might cure that too, just as it might cure a physical ailment,' I had to admit.

'Absolutely. I'm sure Our Lady will look upon him with great favour. After all, problems of the mind are illnesses just like any other. So, if his condition is due to some deep internal anguish, then he qualifies, Nick. I'm not saying he's mentally ill, though! Whatever his problem, he must be cured, miraculously or otherwise.'

'It seems you are determined to get him there. So what's my part in all this?'

'We need to raise funds, Nick. The Guild doesn't pay for pilgrimages to Lourdes, it pays for funerals. Raising the necessary money very quickly means raffles and tombola, or any other method we can utilize.'

'Bingo's always a good money raiser for Catholics!' I laughed.

'Yes, there'll be bingo too. Now, I know there are rules and regulations about organizing lotteries and sessions of bingo when the tickets are on sale to the public and when the cash value of the prize is considerable. So I am here to seek your advice on that aspect of our fund raising. We'll also be having special collections in church, a sale of work and even a church fete if we can organize one in time.'

'It sounds as if this is a rushed job?' I put to him.

'It is rather. For one thing, we have no idea how long Joseph is going to be with us in this world, but in addition most of the pilgrimages from England to Lourdes are booked up well in advance, months in advance in fact. Fortunately, there is a one-week diocesan pilgrimage from Middles-brough which leaves the UK on Sunday July 26. It returns on Sunday August 2. It's a coach trip with hotel accommodation *en route*, including meals and on-going expenses.'

'That sounds ideal,' I muttered.

'Yes, but there is only one seat left. Just one. It's due to a cancellation – I managed to stake a claim before anyone else heard about it and I've made a provisional reservation for Joseph. That has the backing of our parish sub-committee, but it means we've got to raise the entire fare, along with the on-going expenses for Joseph, and it's got to be done by July 11.'

'You say there's only one seat left. That rules out Mabel, or any helper who ought to accompany Joseph?'

'I'm afraid so, but the diocese does provide a party of volunteer helpers who look after everyone on the pilgrimage. Some are medically qualified. Most of them pay their own fares too. Very noble people, Nick. Joseph won't be left to his own devices.'

'That's reassuring. So how much money is needed?'

'We haven't got an accurate figure, but something in the region of £65 to £75 wouldn't be far off the mark. That should cover all the costs with a little surplus for parish funds perhaps, or to provide the means of helping someone else.'

'It's a lot of money but I'm sure it can be done,' I said. 'So, Father, how is all this going to be arranged without Joseph knowing about it? He's one of your most faithful parishioners, an ardent mass attender and constant church helper. And he'll need a passport. He never goes anywhere so he won't be prepared for a trip overseas.'

'I'll see to that. But so far as the fund

raising is concerned, we've had to be a wee bit devious. We've decided to call our scheme the St Aidan's General Purpose Fund, to hide the truth from Joseph.'

'That sounds very official!' I laughed.

'It is. We'll let it be known to him that it was established rather swiftly while he was in hospital.'

'Which it was!'

'True. We had to move fast and with considerable secrecy,' he admitted.

'Well, you did that – not even I knew about it until now.'

'When we mention it to Joseph, we say the roof needs some expenditure – which it does – and one of the windows is leaking – which it is. And so we shall ostensibly raise the money for that sort of thing, a catalogue of small items of unexpected expenditure in other words. Joseph's trip to Lourdes will come under that general heading.'

'Well, so long as the people contributing know what their money is going to be used for, I see no problem. After all, we wouldn't want the church prosecuted for obtaining money by false pretences, Father!'

'Which is why I am here, Nick. You reckon you can help us from the legal aspects?'

'Give me a day or two with my various

reference books, and I'll come back to you. But yes, go ahead, Father, start your fund raising and I'll find a form of words or a name for something that will comply with the law. And you'll need to register the raffle with the local authority – it's known as a registered lottery. If you do that straight away, I'll see to the rest and will come back to you in a day or two.'

'And not a word to Joseph!' he smiled.

'Would I dare suggest he's suffering from an incurable illness?' I said.

'I'll have words with Dr McGee,' promised Father Simon as he turned to leave. 'Just to clarify, if I can, the facts of his real condition.'

Father Simon's wish to run lotteries, bingo and tombola for the benefit of one man might prove tricky; it could be argued that such a purpose was not a true charity. It was not permissible for a person to run a raffle which would benefit himself – the law said that small lotteries, i.e. raffles and tombola, should be devoted to purposes other than private gain, with the proceeds going to charitable, sporting or other suitable purposes arranged by genuine clubs, associations or *bona fide* organizations. If money was raised for a church fund, however, then the administrators of that fund could decide how to spend the money. If they decided to send Joseph to Lourdes, then that was quite legal. But the money could not go directly to Joseph – that was the crucial point because it might be construed as private gain.

Before checking those facts, however, I decided to put into action my ideas about the cycle thefts and although I felt that the new sergeant, Raymond Craddock, would be the best person to advise me, I was aware that a direct approach might be construed as a snub to Sergeant Blaketon. After all, he was my sergeant and the officer in charge of Ashfordly Section. Internal police politics had to be considered, so I rang Blaketon and explained I would like to discuss a somewhat urgent matter with him.

'Today?' he asked.

'Yes, that would be very helpful, Sergeant,' I agreed.

'Right. Meet me outside the village institute at Briggsby,' he told me. 'I've an appointment in the village at two-thirty p.m. A potential recruit to interview. It won't take more than an hour. How about three-thirty?'

'Fine,' I agreed.

When we met, I outlined everything that had occurred during my stolen cycle investigations, showed him my sackful of paint tin lids and told him about the former cycle shop in Eltering. He listened carefully, clearly impressed by the results of my dogged determination to capture the thief, and then said, 'Sergeant Craddock's really the man for this, Rhea. He was based at Guisborough before being posted to Brantsford. He's very knowledgeable about the cycling scene, especially on Teesside, and he might know how your villain is getting advance information about those meetings. I think a discussion with him is called for. You, me and him, Rhea.'

'A good idea, Sergeant.' I was delighted at his commonsense approach.

'I'll radio Brantsford. He's on duty this afternoon because I had a telephone call from him earlier,' and with no further ado he lifted the handset of the radio in his car, made contact with Force Control Room and sought a talk-through with Brantsford Police Station. He was connected within a few moments and, over the air, I recognized the Welsh tones of Sergeant Craddock. After Blaketon had explained our purpose,

Craddock said he would be happy to meet us.

He suggested there was no time like the present and proposed Ashfordly Police Station as the most suitable rendezvous point. Blaketon and I, in our separate vehicles, found ourselves heading into the little market town and half an hour later I was sitting in Sergeant Blaketon's office with a cup of Alf Ventress's strange-coloured tea at my side, and two sergeants listening to my words.

When I had finished, Craddock smiled. 'Well, PC Rhea, I think you have done very well indeed, and I agree that we should try to co-ordinate the enquiries. I am sure, based on what we know, that our leaders would agree to a trap of some kind. The trouble is that several police forces are involved through crimes in their area. That could cause complications.'

'What about cycle shops, Sergeant?' I asked. 'It's fairly obvious he's got an outlet through the cycle shops of this region. Should we make individual enquires at every one in our area?'

'The minute any of us go asking questions from dealers, they'll close ranks, PC Rhea. They'll close ranks because they think we'll prosecute them for receiving stolen goods – I mean, if they're buying those stolen bikes at prices way below the normal, that's good evidence of their criminal knowledge, isn't it? That's what we were taught at training school. And, of course, if we go poking our noses into their business, then one or other of them might alert our man and he'll go to ground. Not all of them will be buying those bikes in their innocence, I feel. So let's leave cycle shops out of the equation just now.'

'A good point,' I conceded.

He continued, 'I think, therefore, on balance, we should set a trap. Have him fall for some device of ours to lead him into temptation, so to speak, and catch him red-handed.'

'But we don't know how he plans his raids, do we? How does he know where the cyclists will meet?'

'I've done a spot of research on my own. I think he reads the newspapers, PC Rhea, or he visits the library. Club secretaries send advance notices of their outings to the *Evening Gazette* in Middlesbrough, and they are published once a week in the sports pages. Copies of the notices are sent to local branch libraries, too. All he has to do is read those notices and decide where to pay a visit.'

'I'm surprised that secretaries are still broadcasting such detailed information, in view of the risks. We've alerted most of them to the thefts.'

'I know, but the risks are small, bearing in mind the number of cycling clubs in the north-east of England. If you get, say, forty cyclists going on a Sunday outing from one club only, then multiply that by, say, thirty, you get an idea of the number of bikes on the road on any Sunday. I know there are at least thirty clubs in and around the Teesside area, some racing clubs, others touring clubs, one catering for trikes, another is run by a large store for its staff, another is for cyclists over sixty years of age ... but the point is, PC Rhea, that on any Sunday in this region alone, you can have over a thousand bikes on the road – and that's not counting family outings and people who don't belong to clubs.'

'There's mass start racing, too, in the summer, and time trials.'

'Exactly. I'd say you could add a further two or three hundred for all those people. We're heading for a total of around fifteen hundred bikes on our local roads every Sunday – and there are fifty-two Sundays in the year. That's over seventy-eight thousand opportunities every year to steal a bike – and he gets away with fifty or so on very special occasions. It's almost a drop in the ocean, thinking along those lines. Fifty thefts out of seventy-eight thousand opportunities might explain why no police force has seen fit to spend time and money in a major offensive against the thief or thieves.'

'I never looked at it in that light,' admitted Sergeant Blaketon.

'Me neither,' I added.

'But I did, you see, especially because I am a victim myself. I'm afraid I became rather defeatist about it.' A sad smile appeared on Craddock's face; he missed his precious racing cycle.

'But we can reduce that ratio,' I submitted. 'All the stolen bikes fit into a particular category – they're expensive racing machines with crossbars, and they're all made with twenty-four inch frames to accommodate tall people. Our man would never steal a touring cycle, for example, or one which has been mass produced, or one for a small person.'

'Point taken,' said Craddock. 'I must admit I had overlooked the tall cyclist aspect.'

'I've done a check in the supplements. If they're ridden away from the scene of the crime, it means a tall man is responsible. A little chap would never get aboard any of those stolen machines.'

'But I thought we were looking for a covered pick-up truck with no doors on the back?' put in Blaketon.

'We are,' I nodded. 'But I wondered if our thief parks his truck a short distance away from the target bikes, out of sight some-where, and then walks to the bikes, dressed in cycling gear, makes his selection and rides the stolen one away – to his van. A man dressed in cycling gear in the vicinity of other cyclists similarly dressed would not raise any suspicion ... and once the bike is in the back of his truck, he covers it up with the tarpaulin and drives off. He can also cover his cycling gear with a sweater or long trousers once he's in his van.'

'Well, it's a feasible theory,' said Crad-dock. 'So, PC Rhea, what do you suggest we do about this?'

'I favour your idea of setting a trap rather than risk anything that will scare him off, or panic him into temporary hiding. He'd just suspend his activities until the heat was off him, and start all over again. We'll never catch him if we let that happen. We need to tempt him to a scene where we have planted some bait and where we are waiting. And it's vital we catch him red-handed.'

'We?' asked Blaketon. 'And who is we?'

'Well, Sergeant, I mean officers from one of the police forces from the area in which he operates. And that includes us. Once we find out who he is, we can examine his factory, or shed or wherever he does his conversion work, and I'm sure we'll find enough evidence to convict him of other similar crimes. Lots of tins of grey paint, for example.'

'Right,' said Craddock. 'If we decide to set a trap, I cannot see that we need to involve any of the other police forces, nor do we need to bring in the CID. Members of this uniform branch – us in other words – are more than capable of catching this fellow. So how do we set a trap into which we can be sure he will fall?'

'We can't be sure he'll fall for it,' said Blaketon. 'If he's avoided capture or detection, or even suspicion for all these years, he might be alert to any likely trap.'

'He must operate on a slight hit-and-miss method,' I suggested. 'He always takes large-framed bikes, but he cannot be absolutely sure there will be one of the right size on the club outings that he targets. So if we want to tempt him, we'll have to make sure we plant a big bike or two.'

'You mean we should advertise an outing of the Police Cycling Club or the Giant Wheelers?' grinned Blaketon.

'Or a reunion outing of the Coldstream Guards Cycling Club, north-east division,' I grinned. 'They're all over six feet tall, aren't they?'

Craddock stopped smiling. 'That's it!' he almost shouted. 'Yes, we could do that. Advertise a reunion of cycling guardsmen, with a lunch at a country pub somewhere, like they would do. I think it would have to be at a pub, to give it an authentic air ... on a Sunday, of course.'

'Is there such a club?' Blaketon looked serious as we enthused over this idea.

'I've no idea,' I had to admit. 'But we must be sure there are big bikes for him to steal.'

'It's just that if there is such a club, you might get them all riding out to wherever you advertise this trap,' smiled Craddock. 'And that could ruin the whole show. This scheme needs careful planning – and secrecy, gentlemen.'

'And we'd all be there, lurking in the

bushes or hiding in the Gents, watching and waiting to catch him with a stolen bike,' laughed Blaketon. 'But seriously, taking all considerations into account, I think it could work.'

'We'll make it work. To begin with, we need to put an announcement in the *Evening Gazette* among the other cycling-club outings, prepare a reception committee for him and then see if he takes the bait?' said Craddock.

'Great,' enthused Blaketon. 'It would be wonderful if Ashfordly section caught him!'

'It would indeed,' agreed Craddock. 'Right, can you leave this with me? I have the contacts on Teesside and will set up something for a week or two's time. On the day, I'll need all available officers, Oscar,' he said to Blaketon. 'If we can persuade our thief to join us for Sunday lunch, we mustn't let him slip through our net, must we?'

'OK, we'll let you make the plans,' agreed Blaketon. 'I will assume that you concur, PC Rhea?'

Blaketon liked to use the word 'concur' but I told him that I did agree with this suggestion and would await Sergeant Craddock's next move with pleasure.

'I hope you get your bike back,' I said to him as I rose to leave.

'That would be a real bonus,' he smiled.

As I drove back to Aidensfield after that meeting, I experienced a feeling of elation because, at last, something positive was being done to catch a cunning and determined thief. I found myself getting quite excited at the prospect of a cleverly laid trap and wondered just what kind of a plan Sergeant Craddock would produce.

In the days which followed, I noticed Joseph, sometimes in his garden, sometimes pottering around the village and invariably at mass on Sundays and during the week. I thought his face showed a little more colour than hitherto but wondered whether that was due to the summer sun beating down upon him as he worked out of doors or sat in his garden with his pipe to keep the insects away. His weight, however, did not appear to increase and his clothes hung from him as if he had shrunk in the wash and they had expanded. Around him, of course, plans were being made to raise funds for his surprise trip to Lourdes, but whenever possible, I stopped to pass the time of day with him.

Invariably I asked about the progress of his gooseberries. On that topic, he was always extremely guarded, usually grumbling that they weren't doing very well because it was too dry or too cold or there was not enough nourishment in the ground or they had become diseased. It was amazing, the number of things that could go wrong with growing gooseberry. In spite of his careful pruning and delicate selection of those he wanted to remain on the trees for the show, his berries weren't swelling anything like they had in previous years and he thought it was going to be a bad berry year, at least for him.

But under all that contrived gloom, I knew that, somewhere behind his cottage, he would be encouraging colossal berries to flourish, well away from the prying eyes of his competitors. And his competitors would be doing likewise. It was around this time of the summer, as the berries were filling out due to plenty of good manure and pruning, and as the sun was pouring its goodness into them, that the berry growers adopted their most competitive and secretive attitude. Big reputations were at stake in the world of big berries but if anyone listened to these characters, there was not even a moderately sized berry to be found in the whole of Aidensfield. Certainly, I never noticed one upon my travels, but I knew the truly gigantic examples were safely hidden from view, being nursed and cared for like new-born lambs and being shown to an astonished public only on the day of the berry show – that's if they hadn't been stabbed by wasps or burst like balloons before the event.

It was during those days that Mary, my wife, mentioned something over tea.

'The wheelbarrow's collapsed,' she told me. 'It's the wheel. The axle's broken. Can we get another from somewhere?'

I told her I knew just the fellow, a specialist in barrow wheels and promised I would measure ours to ensure I obtained a perfect replacement. After tea, therefore, I went down to the bottom of our garden with Mary. Armed with a tape measure, I checked the size of the barrow wheel. It was of solid metal with a rubber tyre and was 15 inch in diameter, and I could see that the section close to the spindle had cracked.

'What caused this?' I asked her. 'Have you been quarrying or something?'

'No, I got a load of horse manure from Home farm. George Boston brought the stuff up for me on his tractor and trailer, and shovelled it over the fence. I wanted to move it and the wheel collapsed with the weight.'

Mary had recently taken an interest in gardening; it was something to provide an interest as the children were now at either school or play-school during the day, and she had a little more time to herself. My interest in horticulture was limited to cutting the lawn and weeding, although at times I managed to destroy flowers and vegetables thinking they were weeds. Consequently – for the sake of domestic harmony – I tended to leave such matters to Mary. Mowing the lawn was something I managed to achieve without too many problems, however; although on one occasion my runaway Flymo made a staggeringly successful job of demolishing a strawberry patch.

'So what's the manure for?' I asked.

'I've put some under our gooseberry trees,' she said. 'And I took off some of the smaller berries and pruned the branches. We've got quite a good crop, you know, we ought to submit one or two for the show. We are members.'

'I know, but I'm no gooseberry grower!' I

had no wish to make a fool of myself in front of the Aidensfield experts. My puny berries were scarcely large enough to make a pie even when used in multiples of hundreds, let alone win prizes.

'Well, there's one berry that already looks like becoming a giant,' she said. 'Come on, I'll show you.'

She led me into a sunny corner of the garden where she had weeded carefully among our half-dozen gooseberry trees, presents from both my father and Mary's, each of them being keen growers. The tiny copse looked so neat beneath their all-embracing nets, and I could see there was an abundance of handsome fruit. The nets would keep away the birds but our problems would come later in the form of war-like wasps.

'There!' She pointed to a small, heavily pruned tree at the back. 'That tree on the right.'

And I could see that it carried what was already a super-large gooseberry. Still green and young, it had several weeks in which to swell with pride as it matured, and during which it would have to fight off mildew, wasps and birds. It was an outstanding berry, of that there was no doubt and I found myself wondering whether it would survive until the berry show day on Monday, 3 August. But, to be honest, although a berry of this magnitude might be a winner if it survived until she show, I did not want to beat poor old Joseph in this most important of all years. I decided not to mention this monster to anyone ... and asked Mary also to keep our secret.

'What sort is it?' I asked her. 'Any idea?'

'An Admiral Beatty,' she told me with confidence. 'I remember Dad telling me. He said there were over a hundred and fifty different varieties in four colours, but this variety was a particularly good one for producing heavy berries, ideal for shows.'

'Well, if we're going into the berry-show business, we'll need that manure. I'd better get that barrow fixed.'

'So where will you get a barrow wheel?' she enquired, as we returned to the house.

'Claude Jeremiah Greengrass has a pile of them,' I said. 'Or if he hasn't then Tin Lid Talbot has. I'll go and see Claude now.'

Half an hour later I was plodding through one of Claude's outbuildings as I followed the scruffy old fellow into his barrow-wheel shed. He told me he'd acquired a few more since disposing of the last selection to Tin

Lid Talbot, and thought he had one which would suit my requirements. Fortunately, he had.

It was in fetching blue with a fitted solid rubber tyre, and when I checked the spindle and the ball-bearing race, everything seemed in good order.

'How much, Claude?'

'To you,' he said. 'A pound.'

'Ten shillings,' I offered.

'Fifteen bob,' he countered.

'Twelve and six,' was my next offer.

He paused and then said, 'Right. Yours for twelve and six. And a bargain, I might add.'

Having done the deal, we were leaving his buildings when I asked, 'How's the berry growing coming on, Claude?'

'Oh, wonderful,' he beamed. 'I moved my bushes like you said. They're at the other side of the house now, in the sunshine, and, by gum, they're producing some whoppers.'

'You'll be pruning and thinning them, to make sure the biggest are ready for the show?'

'Oh, aye, I've done all that. I'll tell you, Constable, I've never had such a berry year as this. A Blackden Gem it is. Joseph Marshall had better watch out, and so had all his cronies on that committee … I've enough big berries on my trees to win every prize this year … mark my words. You name it and I can win it! And that includes the Supreme. I can see it now. Supreme Champion – Claude Jeremiah Greengrass! That has a lovely ring to it, hasn't it? World Champion even! You know, I might even send one or two of my best ones to Egton Bridge. I reckon I could win the Aidensfield with my second-best ones, knowing the sort of second-rate competition I'm up against.'

'It's all to do with weight, not size, remember,' I reminded him.

'Mine're all good solid berries, Constable, not full of wind like pigs' bladders that are used as footballs or so full of water they burst like paper bags. They'll weigh enough to win everything, just you wait and see. Anyway, come and have a look for yourself.'

Claude's little forest of berry trees now basked in a sunny corner of what was mainly a wild and uncultivated patch of moorland. A feeble attempt had been made to convert some of the adjacent ground into a vegetable patch and a few straggly potato plants, cabbages and broad beans were pushing through the couch grass, nettles and briars. Without any further help from the owner of this place, they would surely have a struggle to survive.

But the berry trees, growing from a patch of cultivated earth which had once borne a midden, looked strong and well tended even if a few strands of goosegrass and a foxglove or two were growing through the strands of the nets which covered them. I could see they had been pruned and that a quantity of the original berries had been removed. It was clear that Greengrass knew what he was doing so far as the cultivation of berries was concerned.

'There you are, Constable.' He pointed proudly towards one of his trees, the one on the most southerly side of his patch. 'How about that for a whopper, eh?'

There was a tree full of very large berries, but among them was the largest gooseberry I've ever seen. Hanging in the evening sunshine like a monstrous plum, I could see the veins beneath the tight, reddening skin and had to admire its beautiful shape. Here was a truly memorable berry, a winner beyond all doubt, I would have anticipated, because it had plenty of time to grow even larger and even heavier.

'Claude, it's a monster!'

'I'll bet it weighs enough to get me the Supreme,' he blinked. 'That's if I can keep it on the tree till show day. That'll be the tricky bit. Making sure it doesn't fall off or get knocked off. It looks happy enough, doesn't it? It must like my soil and my treatments.'

'Treatments?'

'Food stuffs. Stuff I chuck around the roots of them berry trees. Some folks use horse manure and others use cow muck or sheep droppings brewed in moorland spring water, or cold tea or sometimes water that's been used for boiling cabbages, and even washing-up water because the soap clears the bugs away. But I use my own secret recipe, Constable, and wild horses wouldn't drag it out of me. So you've no need to ask, have you? All you have to do is look at the berry and agree I've come up with a recipe that works. Berries that size are the work of a genius, and no mistake!'

'Well, I must admit it's the biggest I've seen for years,' and I spoke the truth. 'You might have trouble keeping it on the tree, there's a long way to go yet.'

'I'll put a little umbrella over it so the rain won't knock it off, and a little hammock underneath for it to rest its weight on. I mean, Constable, the weight of a berry that big can soon snap its stalk, can't it?'

'You'll have to care for that berry day and

night, Claude, treat it like a new kitten. I think you've a potential winner there, provided it's as heavy as it looks.'

''Course it's as heavy as it looks, and I'm not going to put a bit of lead shot inside to increase its weight! Just in case you were thinking I might be thinking of doing summat like that.'

'The judges know all the tricks, Claude. Just look after your berry and make sure it stays on the tree till show day. And the best of British luck, as they say.'

'Aye, well, I thought you'd like to see it, then you might feel like guarding it for me; you know, stopping jealous rivals from nobbling it.'

'I'll certainly look out for berry bashers whenever I patrol past your premises, Claude, but I can't offer more. Hiring the police for special guard duties is a very expensive operation too, as you might know if you attend race meetings. But I will be happy to keep an eye open for mischief-makers.'

'Well, if you're counting me as a possible mischief-maker, Constable, thinking I might be going into the village to nobble rival berries, then you're mistaken. I mean, with a berry this size, I've no need to demolish any of the opposition's berries before the show, have I?'

'No. You'll simply demolish the opposition, Claude!' I laughed.

'I know I will. All I have to do is keep my berry safe and sound, and keep feeding it with my secret potion.'

'Don't give it too much or it'll burst,' I warned him. 'There's many a good berryman lost a potential winner through having it burst, even on the morning of the show. I've even known some burst on the way to the show or even in the show itself, the minute they're handled ... so be careful.'

'I used egg-boxes, Constable, they're just the right size, although this whopper might be too big. I might have to put it into a coffee cup.'

'When it's fully grown, you might need a muslin bag to carry it in, or something large and soft enough not to damage it. How about my crash-helmet? I don't need it now....'

'Coppers' crash helmets are for big, hard heads, not tender, juicy berries of giant dimensions ...' he chuckled.

'Whatever happens, I wish you the best of luck – and thanks for the barrow wheel,' I told him.

'I might have to put my berry in a wheelbarrow, eh? Lined with cotton wool. And push it to the show like a giant pumpkin!' he chuckled. 'You heard about the berry that was so big, a sheep ate its way inside and slept there? Or those that were so juicy the salmon came up the river and hobbled across the land on their fins so they could enjoy the juice ... there's some good tales about berries, Constable, but this beauty will astound everybody.'

'Once they see that berry, they might want to buy your magic potion, Claude. Maybe you ought to patent it and sell it.'

'How about Greengrass's Berry Beverage then? Patent applied for. Produces wonder berries and enriches the earth,' he laughed.

'Did you know they are called thapes in the south of England?' I began 'And grizzles in Scotland. In some parts of Yorkshire, they're called carberries or even day berries, and goggles in Lincolnshire. Think of Greengrass's Goggle Juice, or Claude's Carberry Cobbler....'

'Cobbler? What's a cobbler?'

'Apart from a chap who fixes shoes, it means a cooling drink, so there's plenty of scope for naming your magic mixture. Anyway, I must leave you now with your pride and joy – and thanks for the barrow wheel.'

'You'll not tell anyone about my big berry, will you?' were his parting words.

'I wouldn't dare!' I called to him. 'They'd all stop trying with theirs....'

And he returned to his sheds chuckling to himself as he took a happy glance at his monster berry.

It was truly colossal, there was no doubt about it, but as I had not seen many of its potential competitors, apart from my own specimen, I had no idea how it compared with the serious opposition. But it was bigger than my largest.

Wondering whether I was silly even to think about competing in the berry show, I returned home with my second-hand barrow wheel. I just hoped it was not the proceeds of crime.

# 8

It was during those long weeks of high summer which preceded the August bank holiday that berry-growing frenzy intensified in Aidensfield. A tangible air of expectancy prevailed as small groups of worried men gathered and muttered in the street and in the pub. They bemoaned the fact that the berries this year were the smallest anyone could recall. There were more gooseberry-pecking birds than ever before. Even worse, the long-term wasp forecast was horrendous with millions of the little airborne black-and-yellow devils expected as the heat of summer continued. On top of all that, mildew was rampant and that there seemed to be some kind of virus which was attacking berry trees. It caused potential prize-winning berries to drop off the bough without reason or to wither until they had the appearance of shrivelled grapes or over-dry prunes.

It was a highly stressful time for the Big Berry Men but, of course, these problems prevailed every year and in spite of them, mammoth heavyweights were produced with astonishing regularity. They materialized in secret places, little Gardens of Eden to which the Big Berry Men resorted in trying times. Wives, families, gardens, dog-walking and even pub visiting were all temporarily abandoned by these growers; their devotion was legendary and their berries were miraculous.

For a brief period every summer, the lonesome struggle to produce the world's heaviest gooseberry emptied the cottages of Aidensfield and district of its men folk – and a few ladies. There were indeed some few dedicated lady berry growers and their activities were observed with great concern because one of them, four or five years ago, had come dangerously close to winning the heaviest twins prize with her Oyster Girl Wilkinsons, two lovely berries moulded on one stem, as someone said, quoting from *A Midsummer Night's Dream*. In their isolation, these berry growers nursed and cajoled their little trees into producing the biggest of big berries, tending the fledgling fruit as if they were newly whelped pups and doing so with all the tender care of a new mother with her delicate baby. Some remained all night, spending their vigil with flasks of coffee or bottles of beer as they warded off predators of various kinds, human and otherwise. Some of the men resumed their annual but temporary bout of pipe-smoking, pipe smoke being a fine deterrent to wasps when blown across the maturing berries. It produced a protective coating of tobacco gunge and it was said that regular dressings of smoke from black twist would deter even the most determined of wasps.

Marauding wasps were the final threat, the one thing that could ruin a berry even seconds before it was removed from the tree in readiness for its perilous journey to the weighing table – except, of course, for the other risks such as the biggest berry in the world dropping off the tree during the night, or being nobbled by birds or other insects, or sabotaged by ruthless competitors, or even bumped off the tree and trod upon by careless families or grandchildren rushing about the garden.

It is fair to say that few Big Berry Men slept a wink during those final days. If I had to call upon any of them during that time, I knew where to find them – but they always met me in that part of the garden which was furthest from their secret berry grove.

Somehow, they knew when anyone was approaching, thus no one achieved a sneak preview of the competition berries. One trick, used chiefly at night by berry growers, was to place a length of black cotton across the entrance to the garden, usually near the gate. This was connected to something like a tiny bell, or a tin can perched on a wall, or even a complicated system of pulleys and fly-wheels, all of which would produce a warning noise if anyone trespassed into the unseen cotton. I must admit I never managed to gain complete access to anyone's genuine berry patch during those final weeks, except, of course, to Claude Jeremiah's moorland haven. I did wonder, though, whether he had a hidden garden, some secret place with a crop of even bigger berries … that was indeed a matter of concern. The cunning of keen berry growers was legendary and I had to admit that Claude had appeared rather too willing to reveal his pride and glory to me. But, I thought, he was not a very sophisticated grower … devious in business but naïve in matters of gardening perhaps?

On a fine sunny morning during this long and agonizing period I was walking, in uniform, to St Aidan's Church for a chat with Father Simon. As I was passing the garage, Bernie Scripps rushed out and hailed me. His urgent windmill-like gestures were highly suggestive of some kind of deviousness and I wondered if he wanted to show me his berries.

He led me into his office; it adjoined the work area and resembled a storeroom for spare parts such as spark plugs, fan belts and windscreen wipers. Once inside, he closed the door.

'I'd like a word, Mr Rhea.' He had a con-spiratorial look about him as he indicated a chair before his untidy desk. He moved aside some boxes of brake linings, shifted the tailpipe of an exhaust off his desk and rescued the blotter from beneath a pile of spare-parts catalogues. Then he sat down.

'I didn't know who to ask about this; it's confidential, I suppose, up to a point, but I didn't want to appear grasping, or seeming as if I was undermining the customs of the village or anything like that ... besides, everyone's too busy these days, they're all so secretive and furtive....'

'It's crunch-time in their berry world,' I told him.

'It's what?' he frowned, and so I explained what was happening in the village.

237

'Oh, I see. I thought summat serious must be happening. Anyway, it'll keep 'em all occupied as I set about learning something about this place. Which is why I asked you in.'

'This sounds interesting!' I wondered what on earth he was leading up to.

'It's about Joseph Marshall. You know him?' he asked.

'I do,' I confirmed.

'Well, I'm aiming to establish an undertaker's business here, as you might have heard, and I'm making fairly good progress with my plans.'

'I did hear rumours,' I acknowledged.

'It's amazing how things get known around here,' he muttered. 'Anyway, I'm in touch with my advisers and have had discussions with the planning department of the council about the change of use for my spare parts of the garage premises, so it seems I will be given the go-ahead.'

'A funeral parlour next door to a garage?' I asked.

'It's all part of life, Mr Rhea, and I don't think there's anything to stop me having a funeral parlour alongside the garage.'

'The planners might feel that new businesses are welcome in Aidensfield,' I said.

'Especially if they create jobs.'

'That's how I see things, with me expanding so I can eventually take on staff such as a qualified coffin-maker or hearse-driver. Now, what I would really like is to start off with a flourish, once I get the go-ahead, that is. For that, though, I need a funeral that's good enough to establish my reputation,' he went on. 'I'm looking ahead, but what I would really like is to be given the chance to arrange one that gets into the newspapers, preferably with photographs and a long report; something big enough to give me widespread publicity, to make my service known to all, so to speak.'

'Like a film star's funeral, you mean, or one for the royal family?' I smiled, tongue in cheek. 'The snag is there are no famous people in Aidensfield.'

'Well, I wouldn't go quite so far as wanting somebody very famous,' he said, rather embarrassed at what he believed I thought he was trying to say. 'I was thinking more of Joseph Marshall.'

'Joseph? But he's not dead!' I cried.

'No, but he is dying from cancer with not long to go on this earth, so I've heard, and I understand he's a member of some guild or other which sees to the funerals of its members. It's one of those Catholic things. They all wear robes and sashes and walk in procession beside the coffin.'

'It's a very historic guild, Mr Scripps,' I said.

'I know, and I've heard it's very spectacular, Mr Rhea, ideal for a picture in the paper.'

'You're talking of Joseph's funeral? When he's dead, that is.'

'Well, he is very well known hereabouts; he'll attract a lot of interest when he goes. He'll get a right good send off, I would imagine. It'll be a good funeral for me to start with, Mr Rhea, especially if it involves the guild in all its finery. It'll be rather like a royal funeral in some ways, I would imagine, with pomp and ceremony and hymns in Latin.'

'But Joseph is not dead, Mr Scripps, and I don't see any sign of him departing this world just yet. There's no guarantee he'll die soon, and he might have other plans for his farewell event. He's very big in St Aidan's Guild, you know.'

'I know about his guild membership, somebody told me about that, that's what set me thinking. But so far as his funeral's concerned, I've heard he's not long for this world. I can't say I know him all that well, Mr Rhea, but folks hereabouts have told me he's only got weeks left. I have seen him pottering up and down the village, looking like a corpse warmed up and, if I'm any judge, I'm agreed he's not got long with us. It's not often I'm wrong in forecasting a passing away, Mr Rhea. The way I see it is that he'd be the ideal customer for me to start my business with, Mr Rhea, if you see what I mean.'

'I do see what you mean, and there's nothing like planning ahead!' I commented. 'But I think you might be a bit premature.'

'Thinking ahead and making plans is the secret of business success,' he returned.

'I can't argue with that. So what do you want to discuss with me?' I asked.

'Two things, Mr Rhea. I want to get things right if I do get the contract for his funeral. For one thing, do you think I need to get the police involved for traffic control or crowd control if it's likely to be a very big affair? I would think it'll generate a fair crowd in the village and I don't want to get in the way of regular service buses, delivery vans and things. So that's the first question.'

'It's always a good idea to notify me of any funeral in the village, large or small,' I advised him. 'It means I can be on hand to make sure there's no traffic congestion outside any of the churches, Catholic or Protestant, when the cortège arrives and departs. So yes, keep me informed; a telephone call will do. And the second question?'

'This business of that guild. I'm not sure what it is, Mr Rhea, and don't know who to ask without appearing as if I'm being too presumptuous. But you see, if I have to plan a Catholic funeral – I'm not one of them, by the way, I can't even make the sign of the cross without getting my arms all tangled up – if I have to plan a big Catholic funeral with those guild members in attendance, I have to know what they do and where they sit or stand or say their prayers or whatever, and who's in charge ... it's a funny business, having to cope with an outfit like that. Who's the chairman or secretary? Mebbe I could ask them.'

'That's Joseph Marshall,' I laughed. 'He does all those jobs.'

'Well I can't ask him, can I? I mean, I can hardly ask what's needed at his own funeral....'

'You've tried Father Simon?'

'I have, but he's fairly new to this parish

and hasn't done a guild funeral, Mr Rhea. The last one was before the war, long before he came, and nobody I've asked can remember what the procedure was. Somebody must be able to tell me because I do want to get it right, you see, and I want to make a big success of my first Aidensfield funeral. And I think Joseph will be just the fellow for that. The hard bit is finding the right folks to ask without stepping on a few local toes or upsetting local interests, if you understand. In my business, discretion is important.'

Even though I thought his attitude rather too mercenary, I explained what I knew of St Aidan's Guild, adding that members would probably act as a choir during the requiem mass, they'd lead the prayers and attend the coffin by marching in procession either alongside or behind it. In addition, they'd care for the relatives of the deceased. But, I told him, in modern times they did not make the coffin or dig the grave, nor did they usurp the functions of the family undertaker.

In these modern times, they worked together with the undertaker, although in the past, they would have probably organized the entire funeral, even digging the grave, making the coffin, securing the flowers and arranging the funeral tea which, by tradition, always included ham.

According to what people had told me since my arrival in Aidensfield, a guild funeral was a spectacular affair, although modern people rarely called upon its funds. They had their own insurance nowadays which meant that guild funds were increasing all the time without any heavy expenditure, but its members, always in their colourful regalia, continued to attend all funerals of deceased members. I added that they attended other events too – at mass on Easter Sunday, for example. They would all attend in their costumes and occupy the same pews as they sang the Easter hymns and made the responses at mass. As I explained all this, I could see Bernie's eyes widening at the thought of all the prestige and publicity he would gain from arranging Joseph's burial.

'You could always ask Joseph, he'll know more than anyone,' I grinned.

'I don't think I'll bother, Mr Rhea, but thanks for telling me all this. I can see the potential of a guild funeral, you know ... done properly, it could establish my reputation for life and if I got a contract for all guild funerals, well, what prestige that would be....'

'It would indeed,' I said, pondering his use of words as I made my move to leave.

'A guild funeral could be the making of me....'

'And,' I said, tongue in cheek. 'You might like to know that until just before the war, the guild used a hearse drawn by four black horses, all with red rosettes on their harness....'

'Did they by gum? Now there's an idea....'

And I left him pondering the merits of a splendid funeral with black horses drawing a black hearse with cloaked guild members walking alongside to a good old Catholic hymn in Latin.

Upon leaving Bernie to his musings, I continued to St Aidan's and went inside to find Father Simon arranging the altar for that evening's benediction and Stations of the Cross. He led me into the vestry where there were chairs.

'So, Nick, what's the legal verdict on my fund-raising schemes?'

I confirmed there was nothing unlawful in arranging lotteries such as raffles or tombola, plus bingo or other events, with or without a gaming element, provided the income was for his proposed church fund, stressing he could not raise money specifically for Joseph. I added that events like whist drives, dances, sales of work, bring-and-buy sales did not require any sanction from the police. I advised him that the accrued funds could be utilized by a committee to send Joseph to Lourdes, perhaps with some of the cash being allocated to church purposes. During our chat, I discovered that the profits from a village whist drive had already raised £19 and a bring-and-buy sale was being planned for a couple of weeks' time in the parish hall. It looked as if there would be enough money to send Joseph to Lourdes.

'Did you manage a chat with Dr McGee?' I asked. 'About Joseph's true condition?'

'I did indeed, Nick,' he nodded vigorously. 'And you were right. He's got a copy of the consultants' reports and although he didn't divulge any of the details, he did say there was nothing physically wrong with Joseph. It seems Mabel's slightly misunderstood the situation, but he said he'd have words with her to explain things. There is, however, some reason for believing Joseph is worrying himself so much about something that

246

he's been shedding pounds – as if he was doing the dance of the seven veils and they were the veils. His loss of appetite is associated with the same problem. But Joseph has told them he had no worries.'

'So if he's not physically ill, how does that affect this fund-raising?'

'We're going ahead, Nick, and we are sending him to Lourdes, if only in the hope we might remedy the cause of his mystery condition. We believe the whole village will support the idea – they all think he's dying of cancer and they want something done for him. So we're doing it. As I told you earlier, the date of his pilgrimage has been fixed and we're going ahead.'

'And he has no idea?'

'No, not a hint.'

'And Mabel?'

'We decided we daren't tell her, not yet. She might let the news slip, so she's being kept in the dark too. Apart from you and I, the only people in the know are the small committee.'

'I'll not mention it,' I promised. 'So what about the red-tape side of things? A passport for Joseph, I mean.'

'He's got one, would you believe. Joe Steel at the post office told me. He had to sign

Joseph's passport application form and sign the back of his photograph. Years ago, Mabel persuaded Joseph to go to Paris to celebrate their silver wedding anniversary, but he cried off at the last minute with some excuse or other. He's never been overseas since; mind you, he's never even been to London or Edinburgh either. He's not one for travelling far, isn't Joseph, in spite of working on the railways. I'm surprised he agreed to go to the hospital in Scarborough! But Mabel makes sure he renews his passport every time it's due, always hoping for a trip overseas, and he always agrees for the sake of peace and quiet even though he won't go anywhere. She lives in eternal hope!'

'So it's all systems go for Joseph, as they say,' I smiled.

'It is, Nick. I've had words with the pilgrimage organizer at Middlesbrough, and she'll make sure Joseph has close attention and support throughout his trip. They're very good like that, making sure folks are never alone.'

'And so we'll all pray for a miracle, shall we?' I asked.

'Privately, yes,' chuckled Father Simon. 'Publicly, we're praying for success in repairing the church roof and windows.'

As I was leaving the church, I noticed Joseph approaching and we stopped for a chat in the car-park. Looking at him critically, I felt that he had a little more colour to his cheeks and that he might have put on a few pounds too.

He was carrying a file containing some papers and was puffing contentedly at his pipe. I thought he looked very cheerful even if his clothes still hung from him as if they were several sizes too large.

'Now then, Joseph,' I greeted him. 'How's things with you these days?'

'Can't complain, Mr Rhea.' He adopted a solemn stance. 'I'm feeling fine, and I think I've put on a bit of weight lately.'

'That's good. No more stomach pains?'

'No, nowt like that. I'm still not eating much, though I'm not forcing myself to try and I'm not touching stuff I don't like.'

'Give it time. I'm sure your appetite will return. So, any further news from the hospital or doctor?'

'No, no news is good news, as they say. Dr McGee pops in quite regularly and gives me a check-up. He still says there's nowt wrong with me and reckons I'm doing fine.'

'So, you're back to gardening, then?' was

my next question.

'Aye, but it's a poor year for berries, Mr Rhea, mark my words. We had a right good start but summat's slowed 'em down and they're not filling out like you'd expect, so this year's show might be full of little berries without much weight on 'em.'

'I might stand a chance then!' I chuckled.

'You're having a go, are you?' he asked with clear interest.

'I might,' I said. 'But my berries are very small compared with those I've seen around Aidensfield lately.'

'You've seen some big ones, have you?' and I noted a hint of concern in his voice. I decided I would play along with that concern.

'Well, I'm sworn to secrecy, Joseph, but I'm amazed at some I've seen, and never thought mine stood a chance.'

'I think you're pulling my leg!' he grinned suddenly, recognizing my tactics as a mirror of his own deviousness.

'Just like you and all the other berry growers!' I laughed. 'If I believed everything they say, you'd think there are no gooseberries bigger than peas. Anyway, it's good to see you out and about, and looking a bit better.'

'I'm a lot better than I was,' he confirmed. 'Now, is Father Simon in?'

'Yes, I've just left him,' I said. 'He's in the vestry.'

'I've a bit of Guild business to sort out with him,' said Joseph. 'The way I see it, the Guild has the power, if it has sufficient funds, to lend or give money to the church for urgent repairs or other matters that arise from time to time. That's what it says in the rules, Mr Rhea.'

'You're thinking of donating something to the church, are you?'

'Aye, it would be a nice gesture. It's because the Guild's not had to stand the cost of a funeral for years. It means there's a fair amount of cash in its bank account just doing nowt. I reckon the Guild should do summat for St Aidan's, like helping to pay for that problem with the roof and yon leaking window.'

'I had no idea the Guild could do that!' I was surprised and wondered how Guild members would react if their funds sent Joseph to Lourdes....

'Oh, aye. It's not only funerals and saying prayers and singing. So, in my way of thinking, if t'Guild would cough up a few quid for them outstanding maintenance jobs, it would save all them folks rushing about raising money with their whist drives and things.'

'I think that's something you should discuss with Father Simon,' I said, hurrying away and thus swiftly passing the responsibility to the priest. Trust Joseph to come up with that idea!

As Mary tended our prize-competition berry trees, I spent a lot of time analysing the Stolen Cycle Supplements which continued to arrive from distant police forces. Although I noticed the theft of a superior racing machine once every week in the north-east, I did not detect any identifiable pattern in the crimes. I had examined maps of the area, I had analysed dates of the crimes in relation to other events and I had even checked the colours of the stolen bikes to see if the thief stole them in any kind of sequence. But apart from all the stolen machines being gents' high-quality racing bikes with 24 inch frames, there was no other identifiable theme or pattern to the crimes.

I telephoned Cumbria Police, as well as the East Riding of Yorkshire Constabulary, York City Police and Newcastle-on-Tyne

City, but with no luck. York, of course, is a city with more bikes than dogs, but their records did not show thefts of the kind that interested me.

It seemed, therefore, that the thefts were chiefly confined to rural areas in Northumberland, County Durham and the North Riding of Yorkshire with an occasional foray into the West Riding. In checking the records, I tried to determine whether our thief had entered the North Riding during a particular time, but after comparing my three crimes with the others, it did not seem that he invaded our area once a quarter or on the first Sunday of the month or at any other identifiable time. Try as I might, I could not discern any kind of pattern in his crimes.

It was while thinking about those thefts that I was summoned to a meeting at Ashfordly Police Station. Sergeants Blaketon and Craddock would be present, but no one else. It seemed that Craddock had produced a master plan for tempting our cycle thief into a trap and he now wanted to implement it. Once it had been aired in this meeting, it would be put into operation and hopefully, we could all rejoice with the capture of a clever and persistent thief.

Fortified with mugs of grey tea produced by Alf Ventress, we sat around Blaketon's desk as Craddock outlined his scheme. He called it Exercise Rat-Trap, a good name, I felt, realizing that racing bikes were fitted with rat-trap pedals and we were attempting to trap a real rat.

'The first objective was to determine a suitable site to put our exercise into operation,' Craddock began. 'Knowing the cycling scene as I do, and being familiar with those who venture into the countryside for relaxation with their cycling friends, and knowing we required a venue within this section, I would like to suggest Craydale. It seems perfect for Exercise Rat-Trap.'

He paused for a moment, extracting a map from his briefcase and spreading it across the desk. He stabbed it with a finger to identify Craydale.

'It is on your beat, PC Rhea,' he reminded me.

'Yes, Sergeant, I know it well. It's a very small village with little more than a shop and a pub, the Moon and Compass.'

'Right,' he said. 'It's the pub that we're interested in. Now, I have established that the Five Lamps Cycling Club from Thornaby-on-Tees has arranged for a club outing across the moors to Craydale in three weeks' time. That's Sunday, the nineteenth of July. There are some fifty members and the club has a good attendance record so most are expected to turn up. They will assemble beneath the Five Lamps – that's the name of a street intersection in the town where the founder-members first gathered for their outings, and where there is a lamp standard with five lights, you understand....'

'I was stationed at Thornaby, years ago,' said Blaketon. 'Five Lamps was one of our rendezvous points.'

'But the bulbs still get vandalized, Oscar!' grinned Craddock.

'Not when I was patrolling the town, they didn't!' snapped Blaketon.

'I'm sure they did not! Well, the club departs at ten o'clock for lunch at the Moon and Compass. It's a routine Sunday outing, gentlemen, but I happen to know that several members are very tall and I can guarantee there will be some fine machines there, big bikes with twenty-four inch frames. And I'll advertise a meeting of the north-eastern section of the Coldstream Guards Cycling Club at the same place that day.'

'That's just what we need. Now, the Moon and Compass,' interrupted Blaketon. 'Does it offer suitable observation points for us? Rhea, you should be familiar with that pub so that's a question for you.'

'It does, Sergeant,' I confirmed. 'There is a large car-park at the rear, with an entrance beside the pub, on the left. There's no room to park cycles at the front of the pub because all the available space is taken up with outdoor tables and chairs during the summer. The pub's always busy on a Sunday and visitors' bikes are parked in the car-park. I've seen them there, Sergeant, on many previous occasions, lined up against the rear wall of the car-park.'

'But can we keep an eye on them?' Blaketon pressed. 'Secretly, I mean, without being observed ourselves.'

'Yes, we can,' I said. 'There's lots of room in the car-park, but it depends how many officers we have on the day.'

'And that depends how many we need to ensure full coverage,' returned Blaketon.

I decided to draw a rough sketch outline of the pub, marking its rear and front entrances, windows and car-park, along with the other features which surrounded it. At the rear, behind the car-park, was a patch of fairly dense deciduous woodland with a country lane running past it; that lane passed the gable end of the inn and joined the road which fronted it. Thus one road ran in front of the pub, with a junction to its right when facing it; the other road ran to the right of the pub, passing the gable end, then some outbuildings and finally the woodland.

To the left, when facing the pub, was the car-park entrance, and that was bordered by a private house with a garden; that garden sported a dividing barrier of tall conifers through which nothing could be seen.

'So.' I pointed to my sketch. 'One way of stealing a bike would be to leap over the wall from the wood, jump onto the bike and ride it out of the entrance. The other method would be to enter the pub, mingle with the drinkers and people having bar snacks and wait for an opportunity to commit the crime. That would have to be when the bike owner's attention was diverted or when he was away from his machine. Then chummy could ride the bike out of the car-park, but he'd have to act very quickly.'

'So the only way to steal the bike is either to take it out of the car-park entrance, or lift it over the back wall and into the wood, then carry it to a waiting vehicle, a vehicle parked in that lane?' confirmed Blaketon.

'I can't see any other alternative unless the bikes are left at the front of the pub, which they won't be,' Craddock told us. 'I've been to visit the scene and agree with PC Rhea. Bearing in mind the way chummy has stolen other machines, both those methods are within his capability.'

'That narrows things down a bit,' grunted Blaketon.

'Yes indeed. And that helps us make our plans,' said Craddock. 'Now, one very important factor is that the public rooms – the bar and the lounge that is – do not overlook the car-park, nor, of course, do those tables arranged at the front. Even the toilets are at the side of the building but in any case their windows are frosted.'

'So are we saying his most likely method is to lift it over the back wall and place it in his van?' Blaketon frowned.

'I think that is the only secure way open to him; it's a bit risky riding a stolen bike out of the car-park and onto the road directly in front of the pub and its customers, even if he has a van waiting nearby,' said Craddock. 'I think he'll park his van along the lane, in the shelter of that wood.'

'So we need observers in the car-park, in the wood, on the tables outside and in both the bar and the lounge,' I suggested. 'And, I would think we need a second man hiding in the wood, to observe his approach along that lane and to immobilize his van while he's busy nicking the bike.'

'Good thinking, PC Rhea!' beamed Craddock. 'Yes, we do indeed need to immobilize his van to prevent his escape ... so how many observers are we talking about?'

I did a quick mental recce of the pub and said, 'Two in the car-park, two in the wood, one in the bar, one in the lounge and one outside on the tables. Seven at least, Sergeant.'

'Seven? To catch a cycle thief?' burst Blaketon.

'I agree,' said Craddock. 'This man has been so persistent, it's time he was halted. We must do all in our power to arrest him – even if it requires a small army!'

'I hope we're not going to accrue overtime on this!' grumbled Blaketon.

'The constables will have to be in civilian clothes and fully briefed as to their roles, even if we do have to pay overtime, Oscar,' grinned Craddock. 'We must not have any signs of a police presence that day, no police vehicles on show anywhere near the village or the pub.'

'And you'll be there?' asked Blaketon of Craddock.

'I shall indeed. I will be in cycling gear, and on my own brand-new racing bike. I am prepared to use it as additional bait – how's that for a show of confidence in our men?' He produced a quick fleeting smile, almost cheeky in fact.

'How can we be sure he will take the bait?' was Blaketon's next question.

'We can't be a hundred per cent sure, but I think our advert about the reunion of the Coldstream club will tempt him,' said Craddock. 'It will announce departure from their homes in time to meet at the top of Clay Bank in Bilsdale at eleven, for a reunion at the Moon and Compass at noon on the same Sunday as the meeting of the Thornaby club. I shall place a telephone number in the advert too. That's in case anyone does ring up asking for information about the outing and even suggesting we do not all descend on the same pub. All callers will be told the guards club consists only of five members in widely different parts of the area and that five extra cyclists at the Moon and Compass will not lead to overcrowding.

Besides, it is not uncommon for two or three smaller clubs to meet at the same place. It adds to the social atmosphere of the occasion.'

'And you reckon the thought of guardsmen's big bikes will be enough to temp him? I might argue the notion would scare him off. He might not want to risk being tackled by one of Her Majesty's finest as he's making off with his property.' I could see that Sergeant Blaketon had some reservations about this scheme.

'On the other hand,' smiled Craddock, 'he might see it as a challenge he can't resist ... like stealing from a policeman! Not that he knew my bike was owned by a police officer when he took it.'

'Perhaps he did?' grinned Blaketon.

'In which case he is more likely to turn up at the Moon and Compass,' countered Craddock. 'And Exercise Rat-Trap will be ready for him.'

'OK. I'll arrange for seven officers to be on duty that Sunday,' agreed Blaketon. 'In civvies and looking like cyclists or day-trippers.'

'We'll need to have radio contact. I can arrange for a CID undercover van with darkened rear windows to be stationed in the car-park, fully equipped with radio. The person in there can observe the cycles the whole time, and alert the other members of the team if chummy removes one.'

'All observers can be allocated personal radio sets, can they?' I asked.

'We have a field telephone we can use. I will make the necessary arrangements for all that,' confirmed Craddock. 'If there is one difficulty, it will be identifying the thief from all the other cyclists, particularly if he is wearing cycling clothes.'

'He'll be the one operating alone,' I said. 'He'll be the one who is not in the pub while everyone else is, the one who pops out to the loo and never goes back. We do know he's around thirty, rather tall and with dark hair. We'll know him!'

'Let's hope so. It would be a disaster if he got away with a bike from right under our very noses! So, Oscar, can we have your volunteers parade here, at Ashfordly Police Station, at ten o'clock that Sunday for a briefing by me?'

'It's as good as done,' said Blaketon, still not sounding very enthusiastic about this scheme.

'And make sure they've all got a description of that maroon pick-up. And PC Rhea should be one of the group.'

'Right,' said Blaketon.

And so we began our determined effort to catch the phantom cycle thief.

# 9

The sub-committee of the St Aidan's Guild of Aidensfield had, in its wisdom, decided to inform Joseph in advance about his forthcoming trip to Lourdes. The necessary funds had been raised, his place had been confirmed in good time and, in the belief they were acting compassionately, members of the sub-committee felt he should be allowed time to become accustomed to the idea. After all, this was his first trip abroad and they realized that such an expedition was not a simple matter for a chap in his mid-seventies.

There was some concern that a long outing to foreign parts might aggravate his condition, so, acting on the advice of Dr McGee, they had to think very carefully about their actions. Even though Joseph had worked on the railways with the availability of concessionary tickets, they all knew he'd never been further south than York; consequently, a visit to a destination where no one had heard of Aidensfield could present serious worries for Joseph and his family. Then there was the practical aspect – as one lady member pointed out, Mabel would want time to prepare things like his newly pressed clothes, clean underwear and shirts, several changes of collars, a few changes of socks and new soles on his shoes in case he spent a lot of time kneeling. He might even want to take a camera with him which meant he'd have to buy one.

Ten days before Joseph was due to board the coach, therefore, he and Mabel were invited to a dinner party at the home of Michael Bannister. Michael, a solicitor, and his wife, Alison, lived in a beautiful double-fronted house at the west end of Aidensfield; Michael had been chairman of the sub-committee which had raised funds for Joseph's trip.

Having guests to dinner was a regular facet of the Bannisters' social life and on this occasion the party comprised Joseph and Mabel, Father Simon and the four members of the sub-committee, plus the Bannisters. Joseph and Mabel were somewhat flummoxed by the invitation to such a posh establishment and wondered if there'd been some kind of mistake, but once they realized the invitation was truly for them,

Mabel began wondering which knife and fork to use, and Joseph asked whether he should tuck his serviette into his collar or his waistband. And there might be food with all kinds of foreign names ... and wine ... and funny bits of food called *horses' doovers* which you had to eat standing up before the meal. In houses like that, they called sherry *aperitif* which Joseph had thought was a set of dentures. Apart from anything else, Joseph's appetite had not returned to its former Yorkshire trencherman level but he hoped he would cope with whatever was placed before him. It was a harrowing time, waiting for that Wednesday evening, and in the minds of Joseph and Mabel, the whole affair would be like treading on broken glass. They were not really looking forward to it.

In preparation, Joseph had a bath on the Tuesday night preceding the dinner, his first for a month or so, and on the Wednesday he dressed in his funeral-going suit, the one he also used for weddings and the annual Gooseberry Society dinner. He complemented his suit with a smart white shirt, dark tie and cuff-links he'd inherited from his father. Some might have said the suit looked like a sack on a scarecrow due to his loss of weight, but Mabel thought it wise not to comment on his haunted appearance. It was made worse by the darkness of his suit because that made his face look even paler than usual. However, he plastered his hair to his head with hair-cream and made sure he shaved off all his surplus whiskers, then packed his pipe, tobacco and matches into his waistcoat pocket and waited for Mabel. She put on a smart flowered dress, the sort she would have worn for official do's if she'd accepted that invitation to be president of the WI, and she found a hat she'd last worn at her niece's wedding eight years ago.

Joseph even consented to her having a hair-do in Ashfordly that Wednesday afternoon, the first she'd had since that very same wedding, and the pair of them set off to walk to the Bannisters' residence, feeling very self-conscious about walking through the village on a Wednesday evening in their Sunday best, particularly as there was nothing happening at the church. That's when I encountered them. I was enjoying a summer evening foot patrol around Aidensfield, due to finish at 10 p.m.

'Hello,' I greeted them. 'This looks very formal, Joseph and Mabel! I'll bet you're not going to the pub, dressed up like that!'

'I wish we were!' grunted Joseph. 'I could use a long cool pint or two after a hot day in the garden.'

'Give over, Joseph,' snapped Mabel. 'We're going up in the world, that's what's happening, and it's all due to you retiring from that gooseberry job. You've made folks aware of what you've been doing on their behalf over the years, and now they're realizing you'll have time for other things. They're getting their invitations in already; sensible folks want to get in first before there's a queue waiting to have us. Leastways, that's how I see it. You're important now, Joseph, so don't you forget it. And mind your manners. Don't reach in front of folks to get the salt like you do at home, and don't start tucking in until everyone's got dished up and don't light that pipe of yours halfway through the main course like you do at home. We're going to the Bannisters, Mr Rhea, to a dinner party.'

And she raised her nose in the air, just a little, but I didn't miss it. Not everyone was invited to the Bannisters – their circle of professional friends was a far cry from folks who'd worked on the railway, even if it was making sure the tracks were always in their right place upon the sleepers. I doubt if the station master himself would have received an invitation to the Bannisters.

I must admit I pondered the reason for this unusual event, not at the time associating it with Joseph's trip to Lourdes, and I wondered if this heralded a whole new social life for Mabel and Joseph. It was still early in the evening, not yet 7.30, and I guessed their meal started at 8 p.m. Not wanting to delay them and wishing them a very enjoyable evening, I left the Marshalls to their evening's fun.

Later, I heard Mabel had made Joseph ring the doorbell, telling him it was a man's job on such occasions. Ladies in smart frocks didn't ring doorbells, she'd told him, adding they mebbe should have hired a taxi rather than walk up from the village. Joseph, on the other hand, would never see the sense of hiring a taxi when you could walk.

Completion of my tour of duty that evening was later than intended because one of the villagers, an elderly lady called Emily Arrowsmith, thought she heard intruders in her back yard and rang to complain just as I was entering the house to finish my shift. When I spoke to her, she claimed she'd heard footsteps and heavy breathing followed by someone knocking over the dustbin. When I investigated I did find the bin upturned and the contents emptied. I thought it was the work of a badger; badgers did live in the hillside behind her house. I made a thorough search of the vicinity of her home and found nothing. I told her I would patrol outside for a few minutes in the dark, just to ensure no one was lurking in the shadows, and suggested she went back to bed while I guarded her house. She did go to bed and I patrolled the area, but found nothing. I felt sure she was asleep before I departed because she extinguished all her lights and they were never switched on during my vigil. I remained convinced she'd been disturbed by a rummaging badger.

On leaving her house, however, around 11 p.m., I caught up to Joseph and Mabel as they pottered home after their evening at the Bannisters.

'Hello again,' I said, trying not to raise my voice too much because some people along the street were already in bed and I did not wish to disturb them with loud voices in the street. 'I'm just heading for home, knocking off time!'

'Hello, Mr Rhea,' and I thought Joseph sounded a bit gloomy.

'How was your evening with the Bannisters?' I asked, as I walked beside them, slowing down to their gentle place.

'Oh, t'grub was fine,' he said. 'I managed to eat quite a lot, didn't I, Mabel? I've no idea what I was eating, mind, but it tasted all right and there wasn't a great pile of it. It was summat I could cope with, and I can say it was enjoyable. I might even have a French meal now, if I go out somewhere.'

'It was Italian,' said Mabel gently. 'Our meal, Joseph, it was Italian, with Italian wine. They'd been to Italy, you see, Mr Rhea, for their holidays, and thought we'd like to try some of the local food. Very nice too, I must say. Very nice indeed.'

'Well, it came from somewhere over there, one of them foreign places, with bits of fried bread floating in t'soup.'

'They're sending him to Lourdes, Mr Rhea. That's what it was for. It seems all those fund-raising efforts for the church were really to raise money for Joseph. They thought a trip to Lourdes might cure him. They've paid for his seat on a bus with expenses for hotels and things.'

'Lourdes, eh? That sounds great! I'll bet that surprised you, Joseph!' I tried to sound cheerful and happy for him as I escorted

271

them along the street, but I could see that he was far from pleased. In fact, he looked really miserable.

'Well, I must admit I was a bit taken aback, Mr Rhea. I didn't know what to say. I mean, they caught me by surprise and although I don't want to appear ungrateful, I'm not one for going that far from home....'

'I can't get him to go anywhere, Mr Rhea. I wouldn't say no to a trip to Blackpool or even to see the sea at Bridlington,' said Mabel. 'As for Lourdes, well, I think it's a wonderful idea and somewhere I've always wanted to see, but now he's got the chance, he should go!'

'You're not thinking of refusing, Joseph, are you?' I asked.

'Well, Mr Rhea, I've responsibilities in this village and I can't abdicate them just for a trip to Lourdes. It's not as if I'm seriously badly; I'm not. You were there in the hospital at Scarborough when them specialists said there was nowt wrong with me, so why send me to Lourdes? Why pray for miracles and things when I'm not ill? I reckon that seat should be taken by someone who's really poorly.'

'But you have lost weight, Joseph, and your appetite has not recovered. Obviously

272

there's something not quite right with you.'
I tried to encourage him, if only for the sake
of those who'd helped raise the money. 'A
trip to Lourdes might just put right whatever it is.'

'Some chance of that, Mr Rhea. That's not
what miracles are for! Miracles are for
curing folks who can't walk or see or hear.
Lourdes is full of crutches folks have left
there when they've been cured in that
grotto. I've seen pictures of them. To be
honest, Mr Rhea, I can't see me going to
Lourdes looking like a skeleton and coming
back looking like I was before I lost all them
pounds.'

'It doesn't work as fast as that...' I tried to
explain.

'It does, Mr Rhea!' said Mabel. 'Those
folks who've left their crutches behind got
cured straight away, and Jesus didn't hang
about when he cured Lazarus after he'd
been dead four days.'

'Well....'

'And that chap who couldn't see was
cured straight away when Jesus spat in his
eye. So why can't our Joseph get his weight
back straight away? You answer me that, Mr
Rhea. After all, a miracle is a miracle.'

'I won't try to answer you in the face of

that kind of argument, Mabel. All I can suggest is that Joseph goes to Lourdes to gain whatever benefit he can. It's a wonderful opportunity and he shouldn't miss this chance.'

'I've got to think it over,' Joseph said quietly. 'My first reaction was to refuse outright, and give the seat to someone more worthy, but those folks said the whole village had worked so hard for me. For *me*, Mr Rhea. I reckon that it would be churlish to refuse. It's that side o' things that's got me thinking.'

'Don't be too hasty in making a decision,' I advised him.

'Nay, I can't be too long making my mind up because there's summat none of 'em have thought about,' he said, pulling his pipe from his pocket. He halted in the street, stuffed some tobacco into the bowl then lit it with much puffing and sucking, making us await his comments.

'Go on, Joseph,' I invited. 'What haven't they thought about?'

'Well, you can tell none of them Guild sub-committee is a Big Gooseberry Man, can't you?' He blew clouds of smoke into the cool night air and I must admit it smelt beautiful. Some pipe tobacco produced a

274

most pleasurable aroma and this was one example.

'How's that?' I asked.

'Well,' he said. 'They've gone and booked a seat for me on that bus. It leaves on July twenty-sixth, Mr Rhea, and doesn't get back until August second. Sunday, that is. The day before the berry show … now, what sort of folks make arrangements like that, eh? Here's me, on my last berry show as president, having to be away when all the last-minute jobs have to be done. And then there's the question of my prize berry … big berries need attention, Mr Rhea, in that final week. How can I see to my berry if I'm away in Lourdes? You answer me that!'

'Oh dear.' I did not know how to react. 'But your new president could do whatever has to be done for the show, he's already promised that.'

'Mebbe so, but that doesn't settle t'question of my own gooseberry, does it? The one I'm aiming will win the Supreme, that is.'

'I thought all your berries were little ones!' I joked.

'There's allus secrets to be kept, Mr Rhea.' He sucked at the pipe and blew more smoke into the night air. 'Now I'm going to think it over pretty seriously, but I reckon I'll have to turn down the Lourdes job. I can't see I've any choice. How can I go off to foreign parts and leave that berry of mine just hanging there, eh? It's like leaving a new-born lamb without any warmth and food … they're tender things, is big gooseberries. They need mothering, especially in them last few days. They can burst at the slightest mistreatment or jolt or get knocked off with raindrops and there's them wasps to cope with. Who's going to do all that if I'm gallivanting around Lourdes saying lots of Hail Marys? That won't do owt for my berry, will it?'

I could see where his priorities lay. By this time, we had reached the parting of our ways. He and Mabel would walk along the terrace to their own little cottage, doubtless talking late into the night about the dilemma now facing Joseph. I could under-stand his reservations, yet I wondered if he was finding excuses for refusing the trip. The short answer was that if he went to Lourdes, he's probably have to abandon any hope of competing in this year's com-petition but he must consider his health. That should be his priority.

'Mabel could look after your berry,' I said.

'He'd never let me near his real berry trees, Mr Rhea!' she retorted. 'It's more than my life's worth to go anywhere near them.'

'I'd say your health was more important than any big berry, Joseph. With good health, you'll be around for lots more years to grow lots more big berries....'

'Aye, but this year's my last as president,' he began.

'That same thought has struck me,' interrupted Mabel. 'If you are very sick, Joseph, without realizing it, then a trip to Lourdes might cure you, mightn't it? You've got the faith, you're not a doubter. It's all them doubters who never get cured. If you go, God might look upon you with favour and make you better. Then you'll be here alive and well with lots more chances to win the Supreme.'

'What are you saying, Mabel?' he frowned.

'I'm saying Mr Rhea's right. If you don't get cured of whatever's wrong, you could die tomorrow, or next week, or next month or next year. From whatever you've got.'

'You mean I should go and leave my berry?' he puzzled.

'Yes I do. If you get cured, you'll be in better health and have more time and energy for growing bigger and heavier berries.'

'You mean you really think I should go?' He sounded highly surprised and even just a little suspicious of her overt encouragement.

'Well, with this trip and with your faith, you've got a chance to have lots more chances at growing a prize-winning big berry, but you've only one chance to go to Lourdes and mebbe get a cure. Without a cure, you might not be able to grow big berries ever again. This is the most important thing that's ever happened to you, Joseph, so don't mess it up, for all our sakes. I don't want you to die just for t'sake of one big berry! Just you think about that!'

He paused, puffed at his pipe and said, 'I'll think on it,' and began to walk home. I left them and walked up to my police house on the hill, wondering what Joseph's decision would be.

The following Sunday I could not attend mass as usual because I had been ordered to attend Ashfordly Police Station at 10 a.m. for our briefing for Exercise Rat-Trap.

It meant I did not see Joseph, consequently I could not have a chat with him about his decision on the Lourdes trip. It wouldn't be long before I did know, I was sure. However, clad in casual civilian clothes as instructed, I reported to Ashfordly Police Station. Outside on the street, I noticed a small white van without any identifying markings upon it; it had darkened back windows and two aerials protruding from the roof: an undercover observation vehicle. Also, parked against the inside of the railings, was a beautiful red racing cycle secured to the rails with a padlock and chain.

I went inside to find a posse of constables clad in all manner of very informal civilian clothing. It looked rather like a ramblers' outing, but not quite as smart. Alf Ventress, himself dressed like a grouse-beater in plus-fours and deer stalker, was busy preparing mugs of coffee, while the two sergeants, Blaketon and Craddock, were in Blaketon's office finalizing their plans. Space within such a small police station was extremely limited, the only large room being the public enquiry office. The sergeant's office was too small to accommodate such a group, and the only other spaces were the cells and the cell passage. This meant our briefing would be open to the public who might pop in to report lost dogs or found purses, but we would cope.

At a nod from Craddock, Ventress disappeared down the cell passage and returned with a blackboard which he set up in the enquiry office; it showed a plan of the car-park and surrounds of the Moon and Compass at Craydale all drawn in white chalk and highlighted with red dots.

The red dots, we were to discover, were the location of policemen in hiding. As Craddock positioned himself before the blackboard and made sure his notes were in order, Ventress went once again into the cell passage and emerged with some field radio sets, our sophisticated communications system for this exercise, and he plonked these in a heap on the floor. Clumsy and sometimes ineffective, we would have to rely on those sets – this was some time prior to the introduction of personal radio sets for police officers. As there were insufficient chairs and insufficient space to accommodate them anyway, we had to stand to listen to the forthcoming words of wisdom.

In looking around at the assembled crime-busters, I had no idea what Blaketon's fashion-sense would dictate although I knew that Craddock would be in cycling gear because I was sure it was his racing cycle secured to the police station railings. After a good deal of banter about one another's sartorial elegance, the door of the sergeant's office opened and Blaketon, dressed in what appeared to be part golfing outfit and part hiking gear, with a small rucksack, emerged, followed by Craddock in his cycling shorts, T-shirt and cycling shoes. Someone produced a wolf-whistle at which Blaketon started to respond with a well chosen put-down about this being a serious police exercise and not an occasion for joking, but Craddock deflated the situation with a smile on his face while taking a deep bow as if performing before an audience. His instinctive response eased the slight tension that prevailed and we all chuckled.

From that moment, the atmosphere was one of friendly co-operation. As we waited for some action from our leaders, we chatted about the thefts, swopped yarns about similar exercises which had gone wrong and pondered the outcome of Exercise Rat-Trap. Even Blaketon smiled and he moved amongst us, and then he said, 'All right you lot, settle down and pin your ears back. This operation is very important, it'll put Ashfordly Section in the limelight if we can bring this cycle thief to justice, so I want your fullest co-operation. Sergeant Craddock will now address you.'

For the benefit of those unfamiliar with the crimes, Craddock first outlined the on-going series, highlighting those in our area and making comparisons with others which had occurred within the jurisdiction of neighbouring police forces. He made reference to my own theories about the large-framed and rather specialized cycles, the lone thief using a maroon coloured pick-up and the fact that the thief might well be dressed as a cyclist whilst committing his crimes. That would make him very difficult to recognize as someone suspicious, he pointed out, trying to ensure that we were all very alert during the forthcoming exercise. He also pointed out that the fellow probably stole the machines by riding them to his waiting vehicle which would be securely concealed but ready for a rapid getaway. The fact he had been operating for more than a year without ever being spotted in action meant he was clever, skilful and determined. It would be like catching a shadow, Craddock smiled, adding, 'But we can do it, lads.'

Having provided the background to the

crimes, Craddock next allocated each of his red spots to a particular constable.

He explained there'd be a further briefing upon arrival at the Moon and Compass although these would have to be done with the utmost discretion, but as a prelude he gave instructions to each officer. Because of my more extensive knowledge of the crimes, my hiding place was in the deciduous wood behind the pub car-park; from there, I had to observe the car-park and the movements of people using it, with particular emphasis on the parked cycles.

'I shall place my target cycle there,' Craddock said. 'Take a good look at it, PC Rhea, it is outside now. If no one else brings a large-framed special, this will be the one he'll probably go for. I will leave it unlocked – either he'll ride it like hell out of the car-park to his truck, or he'll lift it over the wall as previously discussed. Or, of course, he might steal any of the other bikes which takes his fancy.'

He went on to say that the road which ran along the side of the pub premises skirted the same trees in which I would be concealed and there were one or two inlet points, places where a small vehicle could pull into the trees and conceal itself from passing traffic. I had to familiarize myself with those, I was told – but I responded by saying I'd already examined the layout of the area and was familiar with the locale.

One constable, PC Harvey, was detailed to conceal himself deeper in the wood so that he could observe the lane and all its likely parking places and then, if the maroon pick-up arrived, alert the rest of us by field radio and immobilize the vehicle by taking off the plug leads.

'The white van parked outside is our communications centre,' he explained. 'PC Grayson, the man at the back wearing the woolly hat with a pompom, will remain in that vehicle, in the rear, out of sight. He will park it so that he has a wide view of the car-park from those rear windows – they're darkened so that no one can peer inside, but he can look out. Clearly, not all of us will be equipped with radio – the sets would be rather conspicuous, but some of us will have them. PC Harvey will have one – he might be the first to observe the arrival of chummy in which case he will alert the rest of us. I'll explain how that will be achieved when we assemble at the Moon and Compass.'

It took an hour to fully brief everyone and I was impressed by Craddock's attention to detail, each constable being given a very comprehensive written order which contained all the elements of the exercise. Afterwards, he asked for comments or questions. There were one or two queries, out of which it emerged that most of us would have to be able to exercise our discretion in the action we took, because plans of this kind invariably failed to cater for some unknown distraction or occurrence. I made the point of describing the maroon van in great detail, asking that everyone made sure they recorded the registration number of any such vehicle, or indeed any suspicious vehicle, seen in the vicinity.

And then I said, 'I think chummy might be a cycle dealer, Sergeant.' I addressed my remarks to Craddock. 'I mean, he might run a cycle shop.'

'And what makes you think that, PC Rhea?' he asked.

'First, he always strikes on Sundays, when the shops are closed....'

'Cycle clubs go out on Sunday, PC Rhea,' smiled Craddock.

'I appreciate that,' I said. 'But some do go out on Saturdays, and some, like those of large concerns, have midweek outings.

Furthermore, the big department store in Middlesbrough, for example, has its own cycling club and they go out on Wednesdays, which is half-day closing.'

'And you are saying there've been no weekday crimes in this series?'

'It looks very much like that, with Sundays only for these special bikes. Every crime we know about has been committed on a Sunday – but the maroon van has also been seen on Wednesdays,' I added. 'Chummy delivered his waste tin lids to Tin Lid Talbot on a Wednesday, and also delivered his machine to that Eltering cycle shop on a Wednesday. My witness saw the van on a Wednesday, and chummy called at the Eltering shop every fourth Wednesday. For all those reasons, I think Wednesday might be his day off, half-day closing in other words.'

'You could be right. OK, lads. Preliminary briefing's over. It's time to visit the Moon and Compass – and I've managed to wheedle some cash out of admin. for each of you to have a pint and a sandwich, seeing that you have to be on duty over a meal break. But don't overdo things – I don't want you to regard this as a party, it's official police duty. Now, I've arranged for unmarked transport to take us to Craydale, and some will go in the communications van – including me and my bike! Right, when we arrive, we should assemble in the corner of the car-park near the communications van, and we should look like tourists or day-trippers or something similar; you'll be further briefed at that stage, but we must make it appear as if we're discussing important things, such as where to go next and who buys the drinks. But most important, we must not look like policemen....'

And so began Exercise Rat-Trap.

Half an hour later, I was lurking behind the stout trunk of a beech tree in the wood overlooking the car-park of the Moon and Compass. From my lofty vantage point, I could also see towards the lane which skirted this wood, and by moving slightly could obtain a good view of the small areas which might be used to park a small vehicle. By moving just a fraction, I could also see PC Harvey – I waved to acknowledge his presence and he waved in return; sadly, we had no direct radio contact with one another and he was well beyond whispering distance. Due to the rising landscape of the wood, however, it was impossible for one constable to keep both the pub car-park and the lane under observation. That required two people and so, having established that visual contact, I returned to my own viewpoint.

It was just noon, opening time for a Sunday, and already the car-park was busy. A few customers had arrived early; some had hung around the car-park in small groups and others sat in their cars awaiting the opening of the doors and so our anonymous white van and our scruffy presence around it during briefing did not look out of place. I felt we mingled well with the awaiting customers. Five minutes later, though, we had all dispersed to our points, the lucky ones inside the premises and the others hidden around the exterior. The Five Lamps Cycling Club had also arrived.

Thirty-five of its members had turned up and they were in the bar, noisily enjoying their pints whilst awaiting mammoth helpings of Yorkshire puddings, roast beef and vegetables, followed by rice pudding and, if required, a cup of tea while their fine machines stood in a line against the car-park wall. I noticed several large-framed racing cycles among them.

They'd be there for at least an hour or

possibly two. Sergeant Craddock's own bike was strategically positioned close to one end of the long line as our undercover officers operated inside the pub, keeping their eyes and ears open for gossip, and their mouths open for pints of cool beer. I must admit I was somewhat nervous about this exercise because so much could go wrong. The fact it was happening at all was largely due to my researches and opinions, although it eased my conscience somewhat to know that Sergeant Craddock had given me his full support – but it was worrying to think that it might all come to nothing.

These efforts to tempt our fly into the web we had created was not bound to be a success – he might not turn up, or he might come and be alerted to our presence, or he might even succeed in spite of our presence. The latter was too dreadful to contemplate, but as I glanced at my watch for the umpteenth time, I began to think he had not taken our bait. From what I had learned from studying his previous crimes, he always struck very soon after the arrival of his target cycle; he committed his thefts long before the owners of the cycles were likely to discover their loss and thus allowed himself adequate time to get clear of the scene before the alarm was raised.

I checked the time again – it was now 12.20 p.m. and the pub had been open for twenty minutes. A selection of desirable cycles was presented in a row, as if on show for a customer, and their owners usefully out of sight.

And then PC Harvey spotted a suspicious vehicle.

'Rat-Trap Two to Control,' he whispered. 'A light-grey pick-up truck has just arrived. Registered number EUB 44C. Single male driver, young looking, dark hair. It is parked in one of the earmarked wooded areas. The driver has not yet emerged. Over.'

In his little white van, PC Grayson received the message; Sergeant Craddock was sitting in the front seat of the van ostensibly reading the *News of the World* and he overheard it and said, 'Tell Harvey to keep it under observation; it might be chummy in a different truck. It's grey, not maroon, but get him to let us know the minute the driver leaves the vehicle.' And so, as I discovered later, that message was relayed to Harvey in the wood.

It was during those few moments that I decided to climb higher into the wood to make contact with PC Harvey. I wanted to see if he had noticed anything; by changing my position just a fraction, I could also keep the car-park under observation. But, as I gained the view I sought, I saw him speaking on the radio and then saw the shape of a stationary grey van. It was a small vehicle, a pick-up with its rear section covered by what appeared to be a wooden structure, and it had no rear doors.

Had it been maroon, I would have ensured that an immediate alert was passed to all our observers but because it was grey ... then I thought of all those tin lids with grey paint on them – and it was the same grey I'd noticed on those tin lids stored by Tin Lid Talbot.

This was our man!

I realized he'd come in the same vehicle but it was now a pleasing grey, having been resprayed. I had no radio. I could not reveal my presence in the wood to alert our men. I could not abandon my post, because if I did, he was bound to arrive during my absence, however temporary. Not realizing that PC Harvey had alerted the others, I knew I had to warn our team without alerting the villain. Taking a quick look at the car-park, I flitted between the trees, feeling rather like Robin Hood hiding from the Sheriff of Nottingham, and when I was close enough, hissed at PC Harvey. He heard me; as he glanced in my direction, I placed my finger on my lips to indicate silence and beckoned him towards me. Happily, he responded. Furtively we crept through the leafy wood until we could talk behind a clump of rhododendrons.

'That van,' I whispered. 'I think it's him, I think it's the maroon one resprayed.'

'Control knows it's here,' he said. 'I've alerted them. I've got to maintain obs.'

'Great. Has chummy got out?'

'Not yet ... he's a young man, dark hair....'

'It all fits; everything says it's our man,' I said. 'Look, I'm going back to my post, the minute he gets out of that van....'

'There, look. He's moving now ... a tall, thin fellow, late twenties, early thirties....'

'Call them,' I snapped with my heart pounding. 'Tell them Exercise Rat-Trap is about to be sprung!'

And as I hurried back to my observation point overlooking the car-park, PC Harvey relayed my suspicions to our waiting team then prepared to immobilize the little grey pick-up.

# 10

In keeping watch for the cycle thief, our instructions were, if possible, to wait until he had placed the stolen machine in the rear of his van and covered it with the tarpaulin. Those joint acts – the taking and the concealing – would prove that he intended to permanently deprive the owner of the machine. These were essential ingredients in the definition of larceny and vital if we were to secure a conviction. If we swooped too early, perhaps while he was wheeling the bike away or even riding it out of the car-park, he might claim he'd selected the wrong bike in error or was just borrowing it to rush to a telephone kiosk to make an urgent call, thinking the owner would not object, or he might produce some other plausible story which a court might believe and which might imply he was merely borrowing the cycle rather than stealing it. Having considered those aspects, the fact we had immobilized his vehicle would assist greatly in catching him red-handed –

further proof of his guilt.

As I sheltered behind my stout-trunked beech tree, I felt twinges of nervousness, wondering whether I could compel myself to stand still while watching him steal a bike. Having seen the present set-up, I felt sure he would ride it out of the car-park and must admit I wondered whether he might still evade us by skilful riding or sheer cunning. But orders were orders. As I waited with heart beating, I began to think he would adopt that route rather than lift the bike over the wall.

I felt sure he'd ride the stolen machine out of the car-park because all the cyclists were inside the pub, unable to keep an eye on their machines – and unaware that a thief was about. I doubted if the people sitting at the tables outside the pub would be bothered about the bikes – they were day-trippers who'd come by car and although we had a constable concealed among them, none would pay any attention if the bike was ridden past. The constable's task, of course, was to observe and if the cyclist passed him, to alert the rest of us – he had not to effect or attempt an arrest.

As I waited during those tense few moments, I wondered if the thief had come to reconnoitre the scene prior to committing his crime. He might have come on the previous Wednesday. Or perhaps he'd arrived early today for the same reason. But the time for speculation was over because I saw him walking into the car-park.

He had walked, unseen by me, along the lane beside the wood, down the side of the pub, round to the front door and then he'd gone inside the premises. Once inside he would have established that the cyclists were all inside too, all busy with their meal and engaged in light-hearted banter, to preoccupied to worry about their machines. In other words, everything was in place for him to steal the cycle of his choice.

As I watched, the car-park appeared to be deserted, apart from our suspect. There was no one to be seen, although I knew that Sergeant Craddock and PC Grayson were concealed in the little white van. They would have seen him, too, and I knew they would have radioed PC Harvey at his remote point with the grey pick-up while keeping him under observation.

Every policeman was on the alert as chummy emerged from the rear door of the Moon and Compass. He walked very quickly and I noted he was a tall, well-built and rather muscular man. He was wearing traditional cycling gear comprising shorts and a T-shirt but with black sandshoes on his feet rather than cycling shoes. I did not recognize him, but with his mass of dark hair, he would be prominent in a crowd. With remarkable speed, he reached the row of parked cycles and selected one – but it was not the red machine owned by Sergeant Craddock. He chose a handsome blue model and in a trice was in the saddle and racing from the car-park with all the skill of a very experienced rider.

Hurrying to my vantage point in the wood, I waved at PC Harvey, but he was already responding to his radio, being told his customer would arrive within a few moments. I reckoned the thief had about 200 yards to cover on the road, a matter of a minute or so for a skilled racing cyclist. I began to move through the trees, heading towards the grey van parked in the lane beyond and I saw PC Harvey had moved too; he was adopting a more suitable position for his ambush. We must not let ourselves be seen, not at this crucial stage and so we both made sure we were concealed from the lane. Then chummy appeared, thrusting hard on the pedals and driving the beautiful bike forward in bursts of fierce speed. Both PC Harvey and I watched as the man raced towards the rear of his van; at the last moment, he dismounted and with a skilful flourish hoisted the bike into the air and thrust it into the rear of his vehicle. I heard it clatter to the metal floor, and then saw the thief haul over the tarpaulin which had been laid aside in preparation.

Then he went to the driver's door, moving momentarily out of our vision. It was time to make our move. I was happy that we had immobilized the pick-up truck and smiled in satisfaction as chummy tried to start the engine; by the time he realized the pick-up would not start without some kind of assistance beneath the bonnet, both PC Harvey and I arrived at the pick-up.

'He's yours, Nick,' said Harvey, and so I went to the driver's door while he approached the passenger side. We'd got him! The driver's door opened and I was waiting.

'Police,' I said, as I seized the door to prevent it opening further. 'You're under arrest for larceny of the pedal cycle which is in the rear of this vehicle. You are not obliged to say anything unless you wish to do so, but what you say will be taken down in writing and given in evidence.'

'Don't be bloody stupid!' he growled, trying to emerge from the vehicle. 'It's my bike, it's got a puncture and the front wheel is buckled. I've come to collect it.'

'You can tell that to the court,' I said, reaching for the handcuffs I had brought with me. 'Come on, out you get, you're surrounded.'

And as I spoke, Sergeant Blaketon and Sergeant Craddock arrived, along with our other officers.

'Good work,' said Craddock, who then smiled cruelly into the eyes of our captive and said, 'You have a cycle of mine somewhere, young man, and I am very keen to know what you've done with it – and I'm not talking about the bike in your truck!'

'I'm saying nothing.' And our prisoner did not say another word as he was placed in one of our vehicles and taken to Ashfordly Police Station. I took charge of the grey pick-up and followed the prisoner to Ashfordly.

The postscript to this tale, which I shall record slightly out of sequence, is that the thief was a man from South Bank, an industrial sprawl to the south of Middlesbrough on the River Tees. He owned a small-time cycle shop and supplemented his income by stealing smart racing cycles and disguising them in premises to the rear of his shop. Because he was a tall man, he'd realized there was a modest but steady demand for expensive machines tailored especially for tall people. He stole selected bikes, refitted them with stolen spares taken from other stolen bikes, removed or obliterated any frame numbers, allocated new ones, resprayed the frames and sold the well-disguised machines through a network of shops and other dealers, all for cash. It was a comparatively simple scheme undertaken by a clever and resourceful thief, but as a result of Exercise Rat-Trap, we traced some of the recently stolen bikes. We found a few in the premises behind the shop, in varying states of refurbishment and repainting, and others which were awaiting customers in shops around the region. Most of those he had stolen weren't recovered and Sergeant Craddock's missing cycle was one we never traced. The thief, a man called Stan Piper, with no previous criminal record, was later sentenced to six months imprisonment. It was a fairly stiff sentence for a first offender but the court imposed it after considering a range of offences we were able to prove against him.

His conviction covered the thefts of several expensive cycles, even if he denied most of our charges.

Meanwhile, the people of Aidensfield were on tenterhooks due to the proximity of their famous berry show, and their berries were swelling with contented growth. But drama came to the village when Joseph Marshall was rushed into Scarborough Hospital once again. He was taken in on Tuesday before his planned departure to Lourdes because he had developed further severe pains in his stomach and Dr McGee had noted some additional weight loss. Joseph appeared to have had a sudden and distressing remission. Mabel asked me to drive her to the hospital to visit him on the Thursday afternoon, acutely concerned about his rapidly deteriorating condition.

'He's still not decided about going to Lourdes,' she told me during the journey. 'I can't get him to make his mind up, Mr Rhea; he's been dithering all this time, worrying about what's the right thing to do. He won't say yes or no. And now this. He started losing more weight a couple of days after that dinner at Mr Bannister's and his appetite went, then he had another carry-on with his stomach, although I think it might have been something he ate there.'

'You called Dr McGee to him?'

'Oh, aye,' she confirmed. 'He gave him something for his stomach, saying it might be nothing more than a touch of diarrhoea, mebbe due to eating that foreign food, but he reckoned it wasn't serious, but since then it's got worse, Mr Rhea.'

'Poor old Joseph.'

'It was very bad pains in his belly, and not eating – and so Dr McGee said it was a hospital job once again. So in he went, and they're giving him more tests.'

'He'll be fed up of going into hospital,' I commented. 'Have you heard any results?'

'Nothing yet,' she said. 'That's why I'm going in again, they want to talk to me this afternoon. I hope they don't keep saying there's nowt wrong with him. It is good of you to take me to see him, Mr Rhea.'

'I'm as anxious as you to find out what's wrong with him,' I assured her. 'So what about this trip to Lourdes?'

'Well, I had a word with Father Simon and they've kept his seat open. He's supposed to

301

go this weekend, you know. Everything's ready, Mr Rhea, I've had his suits pressed and bought him a new shirt and a set of collars, and he needed a new pair of shoes. It's a lot of expense if he can't go but the state he's in now....'

'Maybe, if he is very poorly, he should be sent anyway, in spite of his condition. Some very sick people do manage to make the trip, Mabel.'

'That's just what I said, Mr Rhea. The worse he is, the more he needs to go to Lourdes, that's what I say. So I've told Father Simon to keep his seat available, because I'm going to make sure our Joseph goes no matter how badly he feels. You'd think those experts would realize he's very poorly, wouldn't you?'

'I'm sure they're doing their best for him,' was all I could say. 'But they'll not want the journey to make him worse.'

'It couldn't make him any worse than he is,' she retorted. 'He's got no strength left, Mr Rhea. You can tell how bad he is because he's neglected his show berries. Mebbe he doesn't like me doing it, but I've been making sure the nets are secure, feeding them and checking his little hammocks and brollies, without him knowing I might say.

But those berries need some care. The poor things do look a bit sad, you know, but it's Joseph we should really be tending, not his berries.'

'I couldn't agree more,' I said. 'The main thing is to get him better whatever it takes, then he'll have lots more years to grow his champion berry.'

'Well, it seems to me Lourdes is his only chance, Mr Rhea, because those doctors in the hospitals don't seem able to do anything for him.'

'Let's see what they say today, shall we?'

Joseph was lying in bed when we arrived and, as before, I was invited to his bedside. I thought he looked dreadful this time, far worse than the previous occasion, for the flesh had dropped away from his cheeks and face to make him look so gaunt and fragile, with his skin almost transparent, and yet his eyes continued to sparkle. I located a couple of chairs and arranged them beside the bed. Mabel didn't sit down immediately, however, because a staff nurse called her away.

'Mrs Marshall?'

'Aye, that's me,' she acknowledged, with a look of concern on her face.

'Can you come with me, Dr Hindmarsh is

waiting in his room. He asked if you could see him the moment you arrived.'

The look of apprehension on Mabel's face was sad to behold, and the fact she'd been summoned so soon after our arrival did not ease the situation, but she crossed quickly to Joseph, gave him a quick kiss on the forehead, and said, 'Don't you go away, Joseph, you talk to Mr Rhea. I'll be back in a minute or two.'

'Sit yourself down, Mr Rhea,' Joseph invited me as his wife departed, pointing to one of the chairs. 'Our Mabel has to have words with the specialist again, so you make yourself comfortable.'

'So how's things, Joseph?' I asked, sitting at his side.

'I've really got 'em flummoxed this time, Mr Rhea.' He managed a small smile. 'But they won't let me have my pipe and have given me all them tests, all over again. Same fellows, same tests.'

'Same results, maybe?' I put to him.

'Nowt wrong, you mean?'

'They couldn't find anything last time,' I said.

'Aye, that's what puzzled me. I mean, losing all that weight and not being able to eat and then that belly trouble ... it's the same, all over again, Mr Rhea. So here I am for a day or two. I expect they'll kick me out soon, tomorrow they reckon.'

'Whatever they say, you're going to Lourdes, though, aren't you?' I decided to ask him in the absence of Mabel. I hoped I might elicit a decision, if only so that I could convey it to Father Simon, perhaps in the hope the seat might be reallocated if Joseph declined to use it, and at least to ease the uncertainty.

He did not answer for a while and at that stage, I did not put pressure on him to respond. Clearly, he was continuing to think hard about his decision even at this late stage, and I guessed it had been worrying him deeply ever since that dinner at the Bannisters. He seemed to have some kind of mental blockage about Lourdes, a deep desire not to go.

'I'm not sure, Mr Rhea,' he said.

'You've got to go, Joseph.' I tried to reason with him. 'So many of your friends want you to make the trip, that's why they raised all that money.'

'I didn't ask for it, Mr Rhea,' he said, with some power in his weak voice. 'If I'd really wanted to go, I would have found the money myself.'

'It's a lot of money to find at short notice,' I said.

'We're not exactly broke, me and our Mabel,' he chided me. 'We have money put by, Mr Rhea, we could have used that. Besides, I'm not really ill. There's no disease or owt like that, and we've got to think about all them cases who are much more deserving than me, invalids, folks with incurable diseases, blind folks, deaf folks – they'd be better off than me taking a trip to Lourdes.'

'If everyone thought like that, no one would go,' I said. 'Now, you'll have to make up your mind soon … it's better to say no now, than keeping everyone guessing until the last minute.'

'I know, Mr Rhea. I'm right touched by what they've done which is why I can't turn it down, but I'll be honest, I don't want to go, Mr Rhea. I mean, I've never done owt like that in my life, been to foreign parts, that is.'

'There's a first time for everything, Joseph! Even for retired people.'

'I'm not arguing about that, but it's not natural, is it, human beings flying in the sky or going across water? God made me an Englishman, Mr Rhea, which means I'm

306

supposed to live here and work here and raise my family here and get myself better here and then die here ... not to go raking off to foreign parts for things like that. If our doctors here can't fettle me with all their knowledge, then I shall have to take the consequences.'

'God doesn't think like that, does He?' I smiled.

'He made me an Englishman, Mr Rhea, a Yorkshireman better still.'

'But he has shown his approval for Lourdes, hasn't He?' I said. 'Think of all those miracles that have happened there, all those crutches you mentioned once before when we talked, left behind by folks who have been cured. Where do you think they came from?'

'The crutches? From cured folks!' he snapped.

'No, I mean, where did those cured folks come from?' I put to him.

He paused and frowned, then said, 'Well, from near Lourdes, I'd say. Somewhere handy enough for 'em to get there when they're not feeling very well.'

'No, Joseph, you know perfectly well they come from all over the world. There's pilgrimages from this country as well you know. Lourdes is not only for local folks, Joseph. The Catholic Church is not only for local folks or just for England, it's a world-wide church which is what God intended it to be, and Lourdes is a world-wide shrine. You'll see people from every nation on earth going there to pray.'

'Aye, you're right, Mr Rhea.'

'I think you're making excuses, Joseph. You don't really want to go at all; in fact, I might even say you're frightened.'

'Frightened? What of? I'm not frightened of dying, if that's what you're saying.'

'You're too good a Catholic to be frightened of dying,' I smiled. 'But I get the feeling that this trip is worrying you....'

He lowered his eyes and licked those thin lips and then said, 'Mr Rhea, there's summat that mebbe I should say to somebody ... not even our Mabel knows ... there are some things you can't tell a woman, but, well, mebbe I can ask you, as a friend, in confidence and all that, without you telling her, or anybody else, or them doctors. Policemen are like priests, aren't they, they can keep secrets....'

'Yes, we're expected to keep some secrets,' I assured him. 'But maybe this secret is something to discuss with Father Simon?'

'I've often thought that, Mr Rhea, but have never got round to it, but, well, seeing what you've just said and bearing in mind what we're talking about, well, yes, there is summat that should be said, Mr Rhea, and now's mebbe the right time.'

'Go on, Joseph.' I spoke softly and leaned closer so that the man in the adjoining bed would not overhear his comments. I would let Joseph get around to his topic in his own good time.

'I am frightened, Mr Rhea.' He lowered his eyes again, and I saw a tinge of redness come to his cheeks.

'Frightened, Joseph?' I asked. 'What makes you frightened?'

'Flying, Mr Rhea. Going up in an aeroplane. It's not natural, flying about up there with nowt beneath to stop you falling out of the sky. If God had wanted us to fly, He'd have given us wings.'

'Or He might have given us enough brains to build aeroplanes,' I added. 'And the means to build them ... which is what He has done. Is that what's bothering you? Flying?'

'Aye, I've never mentioned it to our Mabel, but she's allus going on about raking off to foreign parts, flying off to Rome or

Spain and such spots. The mere thought of being up there with nowt beneath me gives me the jitters, Mr Rhea.'

'Is that why you cancelled your silver wedding trip?'

'Aye,' and he sighed. 'It scared me rigid, the idea of flying. It made me sick. I was as sick as a pig one day when Mabel was out, but I never told her, she just thought I was off colour. We had to cancel the trip ... I was sorry, really, but I couldn't have gone, Mr Rhea. There's no way I'd have got on to that aeroplane.'

'But the trip to Lourdes is not in the air,' I said. 'It's a coach trip, it goes across the English Channel on a ferry. Across the sea.'

'That's just as bad,' he admitted. 'Sailing, flying. Neither's got solid ground under them, that's what scares me. I do like to have solid earth under my feet, Mr Rhea, and the thought of sitting on top of a lot of water too deep for me to put my feet down is very scary, I can tell you. I never learnt to swim, you know, too scared of deep water, I was.'

'So is that what's bothering you about the Lourdes trip?' I asked.

'Aye, it is,' he said meekly. 'Sailing, flying, it's all the same to me. Now, if there was a

310

tunnel between here and France....'

'So you've been holding back, have you? Not admitting your fears to anyone and worrying yourself sick about it, getting yourself into a right tizzy and finishing up here, in hospital?'

'Mebbe that's it, eh, Mr Rhea? Like the specialist said, it's mebbe all in my mind.'

'If you go to Lourdes, you might be cured of this,' I said. 'And then you could be happy about flying or sailing, and you could take Mabel off to Rome to see the Pope or wherever she wants to go.'

'That's what I was thinking, Mr Rhea. If only I could persuade myself to get on that bus to Lourdes, I might be cured of all this worry about travelling. That's why I'm taking so long thinking about it ... it really scares me, Mr Rhea, but I want to go, you see, deep down.'

'Then you'll have to make a real effort and go, Joseph. Besides, it is an act of faith, isn't it? Going to Lourdes, I mean. It's not a holiday or just any other trip overseas. It's for God, for the Church, for you, too. A pilgrimage, if the truth was told. Even a penance. I think some Lourdes pilgrims consider it a form of penance ... so there you are, think of it as a penance for all your past worries about travelling, a way of doing something for Mabel, a means of ending all your fears, once and for all.'

'Mebbe you've got summat there, Mr Rhea. Thanks for listening. Ah, here she comes now, with Dr Hindmarsh.'

'I'll leave you alone.' I got up from the chair. 'So shall I tell Father Simon to keep that seat for you?'

'Aye,' he said. 'You do that. I'll take it even if they have to strap me into it and dope me with summat to send me to sleep.'

'So what about the gooseberry show?'

'I've been thinking about that, an' all. I reckon Jacob can see to things while I'm away, and as for my big gooseberry, well, I might not worry too much about it this year. I won't submit any berries this time. I think it's best if I get myself better before I do owt else. Besides I didn't really think this year's berries were heavy enough. They've been neglected too much. But next year, when I'm fit and fat again, well, everybody had better look out!'

'Joseph, you're a new man!' I said, turning to leave.

'Not a word to a soul, Mr Rhea.' He put his finger to his lips.

'Our secret,' I smiled, as Mabel came to

Joseph's bedside with her news.

On the journey home in the car, Mabel told me that Dr Hindmarsh had reiterated his previous diagnosis, i.e. that Joseph was not suffering from any physical illness or disease. His stomach upset was not associated with his major condition – it was nothing more than a fairly normal stomach upset due to something he'd eaten. Hindmarsh had told Mabel once again, that it was his belief that Joseph's problems were entirely psychosomatic.

Having listened to what amounted to a confession from Joseph, I tended to agree and could now understand what might be at the root of all his recent trouble – it might be associated with Mabel's continuing insistence that once he'd retired from his gooseberry duties, they might travel more and might include some visits overseas – something that literally terrified Joseph into making himself ill. He was too frightened to go, but daren't admit his phobia to Mabel. I hoped that Lourdes trip would put an end to all that.

'Has Joseph been like this before?' I asked. 'Losing weight, I mean, and not eating?'

'Only when we were making plans to go to Rome for our silver wedding,' she said. 'He was very poorly, so we had to cancel it. We went up Wensleydale instead, a few days in Middleham, but it wasn't the same. And he has got himself right worked up about going to Lourdes, Mr Rhea. It's almost a torture for him, but as I said, he had to think of it as a penance for all those missed opportunities...'

'It's funny you should use those words,' I smiled, adding, 'Did you mention that to Dr Hindmarsh? About him losing weight when you were thinking of going to Rome?'

'No, that was such a long time ago, Mr Rhea. I don't think it has anything to do with his present state.'

I did not think it wise to refer to Joseph's phobia, after all, he'd told me in confidence, so I said, 'I think Joseph should go to Lourdes. It could be the best thing that ever happened to him.'

'That's just what I've told him, Mr Rhea. Mind you, talking to him just now, it seems he has been thinking about making a decision. He said he wanted another day to think it through. He said you and him had had a long heart to heart about it, and you'd said it was a religious commitment, a pilgrimage, not a holiday. If he can think of it as a church matter, that might just convince him, Mr Rhea. Anyway, he's due out of here tomorrow and our Alan's free to bring him home from the hospital.'

'So by tomorrow, we might know his decision?' I smiled, accelerating as we headed across the open expanse of moorland on our way back to Aidensfield.

Joseph returned the following afternoon and the first thing he did was to visit Father Simon with the announcement that he had decided to go to Lourdes. The parishioners and indeed the entire population of the village were delighted, many believing this heralded some kind of miracle by which Joseph would be cured of whatever was killing him. Joseph's rumoured cancer continued to be a hot topic in Aidensfield and district, and his most recent spell in hospital had served only to strengthen that belief. We learned that in order to catch his coach from Middlesbrough, which left at 6 p.m. and travelled overnight to Dover, Joseph would have to leave Aidensfield just after 4.30 p.m. on the Sunday. He would travel in Father Simon's parish car, and Mabel would accompany them to the departure point near Middlesbrough Cathedral. Word of this spread around the village and surrounding district with a speed that would have surpassed the most sophisticated of communications methods and it is fair to add that several highly competitive Big Berry Growers welcomed Joseph's decision.

It seemed they had not been taken in by his eminently visible garden of trees bearing mediocre berries – they knew his capabilities and guessed he'd been planning a *coup-de-grâce* with monster fruit on trees concealed behind his cottage. Until this moment, they'd all been expecting him to produce a majestic specimen for the Supreme but his decision to go to Lourdes suggested he had abandoned any idea of competing at all this year. That, in itself, was an indication of the seriousness of his plight. Never before in the history of serious berry growing had a competitor abandoned his berries to God, the weather and wasps in the final week before the competition. Stories were told of family funerals being delayed because of the needs of maturing berries, of men continuing to guard their berries while their chimneys were on fire and men sitting up all night with their berries while their wives were giving birth to babies. In short, berries were never abandoned during those final days.

In Aidensfield, therefore, Joseph's condition was regarded as extremely serious – that he had actually decided to abandon his berries was destined to become part of the local berry lore. Even non-Catholics believed that Lourdes was the only solution to his problems, but his absence meant that anyone might win the Supreme without being castigated by the villagers. It had been an unspoken wish that Joshua should be allowed to win the Supreme, most berry growers retaining their biggest berries for the other classes. But as potential winner of the Supreme, Joseph was no longer a consideration. Anyone could win any of the prizes in the show.

Joseph's forthcoming absence meant that more growers decided to spend additional time with their berries in those final days; whereas they might have aimed for one of the many minor prizes, now they began to focus on the Supreme. Nonetheless, most of them found time to assemble outside Joseph's cottage to wave him farewell that Sunday afternoon. I was there too and I must admit it was a rather emotional occasion, with lots of parishioners and villagers all coming to wish Joseph God Speed for his forthcoming journey. With his full suitcase and a new camera bought by his children, Joseph settled in the front seat of Father Simon's Hillman Minx as Mabel clambered into the rear. Their family was there too, kissing Joseph farewell as the villagers produced a rousing cheer to accompany the car as it moved away. I noticed one lady with a rosary, praying for a miracle as Joseph was carried up the hill and over the moors to catch the pilgrims' coach. I thought it was a miracle he was going at all – but he wasn't on the bus yet! I wondered if poor Mabel would have a struggle with him in Middlesbrough, a battle to get him to board the coach. As I turned away from the small crowd, I bumped into Claude Jeremiah Greengrass who'd been lurking at the back as the little drama had unfolded.

'What brings you here, Claude?' I asked him.

'I just wanted to be sure Holy Joe Cut-Stalk was on his way, that's all. I wanted to see it for myself; I couldn't believe a Big Berry Man like him would abandon his show berries just when they needed him.'

'He's ill, Claude. He's going to Lourdes.'

'Well, I hope he prays for a miracle because he'll need one if he hopes to produce a Supreme. Well, I mean if he was competing, he'd need a miracle. He's finished now, isn't he? While he's away, his berries will shrivel and wither away, and without that pipe of his to keep 'em off, all the local wasps are going to go berserk and there's nowt they love better than a big, fat, juicy goosebeerry that's being plumped up for the show. But even if he did grow the heaviest he's ever seen, I've got a world beater at Hagg Bottom. Just you wait and see!'

But I thought the berry that Mary was tending in the police-house garden was larger than Greengrass's. But would it be heavier? And would it survive the dreaded wasps?

We'd all know in just over a week from now.

# 11

The enforced absence of Joseph Marshall
prompted a surge of gooseberry mania in
Aidensfield. Berry growers know that such a
lot can be achieved in the final days,
although total success depends upon a
lengthy period of protection from the
elements along with oceans of tender loving
care. All this must be supplemented by the
very best of farmyard muck spread in the
right places at the right time, fine weather
which is not hot enough to shrivel the fruit,
a dearth of wasps and a vital spot of good
fortune. Those factors, plus the unknown
magic that somehow elevates this winning
combination into a powerful formula, can
turn a fairly modest berry into a fabled
prizewinner. The secret is to ensure that the
berry gains those extra minuscule portions
of weight, hardly more than the imponder-
ableness of a barn owl's breast feather,
which make the vital difference between a
winner and a loser. The splendid, delicate
scales used by the berry weighman are

placed in the show room on the previous day to ensure they adapt to the prevailing temperature so that they are perfectly balanced to record the tiniest of distinctions. Weight is all important; the size or beauty of the berry counts for nothing in the final judgement.

During my forays into Aidensfield in those final days, I learned that the true berry men, friends and competitors of Joseph over the last four decades, had honestly wanted him to win the Supreme this year.

For that reason, some had decided to withhold their finest specimens from the Supreme contest, but with Joseph's absence all that had changed and so the berry growers of Aidensfield got down to some serious work in that final week.

There were the inevitable dramas and sorrows, however. Old Jack Youngman's lovely red berry, a Lord Barney Weston, was pecked by a blackbird when it was a sure winner; Fred Singleton's whopping Wonderful Saunders fell off the bush because his neighbour's golden retriever wagged its tail against it; the Reverend Chandler's white Lord Kitchener burst on the bough and the wonderful yellow Wakefield Wardle twins reared by Austin

Sheffield were fatally attacked by a pair of raiding wasps. Austin had witnessed the attack – he said it reminded him of wartime pilots engaged in dive-bombing missions because accuracy and determination of the wasps was a lesson in itself. In that final week, dozens of similar stories circulated about potential prize-winning berries being nobbled in some devious way – it was far worse than the fish which got away.

I must admit that our berry, a splendid green called Admiral Beatty, remained on the tree and it was responding wonderfully to Mary's love, devotion and loads of manure delivered from her barrow with the replacement wheel. The night after Joseph departed to Lourdes, I went to examine it with her.

'You know,' I said, squatting on my haunches to locate the berry under its canopy of leaves, 'I reckon that berry stands a chance. I don't think it's capable of winning the Supreme but I think it could win one of the other awards, such as the Maiden Prize. And we qualify as competitors, Mary.'

'Have you seen any of the competition?' she asked.

'Well,' I had to say, 'I've seen Greengrass's

biggest berry and it's huge, but I think ours might beat it. But every time I've visited the home of any other berry man in the last few weeks, they've always been down the garden, out of my sight, doing something very important and very secretive with their berry trees. If I attempt to enter that part of the garden, I'm always escorted to a safe distance, to some remote patch where I can't see the berries. And then they complain about the small size of this year's berries, blaming too little rain, not enough sun, poor ground conditions, wasps ... you name it, their berries have got it.'

'So that means we're in with a chance?' asked Mary.

'No,' I said, 'it means just the opposite. It means they're all hiding gargantuan berries. The deviousness of berry men when they're under threat is astonishing, Mary. But having said that, I still think ours has a chance.'

'So what do we do? Do we have to register our entry now, pay a fee or what?'

'No, just take it along on the morning of the show. It will be weighed in your presence and cared for ... but you'll not know who's won until the very last berry has been weighed. And some cunning old devils leave theirs on the tree literally until the last minute, to get every available piece of succour from it. And it keeps the opposition guessing. So there's a tip I've learned since coming to Aidensfield.'

'So we enter our berry?' she smiled.

'We do,' I agreed.

Next day, I regretted my decision because I had to visit the Greengrass ranch to interview Claude Jeremiah about a parking infringement in York.

He denied it vehemently while leading me to his grove of gooseberry trees. He lacked the sophistication and guile of the true berry men, for he wanted to boast about his berries way ahead of show day. I know he was proud of his crop and I could see his trees bore lots of massive berries, reminding me of giant plums as they dangled temptingly in the sunlight. Each one seemed large enough to win a prize and I felt sure he wasn't hiding a crop of secret monster berries elsewhere on his ranch.

'I don't know how you do it, Claude!' I was genuinely amazed.

'Sheer skill,' he grinned. 'Mind you, there's years of berry expertise in my blood, going back to my great-great grandfather. He was good at growing rhubarb an' all, and his parsnips weren't tiddlers, but his berries were the best for miles around. Anyway, that patch of land is virgin soil, Constable, reclaimed from the moor, enriched with all manner of things and laced with special food whose recipe I cannot divulge. But you can see what a crop I've got! And just you have a look at that tree in the far corner on the right, under them leaves at the back ... I'll bet you've never seen such a whopper! That's a berry and a half! You know, I just wish Holy Joseph was entering because that berry of mine would make his look like a pea on a drum.'

'Well, I wish you luck, Claude. All you've got to do is make sure that berry stays on the tree till show day – no wasps or birds. You know the risks.'

'There's not many wasps on these moors, Constable; the smell of heather mixed with sheep muck keeps 'em away. And I know my berries. See you at the show then? With me holding the Supreme trophy, eh?' and he chuckled as he wallowed in thoughts of future success.

As I toured the village, I did not encounter any berry, of any class or colour, which compared with Claude's Herculean red Blackden Gem and I reckoned it must crush any competition – except ours! But, as I constantly reminded myself, it was weight not size which determined the winner. A good solid berry was better than one full of fluff and wind, and in spite of Claude's overt confidence, I felt the result was wide open. After all, I had not seen any other large berries, apart from my own, although I guessed they were all being kept out of sight. But, I told myself, people would hide little berries too, out of a sense of shame....

It was on the Saturday preceding the show that Mabel received a postcard from Joseph. She told everyone about it, saying it bore a picture of the shrine where St Bernadette had experienced her visions, that he'd bought some bottles of holy water, was having a wonderful time and that the pilgrimage organizers had had to dose him with something to put him to sleep before they crossed the Channel because he'd started to shake a lot, but now that he was in Lourdes, he felt fine and had never seen so many foreigners, and he couldn't understand a word most of them were saying. But on the bus he'd met a chap whose cousin's wife knew a man whose grandfather's brother had once lived in Aidensfield, so Joseph reckoned he was not too much of a stranger among the English pilgrims.

As postcards from abroad tend to do, this one arrived only a day before Joseph's triumphant return; several friends, including Father Simon and Dr McGee, called at the house to admire it and some came to ponder the fact that this card had actually come all the way from Lourdes. One or two pointed out that it didn't mention his berry trees nor did it say whether or not he had been cured.

Not that anyone really knew what was wrong with him, but they appreciated that the whole purpose of going to Lourdes was to receive a miracle cure. However, as Mabel told them, he was due back on Sunday night, disembarking at Middlesbrough around 8 p.m. if the bus was on time. Father Simon had offered to go and collect him from Middlesbrough, but Mabel had declined the offer of a trip to meet him off the bus, saying she'd better stay at home and make him something to eat. If he'd not had any Yorkshire puddings for a week or more, he'd be famished, whether or not his lack of appetite had been cured.

Due to the lateness of the hour, there was no welcoming party for Joseph but one of the committee who'd organized the fund to send him to Lourdes had suggested he gave a talk about his experiences. She suggested a meeting in the village hall a week on Friday and said she would approach Joseph to seek his co-operation. And so Joseph returned home quietly – Father Simon dropped him outside the front door of his cottage, saying he'd not come in because Joseph would want to be alone with Mabel. Later, we were told that Joseph was so thrilled with his trip that he hugged Mabel with the front room curtains standing wide open and kissed her passionately the minute he put his suitcase down. And then he never stopped talking.

She tried to say his dinner was in the oven and the table was set ready in the kitchen, adding it was a bit late for supper and very late for dinner, but she'd done some Yorkshire puddings and hoped he'd got his appetite back. He said he'd never enjoyed himself so much in all his life. And the food! He'd never stopped eating once he got across the Channel. Then there was all those masses with sermons in hundreds of different languages with a special international mass attended by 30,000 folks, and the processions by candlelight, and non-

Catholics getting baptised because of the atmosphere and all the abandoned crutches and folks saying the rosary. There was the anointing of the sick in the underground Basilica, confessions in a tent on the Prairie, mass at the actual grotto where Bernadette had seen Mary, Stations of the Cross, places to get a bath and lots of hymns and a mass in a hospital for sick folk. Somehow the priests had managed to distribute communion to everyone without long delays. The Middlesbrough Diocesan Pilgrimage had its own mass before leaving ... oh, and he'd brought her a statue of the Blessed Virgin Mary and a few bottles of holy water, they were in his suitcase with some medals and rosary beads he'd brought back for family and friends. And had Jacob got things organized for tomorrow's show? Notices out? Tables set up and chairs around the sides of the hall? Car-parking arranged? Scales taken into the room to adapt to the temperature? Raffle tickets set up on a table inside with someone to sell them? Prizes laid out? Spare pens and paper for listing winners and competitors? Newspapers telephoned in case they wanted a picture?

And to each question, Mabel had nodded

– she'd assured him that things were in hand, everything that needed to be done had been done by Jacob Butterworth who'd even found a new weighman, someone who was not a competitor and therefore unbiased when it came to accusations of cutting off stalks or favouring friends.

'You know, Mabel,' he said, as he settled down to a late-night meal of Yorkshire pudding followed by roast beef and vegetables, 'I feel like a different chap!'

'You look different,' she'd told him. 'You've got a bit of colour and you've put weight on as well, and your appetite has returned ... that trip did you good!'

'Aye,' he said. 'It did. I've never had such a time.'

But Mabel thought he had changed because he did not mention the berry he'd left behind. Maybe he'd come to realize there was more to life than growing big berries and winning the Supreme? Perhaps it meant he would take her to Rome or somewhere? She felt very happy as she gave him a second helping of mashed potato, some more carrots and another Yorkshire pudding smothered in onion gravy even if it was well past his bedtime.

Joseph's first outing after his return was to

morning mass the following day, 7.30 a.m. on Bank Holiday Monday. The service had attracted a congregation slightly larger than normal because so many people wanted to inspect Joseph to see if he had the appearance of being cured and to hear something of his time in Lourdes; apart from that, of course, people had a day off work which meant they could attend mass. Perhaps the most important factor was that a lot of men came to mass to pray for success at today's gooseberry show – provided God wanted them to win.

On that occasion, no one knew what Joseph would be praying for now that he had no berries to show, although some felt he might be giving thanks because he looked so much better. Lourdes did appear to have made him better. I did not attend mass that a morning, chiefly because I had to prepare for duty and I had some paper-work to complete; it had to be taken to Ashfordly Police Station before 9 a.m.

That Bank Holiday Monday was a duty day for me – apart from supervising traffic and paying some attention to the security arrangements at the Gooseberry Show, I had a brief to patrol the district to cope with the influx of tourists, trippers and litterdumpers. But the show would occupy me for most of the day – and, of course, I had my own berry to contribute to the proceedings. Mary had said she would convey our specimen to the show in an egg box; I thought she might have a more delicate touch than I because I did not want to burst our berry upon being handled.

Meanwhile, the other contestants were harvesting their berries, many using delicate nail scissors and tweezers to remove them gently from the trees. Great care was taken when harvesting them because a spike from a branch, a nick with a fingernail or a grip too tight for the tender flesh to resist could ruin a potential champion and I know that tears of frustration, sorrow and even rage were not uncommon during those harrowing moments. Another rule was that the berries had to be dry upon being submitted, wet berries weighing more than dry ones due to the water which clung to them, rather like unscrupulous coalmen selling wet coal by weight.

But most of the berries did get harvested safely and packed into cotton-wool lined boxes, or egg-boxes or even egg cups and other suitable containers for their precarious journey to the show. It was not unknown for a berry to burst during that hair-raising trip – these berries were far more fragile than eggs – but, invariably, a suitable complement did arrive at the weighman's table. His task, of course, was critical – if he burst a berry due to careless handling, he could be accused of sabotage or malicious damage.

In uniform, I went along to the show room prior to the 1 p.m. closing time for submissions and saw the new weighman, appropriately named Barry Scales, carefully weighing those berries already submitted. As he worked, I saw that both Joseph and Jacob were present, along with other members of the committee. It was a rule of the society that the berry weighing was supervised by at least two persons independent of the weighman – currently, they were Joseph Marshall and Jacob Butterworth, the latter resplendent in his famous red waistcoat.

Joseph looked different – his skin was more rosy in colour with just a hint of suntan, his cheeks and face were fatter than they had been for weeks and his clothes seemed a better fit because he had put on some weight. Everyone commented on how well he looked. It was amazing, the transformation a week could make. Clearly, the Lourdes trip had been of benefit and I managed to have a quiet word with him as he was replaced at the weighing table by another committee member.

'You're looking good, Joseph,' I smiled. 'Nice to have you back.'

'They've asked me to give a talk about my trip,' he said. 'By gum, Mr Rhea, it was good. I never thought the world was such a big place, all them folks with different coloured skins and ways of dressing. None of 'em had heard of Aidensfield, mind, but I'll tell you what, it made me realize there's a lot going on out there, things to see and good food to eat and nice folks....'

'You're quite taken with the idea of travelling, then?'

'I am, and no mistake about it. I want our Mabel to see what I saw, Mr Rhea, and they say there's mountains in Switzerland that have snow on all the year round and spots so hot you can fry eggs on the pavement and sands in deserts that stretch for hundreds of miles without a drop of water. You'd never grow big berries there, would you, Mr Rhea?'

'I thought you were frightened of flying and sailing?' I said quietly.

'Don't you go telling folks that, Mr Rhea! It's not true, not any more. They had to give me summat to make me sleep on the way to Lourdes, across the water that is, but on the way back, I wanted to see what was happening – all them ships cruising up and down the Channel, big enough to put all the folks in Aidensfield on board, some of 'em were.... No, Mr Rhea, I'm not frightened of travelling, not any more.'

'So you were cured then?' I said.

'Aye, I was. Yes, I was cured, Mr Rhea. Is that a miracle?'

'I'd say it was, Joseph. Just think if you'd never gone to Lourdes....'

'Aye, I'd still be frightened of our Mabel wanting to take off to foreign parts and now I can't wait to go.'

'You have changed! And that reminds me, what about your own berries, this year? You've not submitted any, have you?'

'Nay, Mr Rhea, I thought it best not to. Being sent off to Lourdes meant I couldn't tend 'em like I should, so I thought it better if I got myself cured first, then I can concentrate on my berries next year. And it's worked out right. I am cured, Mr Rhea, I know it – so look out next year, all you Big Berry Men, that's what I say! I'll aim for the

Supreme next year, my first year of not being president.'

'That's provided you are not too busy touring all those places you've wanted to see!' I laughed.

'Well, even though I might be travelling, I shan't go away during the berry season, Mr Rhea. Besides, who wants to go travelling in August when all them tourists are about?'

'So you can plan your year now?' I said. 'But I'm pleased you're continuing with your berry growing. At least, it might knock Claude Jeremiah Greengrass off his perch!'

'Why, is he growing again? He never forgave me for telling him to chop some of his stalk off. It was half a branch, Mr Rhea, not just a bit of stalk. It was enough to take any berry off the scales, but he wasn't very pleased. He said I cost him the prize that year. But he wouldn't have won, not with the tiny specimen he produced.'

'Well, he's got a monster this year, I've seen it,' I said. 'And he's going to submit it.'

'A big berry? On those trees of his? He had 'em growing in the shadows, out of the sun. They'd never do any good!'

'He's moved them,' I said. 'He's transplanted his trees, moved them to the south of his house, into the sunshine and onto a patch of land that seems to be rich and fertile. He's got some lovely berries, I must admit.'

'Moved his trees? But that means he must be disqualified. Anybody who moves his trees must do so with committee members watching, otherwise how do we know those trees are originals? And nobody's reported it to committee, so it looks as if he's broken the rules. Well, thanks for telling me that, Mr Rhea, I'll see that his berry is disallowed. I don't care how big it is! After all, rules are rules.'

'That'll be worse than cutting his stalk off!' I muttered with some remorse. I hoped I wasn't responsible for having Claude banned from the show but reconciled myself to the thought that if he was a committee member as he'd claimed, he would be familiar with the rules.

As Joseph returned to his duties to observe the weighing, I decided to remain in the room until the time for submissions had closed – chiefly because I wanted to see the competition faced by our modest berry. From what I could see and hear in the room, this year's berries were about average, with no massive ones and no surprises. Many growers had submitted berries for the various classes while keeping their biggest and best – the Supreme contenders – on the bush until the last minute.

The range and variety of berries was fascinating – there were classes for the heaviest dozen, the heaviest twins, the heaviest maiden, the heaviest maiden twins, the heaviest half-dozen, the maiden half-dozen and the heaviest four colours. There were more entries than usual, it seemed, certainly an increase upon last year and the berries already submitted including some wonderful names, such as Just Betty, Kathryn Hartley, Delves Derby, Fascination, Leveller, Transparent, Firbob, Castle Rock and dozens of others. In my untutored mind, they all looked green or red, although I knew that some were classified as white and yellow, in addition to green. But it took an expert to distinguish them and every one of them looked huge to me, even if the experts did not regard any as particularly impressive. I felt rather sad that Joseph had not been able to compete – he hadn't entered any other class and surely he would have beaten these very average specimens.

I was becoming quite excited because Mary had not yet brought in our sample. I had suggested she bring it around after quarter to one and, as I waited, she arrived clutching an egg box containing our pride and joy. We had decided to enter just the one berry and she handed the box to Barry Scales. She and I watched as he carefully extracted our Admiral Beatty, checked the stalk length, made sure the berry was dry and then gingerly placed it on the scales. It weighed in at twenty drams and five grains, a very commendable weight.

Joseph smiled at Mary. 'Your first time, Mrs Rhea, isn't it?'

'Yes,' she told him. 'Really, we've no idea about growing big berries, but Nick thought I should submit this one....'

'It might be the heaviest maiden,' said Joseph. I knew that maiden was the term used to indicate a first-time submission. 'In fact, I'm sure it'll get the maiden prize ... but there's a few minutes left before closing.'

Mary came across to me and gave me a hug. 'Wouldn't it be wonderful if we won something,' she said. 'Dad will be so proud.'

And then the door crashed open and in breezed Claude Jeremiah Greengrass clutching an egg box. 'I'm not too late, am I? My truck wouldn't start....'

'You qualify to submit an entry, do you,

Claude?' asked Joseph pointedly.

'Qualify? Of course I qualify. I'm a fully paid-up member, like my father before me....'

'I mean, you've not broken any rules about moving trees, have you? I understand you have moved your trees from one place to another. Those trees previously belonging to your father...'

'I have,' snapped Claude, still clutching his box. 'And I've not broken any rules. It says in rule sixteen that I can compete from trees belonging to another member – my dad that was – if the trees are moved in the presence of one or two committee members.'

'Right,' smiled Joseph.

'Well, in case you'd forgotten, I am a committee member. I was present when I moved my trees. It says nowt about who the committee member must be. According to that rule, I've done nowt wrong – except I might have grown the heaviest berry seen in Aidensfield and it's not all stalk, like some have said my berries are.'

'He's right,' said Jacob Butterworth, coming forward with a rule book in his hand. He had checked the relevant rule and announced, 'According to the wording of this rule, he does qualify.'

'Fair enough,' said Joseph. 'We might have to reconsider a rewrite of that rule to make it clearer.'

'It's clear enough to me!' blinked Claude.

'We might rewrite it to say the committee member who is present has to be in addition to oneself,' said Jacob. 'Anyway, you're OK this year, Claude, so let's see what you've brought.'

He opened his egg box to reveal a colossal red Blackden Gem and beamed at the various officials. 'How about that, then? I'll bet you've seen nowt like that one this year. Come on, Barry, get it on the scales and see how much it weighs.'

After carrying out the necessary checks for dryness and stalk length, Barry Scales placed it on the delicate weighing machine and it recorded twenty-five drams, twenty grains.

'Open class, Claude? You're not a maiden, are you?'

'A maiden? Me? I've shown more berries than you've had apple pies. And you'll see I've entries in for other classes, some I brought earlier. But this one's for the open. How about it for the Supreme, eh?'

'It's a beauty, Claude,' Joseph congratulated him. 'I must admit you've done well …

not world champion class, but well in the running for today's prize list.'

'Well, can't I know now? Is it the heaviest in the show?'

'It's not closing-time yet,' said Jacob. 'There's a few minutes left before we close the weighing. There's time for somebody to fetch a heavier berry in.'

'There's still time for a big one to arrive,' muttered Joseph, and I thought I detected a certain amount of guile in his facial expression.

'It'll have to be weighted down with lead shot to beat that 'un,' chuckled Claude. 'So what about you, Joseph? I've heard you've not entered this year?'

'That's right,' admitted Joseph. 'I didn't get back from Lourdes until late last night and didn't bother to check my berries; there's no point, with me being away. A week without being tended condemns them to the rubbish tip, as you know. I've not fetched any to the show, not for any of those classes.'

As Claude hung around with the clock slowly ticking towards 1 p.m., I decided there was no point in waiting any more; I would leave. But just as I reached the door, Mabel Marshall came hurrying across the forecourt with an egg box in her hands.

'Oh, dear, Mr Rhea, am I too late?'

'For weighing, you mean?' I was surprised at this development.

'Yes, I've brought this along for Joseph.'

She opened her egg box to reveal a huge yellow Firbob.

'You're just in time,' I smiled. 'You must take it in!'

And so Mabel closed the lid of the box, then rushed indoors with about a minute to spare, handed it to Joseph and said, 'There you are, Joseph, your big berry.'

Without opening it, he smiled at everyone and said, 'Thanks, lass. I think this might do the trick.'

'If there's owt in that box, you might as well chuck it away because you know mine's heaviest!' grinned Claude. 'So come on, Joseph, get it out and let me see what your abandoned fruit weighs!'

Joseph opened the box with all the tenderness of the enthusiast to reveal a massive berry which one of his trees had nurtured. It sat in the box like a large egg, dry and clean, with its ripe yellow skin taut and revealing the veins beneath. It was magnificent.

'Give us it here!' said Barry. 'We're nearly

343

out of time.'

And so Joseph's berry, submitted in the open class, was placed on the scales and it recorded twenty-six drams eighteen grains.

'I reckon this is the winner,' said Barry Scales. 'It beats yours, Claude.'

And so Joseph won the Supreme Championship that year. He said it was all due to Mabel's secret attention to his berry during his absence. She claimed she hadn't done a lot, saying it was all due to the carrot water she used, perhaps with a mixture of onion gravy and some cold tea, not to mention the bottle of Holy Water from Lourdes she poured over the roots last night. In spite of that, word got around Aidensfield that when in Lourdes, Joseph had prayed for a miracle to happen to his berry, praying that it would survive without his close ministrations, and the whole village thought two miracles had happened because Joseph's appetite had returned and his energy levels had been restored. That was the first miracle.

The second was that he had clearly put on weight – and so had his berry. Did that mean he'd got the wording of his prayers muddled up?

At 2.30 p.m. that afternoon, Bank Holiday

Monday, the berry show opened its doors to the public and they flocked in to admire Aidensfield's renowned annual show of huge berries. Claude got second prize in his section, Mary won the maiden but Joseph Marshall won the Supreme fair and square. The committee also made a presentation to him to mark his retirement; it was a silver cup engraved with his name and the date of his lengthy term as president. Afterwards we all adjourned to the pub for celebratory drinks and the inevitable inquest on the results.

'I never thought I'd win anything!' Mary said, as we enjoyed the atmosphere as winners and losers relived their experience, blaming wasps, frosts and a host of other outside influences for failing to scoop the Supreme, or just failing in any of the other categories.

'Oh, but I've always regarded you as Aidenfield's heaviest maiden!' I laughed, as we thought about her prize, a new ironing board.

'It's funny that both a Joseph and a Mary won prizes,' she laughed. 'It must be the Lourdes influence!'

Joseph was nearby and laughed at her remark saying, 'It was, Mrs Rhea. Due to

Lourdes, I mean. I haven't told anybody yet, but I think I had a vision there.'

'A vision?' I smiled.

'Mebbe it was just a dream,' he capitulated.

'Really? So what happened?' I was intrigued.

'It was Our Lady clutching a rosary, Mr Rhea, one night while I was asleep.'

'That sounds like a dream, quite normal under the circumstances.'

'Aye, but her rosary was made up of big gooseberries, Mr Rhea. What about that, eh? A gooseberry rosary made up of all four colours. I've never seen owt like that before. And by gum, they were whoppers. She must have some secret recipe for growing 'em. They'd have won a prize or two in our show, make no mistake about that.'

'Perhaps there's no wasps in Heaven, Joseph!' I laughed.

'Now, I wouldn't be too sure about that.' Joseph puffed at his pipe. 'That's summat I can ask Father Simon about, isn't it? And if there is wasps in Heaven, will I be allowed to smoke pipes there, to keep 'em off my berry trees?'

'You intend growing berries in Heaven then?' I put to him.

'I do, when I decide it's time to go,' he smiled. 'But it's Heaven here just now, isn't it? Me with my Supreme and my pipe and my berry trees – and Mabel.'

It was afterwards that I pondered the deviousness of Big Berry Growers, but if Joseph had gone to Lourdes to wrong-foot the opposition, he'd succeeded. Would a Big Berry Man who was a Big Catholic do a trick like that, I wondered?

The publishers hope that this book has given you enjoyable reading. Large Print Books are especially designed to be as easy to see and hold as possible. If you wish a complete list of our books please ask at your local library or write directly to:

**Magna Large Print Books**
Magna House, Long Preston,
Skipton, North Yorkshire.
BD23  4ND

This Large Print Book for the partially
sighted, who cannot read normal print, is
published under the auspices of

**THE ULVERSCROFT FOUNDATION**